MOTHER OF MINE

IAN GIELEN

ISBN: 978-1-7640126-3-8
Cover designed by Adrian Medina
Edited by Stephanie Huddle
Formatted by Jyl Glenn
Published by Ian Gielen

For all the mothers in my life, both past and present, whose love, support and strength have helped shape me into the person I am today.

"She was not a mother, but a monster in a mother's shape."
— Ann Radcliffe, The Mysteries of Udolpho (1794)

CHAPTER ONE

Stockbridge, MA

"Julia? Julia dear, are you there?"

The phone line crackled, the sound making Julia wince as she moved the receiver away from her ear for a moment. She really needed to get a technician to look at her mother's phone line. She made a mental note to add it to the list of things to follow up on for her mother, which was adding up unusually fast.

"Yes, Mother, I'm here," Julia said, her tone thick with love.

"Oh, good. I was afraid you weren't going to answer the phone. You know how I get stressed when you don't answer the phone," her mother said with an undercurrent of disapproval in her voice.

"Yes, Mother, sorry. I was just saying goodbye to Ron before he left for work."

"Oh, I'm sure he would've understood if you'd

answered a bit sooner, dearie. You know your mother needs you."

"Yes, Mother, I know."

The sound of an obvious, annoyed sigh came through over the phone, making Julia cringe. With it came an immediate sense of guilt, a heavy weight she knew she deserved. Her mother, Mary, had always been her biggest supporter and her best friend. She was always there with advice, ready to weigh in when problems cropped up, offering direction, and helping her navigate life's challenges. Even if it was often laced with judgement. Disappointing her filled Julia with instant feelings of shame and guilt. In Julia's eyes, there was nothing worse. Tears began to well up as she berated herself. She needed to do better. She had to.

"I'm... I'm sorry, Mother, it won't happen again."

"You say that, dear, but it does. Too often now that you're with that man."

"But Ron is my husband, Mama. I love him. You said I should marry him, and I did."

"Don't you dare talk back to me and tell me what I said. I know very well what I said," Mary snapped, anger coursing through her voice.

Julia trembled with sobs, struggling to contain them from spilling through the line. Her chest tightened as her thoughts spun out, anxiety surging like a tide she couldn't hold back.

"I'm... I'm sorry, Mama. Please don't be angry. I'll try harder, I promise."

"There's my girl," Mary said, her voice regaining its previous warmth.

Julia smiled brightly. She loved making her mother

happy. There was nothing in the world like it. Her body was in full tremble mode now, her nerves shot, but she knew how to hide it over the phone. She'd had plenty of practice. The hardest part was always the beginning, when her anxiety surged faster than her ability to take control of it.

"Now, darling, I need you to do something for me."

"Yes, Mama, of course, anything you need."

"Good girl," she said, affection colouring her voice. "I need you to come pick me up and take me to the doctor to get a prescription for my medication. Then you can take me grocery shopping and to the library so I can get some books. Afterwards, you can drop me off. Oh, and then I'll need you to pay some bills for me. Can you do that for Mama?"

"Of course I can," Julia gushed. She had arranged to meet Ron for lunch, but she would have to tell him she couldn't make it. He would understand. He would have to. Her mother always came first.

CHAPTER TWO

Ron took a left into the employees-only car park at the back of Crescent Capital Bank and pulled his Lexus ES into his allocated parking space in the coveted position next to the back entrance. The bank sat among a strip of tired-looking shops, its sleek modern design jutting out, like it didn't belong. It was the newest of the buildings, replacing the old council hall that had been condemned in favour of a shiny new one built further up the road. Word was the whole stretch was slated for redevelopment, but Ron didn't buy it. Not in the current economy. Why would they when the town was barely surviving as it was?

Flipping down the sun visor, he studied himself in the mirror, noticing the increasingly large bags under his intense green eyes and the stress lines on his forehead. The year since he'd married Julia had seen them become a regular staple. Though he loved her dearly, the threads of their marriage were on the verge of snapping, at least from his perspective. Julia's unhealthy relationship with her mother was the source of all their arguments, of which there had been and continue to be many. If only she could step outside her mother's shadow for once, see things from his side instead of being consumed by the need to please, to sacrifice everything for a woman who never seemed satisfied.

He sighed as he adjusted his tie and swept a few unruly curls of his brown hair back into place. He was tired just thinking about the whole thing. The last hope for them at this point was having a child. Pinning the relationship's success on that wasn't exactly healthy either, but he was out of ideas. Maybe if Julia had someone of her own to care for, she'd finally be forced to put them first. Maybe it would break the cycle, her endless need to please, to orbit her mother like a satellite that never got to land.

Checking his watch, he figured he had just enough time to grab a coffee from Bochello's Cafe next door before he had to start work. Although technically, as the branch manager, he could start whenever he wanted. It wasn't as if the boss would pull him up for walking in ten minutes late; he WAS the boss.

Folding away the sun visor, he retrieved his briefcase from the passenger seat and slid out of the car, closing the door gently behind him. With a frown, he noticed there was a thin film of dust on the roof. He would have to give it a wash soon. With all the free time he had on the weekends with Julia tending to her mother's demands, that wouldn't be a problem. The thought soured instantly, a flicker of irritation tightening his jaw, his teeth grinding in quiet protest.

The moment he locked the car and turned toward the cafe, his phone vibrated insistently in his pocket. He walked on and pulled it out, the morning sun catching the screen with a glare. Julia's name flashed across it, halting him in his tracks.

With another frown that seemed to be perpetually etched on his face these days, he pressed accept.

"Hey, sweetheart, is everything okay?" he asked, keeping his tone warm and light despite feeling anything but.

"Um... Yeah, it's just... I can't make it to lunch with you today." Julia's voice was hesitant and nervous. The way it always sounded when she had to cancel plans because of her mother.

"Oh? You don't sound too good, baby. Did you forget to take your meds this morning?"

"No... I mean, I haven't taken them yet, but I will. It's just that... my mom... she called me just as you left, and she needs me to take her to the doctor to get a prescription and do grocery shopping." As if she couldn't wait to get it out, the last part of the sentence was delivered in a breathless rush.

As soon as he heard her mention her mother, Ron felt a surge of anger start to boil inside him. He managed to suppress it, instead letting out a sigh.

"Julia, you know she's quite capable of doing that herself. She's not an invalid as much as she'd like to make you think she is. She can walk and drive just fine."

"She needs me, Ron, she's not as capable as you seem to think she is. Plus, I'm her daughter, I can't just say no."

"You can and should say no to her more often. I don't know how many times I have to say that. You can't just drop everything and run to her every time she snaps her fingers. Especially when it's every damn day, for hours at a time. It's unreasonable, not to mention selfish. What about me? What about us? Do we have to come second all the damn time?" Ron's voice rose the more he spoke, and he looked around the parking lot nervously. Thankfully, no one else had arrived yet, but he knew it wouldn't be long before they did.

"Ron, I'm not going to get into another argument with you about this. She needs me, and I need her. One day, you're just going to have to accept that."

"Oh, really? So that's how it is, is it? You know if we end up having a child, you can't just run off and do her bidding."

The line was quiet for a few seconds before Ron could hear quiet sobbing through the speaker. He felt his anger instantly crumble. He hated making Julia cry, and lately it felt like that's all he'd been doing. His heart ached, a dull throbbing in his chest, as shame and guilt began to twist inside him like a venomous snake.

"Julia, I'm sorry. Listen, it's okay. Go and help your mom. We can do lunch another day." He paused, taking a deep breath before continuing. "Let's talk about things when I get home, okay? Maybe we can plan some us time together. A weekend away, some wine, long romantic walks along the beach, a candlelight dinner, a bath, and then... perhaps we can try for a mini-Mathews."

Julia's sobs turned into shaky laughter. It was a brittle sound. Despite everything—the fights, the distance, the exhaustion of dealing with her mother—Ron felt a spark of hope stir inside him. Maybe they weren't beyond saving. Maybe, just maybe, they had a shot.

"Oh, really? A girl Mathews, or a boy?"

"Either, as long as they have your smile," he answered,

feeling his spirits begin to lift. When the subject wasn't her mother, Julia was the woman he had fallen in love with. Sensitive, caring, empathetic, and easy to talk to. Ironically, it was those very qualities that turned every conversation he had about Julia serving her mother into a battlefield.

"You're a charmer, you know that," she said, sniffling between giggles.

"I know. It's a burden that I carry heavily," he replied with a theatrical sigh. "Okay, sweetheart, I have to go and grab a coffee before I start work. Have a great day, I love you."

"I love you too."

The call ended, and he stared down at the dark screen of the phone for a few moments. A heavy weariness settled over him, compounding the fatigue that had already taken root inside. He needed the coffee more than ever now. He let out a sigh, gave his head a slow shake, and turned down the narrow alley between the bank and Bochello's. The shadows clung to him as he walked, long and heavy, mirroring the weight in his chest. He reached the cafe door and pushed through.

A cheery jingle of bells, accompanied by the familiar scent of fresh coffee, greeted him as he entered. Besides an elderly couple seated at a table with their hands around their steaming mugs, murmuring softly to each other, the cafe was otherwise empty.

Behind the counter, Amanda looked up after giving the coffee machine a final wipe-down. She met his gaze with a bright, easy smile, the kind that lingered just a moment too long and was tinged with a hint of flirtation.

"Hey, you, I was beginning to think you'd skipped out on our coffee date." Her voice was warm and playful.

Ron laughed, brushing off her flirting like he usually did. "Yeah, I just had a call from Julia. She's skipping out on lunch with me to help Mary."

Amanda rolled her eyes at the mention of Julia's mother. "You did tell her that Mary doesn't really need her, right? That she's just using her?"

"Yeah, I said that, alright, for about the millionth time," he said, the weariness in his voice echoing the slump of his shoulders and the lines etched on his face.

Amanda's tone softened. "Well, I can only imagine how hard it is. All I can do is offer you my sympathy. Oh, and my coffee, of course. The usual?"

"Please and thank you," Ron replied, offering a faint smile. He glanced around and caught the older couple watching him. He gave them a polite nod. They didn't return it; instead, they turned their attention back to the newspapers that were now before them. Typical small town, there was always someone watching, someone ready to stir the pot if there was a hint of drama in the air. Thankfully, these two looked like out-of-towners, so in this case, he had dodged a bullet.

He approached the counter and sat down on the stool whilst Amanda busied herself with the coffee machine. Amanda knew the happenings in most people's lives, and she took a much more noticeable interest in his than most. She was quite familiar with the goings-on between Julia and Mary. Mary used to visit the cafe often when the owners, the Bochellos, ran things.

In her early thirties, Amanda had been at the cafe for a

few years before Ron had started at the bank. She had been just an employee then, but the Bochellos had decided to retire eighteen months ago and handed the business over to her. With short brown hair parted at the side that showcased her elegant features, she wasn't striking in the way that turned heads in a crowded room, but she was confident, and there was something quietly magnetic about her. People came for the coffee, sure, but they often stayed just that little bit longer for Amanda. Her presence made the cafe a safe harbour for people to dock in, a temporary escape from life's chaotic demands. The only other option in town was run by a grumpy father-and-son duo. To be fair to them, their food was better. But the atmosphere left a lot to be desired.

Amanda gave him a side-eyed glance and a half-smile while getting his coffee ready. She had made it obvious over time that she was interested in him, but he had never encouraged it. He was faithful to Julia through and through. Whatever cracks and fissures that had formed in their relationship, he wasn't the kind to look elsewhere.

He slipped out his phone and scrolled through his social media feed. Nothing there but the usual spread of food, smiling faces, and vacation pictures. A pang of jealousy hit him before he put it away. He and Julia were lucky in that his job paid well, and they could easily afford a vacation, but whenever he'd suggested it, he was shot down. It was always the excuse that she couldn't be away from her mother too long or be too far away in case she was needed. Perhaps he would have better luck tonight, but he highly doubted it.

"Here you go," Amanda said with a wink, placing the large takeaway cup in front of him.

"Thanks. First of many I'll need today," Ron replied, standing up and reaching for a lid. When he looked down to snap it on, he saw the milk foam had been formed into a love-heart design.

He glanced up and gave her a quiet nod and a small smile, enough to show his appreciation and nothing more, before he sealed the lid, paid for the coffee, and turned toward the door.

"Enjoy your day," Amanda called out after him in a radiant voice, as he stepped out into the morning.

"You too," Ron called back as the door closed softly behind him.

He approached the front of the bank and gave a wave to Stanley, the security guard, visible through the glass doors. Stanley was a constant, always there like clockwork, at least an hour before opening to perform his security checks. Ron swiped his access card at the panel beside the door and stepped inside, giving Stanley a smile.

"Good morning, sir. Ready for another day of wheeling and dealing?" Stanley said with a grin.

Ron chuckled and clapped him on the shoulder as he passed. "None of that," he said. "Just ready to turn transactions into smiles as always." He delivered the slogan of Crescent Capital Bank with practiced ease. He privately loathed corporate slogans, especially this one. *Turning transactions into smiles.* As slogans go, it left a lot to be desired. Still, he would do his corporate duty, use it, and even mandate its use by his employees, despite the sugary words sticking in his throat. Anything to appease the corporate gods.

He strode towards the roped-off stairs at the far end of the office, passing the glassed-in teller cubicles and neatly arranged brochure stands.

He tried to focus, to mentally prepare for the day ahead, but his thoughts drifted, as they always seemed to do these days, to Julia. Something had to give. He needed things to change, and soon. He felt stretched too thin. The pressure inside was approaching boiling point, and he could feel his patience was nearing its limit. Perhaps the thing that needed to give wasn't the relationship but his own stubborn refusal to admit it was already gone.

CHAPTER THREE

Mary placed the receiver back into its cradle with a clunk, its coiled cord swinging like a lazy pendulum beneath. Julia had offered to buy her a mobile phone, but Mary wouldn't hear of it. She liked things as they were—familiar, tactile, dependable. Technology was best left for the young and had no place in her life; it only stood in the way of her comfort and rituals.

She shook her head in frustration as she walked to the kettle to flip it on. Retrieving a mug from the cupboard overhead, she plucked a teabag from the tin beside the kettle and dropped in a spoonful of sugar. Leaning back against the kitchen counter, she let her thoughts drift to Julia. Like clockwork, the familiar sting of disappointment settled in, the type that was deep, filled with a lifetime of failed expectations.

Things used to be different before Julia met that man, Ron. Though if she was being honest, Mary knew part of it was her own doing. She'd given her blessings to Julia to start dating him after Julia had met Ron at a friend's BBQ and learned that he was a branch manager for Crescent Capital Bank in town. When Julia had brought him over to meet her after the first date, Mary had initially been charmed by him. He was attractive, well-dressed, smart, and presented himself well, and, most importantly, was well-off financially. That was the tipping point for Mary; the rest was just icing. But the charm didn't last. Ron started questioning Julia's close relationship with Mary. At first, it was subtle, then not so much. Julia still came when Mary needed her, but the strain was increasingly visible. Mary could see it on her face. How tired Julia looked, the guilty glances whenever she spoke of Ron. It clung to her every time she walked through the door.

As far as Mary was concerned, that simply wouldn't do. Julia was her daughter, and if she needed her, she expected her to show up and be happy to do so. She had raised Julia, given her everything she ever asked for, and prepared her for a good life. Now that Mary was sixty-four, she saw no reason why that debt shouldn't be repaid in full. Family should be simple that way. Loyalty in, loyalty out. Which is why she'd cut off her brother, her sister, and their smug little families years ago. Their constant judgement, their unsolicited advice given under the guise of care. She hadn't needed it. Never needed it. Both Ella's daughter, Belle, and Bryan's son, Andy, had always kept their distance. The few times she'd seen them, their glances were enough to confirm what she already knew. They held nothing but disdain for her. Over time, the disappointment she felt at her treatment had curdled and hardened into hate. Even now, just the thought of them all made her blood boil.

She huffed in annoyance, irritated by the sudden flush

of emotion. She'd have to get Julia to give her a massage later to help take the edge off. One more thing to blame them for.

The kettle clicked off with a snap, and Mary poured the steaming water into her mug, stirring the tea in slow, deliberate circles. She glanced up at the clock above the kitchen sink, its soft ticking a reliable, calming presence alongside the aroma of the Earl Grey tea that wafted from the cup below.

Julia would be here soon. Mary took a sip, letting the warmth settle in her chest. She would have just enough time to finish the tea and fetch her wheelchair. She could walk if she had to, but she'd done quite enough for one day. Julia could just as easily wheel her around and do the work for her. It would save her from having sore feet later.

A few minutes later, she was down to her last dregs of tea, and she set the mug down in the sink alongside the other dirty dishes she'd left there since Julia last cleaned. No point in doing them herself when she could get her daughter to do them for her.

She made her way down the hall to her bedroom, retrieved the library books from her bedside table that she wanted to return, and placed them on the seat of the wheelchair. Pushing it ahead of her into the lounge, she transferred the books to the coffee table, where Julia could pick them up once she arrived.

Next, she fetched her purse from the kitchen table and returned to her wheelchair. She settled into it and picked up the latest issue of her favourite gardening magazine, leafing through it as she waited for Julia to arrive. Her garden was overdue for a makeover. With any luck, she could find something that piqued her interest. Something that Julia could tackle next.

Living alone was something she was used to, but as she'd gotten older, she found herself getting increasingly lonely. Julia was the only one in her life now with whom she truly felt at ease. Her moods, her rhythms, her needs, Julia understood them all. If she could find more ways to keep her daughter close, keep her busy, then things would be even easier. Happier.

In the next few months, she planned to ask if she could move in with Julia and Ron. She already knew Ron would object. But Julia? Julia could be persuaded. Mary was confident of that. If Ron didn't like it, well, he could always leave.

She paused on that thought for a moment. Perhaps it would be better if he did. Grandchildren would've been nice, sure, but not if Ron was going to be a constant obstacle, always questioning, always interfering. Anyway, Julia was an attractive young woman. She could easily find someone else. Perhaps it was time to start planting a seed in Julia's mind, a gentle nudge here, a quiet suggestion there. Nothing direct. If she could get them to part ways, her proposal would be far easier to accept and far harder to refuse.

She continued to flick through the pages of the gardening magazine, shooting a quick glance at the clock. Julia was late again. She hated it when Julia was late. She considered it a sign of disrespect. A quiet insult. As if her time didn't matter. As if she didn't matter. She could feel her jaw tighten at that thought. Another thing to raise with Julia. She'd add it to the list.

She returned her attention to the magazine, trying to refocus, and her eyes caught sight of a garden spread that instantly captured her imagination. Flowers of all colours popped out from the page, and she found herself sniffing at it, half-expecting the scent to rise from the paper. Yes. This was what she wanted. The plant types were irrelevant; Julia could sort that out.

The crunch of gravel outside finally announced her arrival. She checked her watch. She was just a little over five minutes late. That would not do. Mary set the magazine aside and drummed her fingers on the armrest of the wheelchair, shooting daggers at the door.

The jingling of keys came from the other side, along with a clatter of them hitting the ground, and a muffled curse echoing through the door. Typical. There was a pause, then another jingle as Julia retrieved them before they slipped into the lock with a soft click. The doorknob turned before the door swung inward with a hurried push, as if haste could erase the delay.

CHAPTER FOUR

"You're late," Mary said coldly, her eyes narrowing at Julia's flushed face as she stepped inside and shut the door.

Julia's heart sank as soon as she heard those words. She'd been dreading them ever since she'd hung up from the phone call with Ron and saw the time, knowing she'd be late.

"I'm sorry, Mother. I was on the phone with Ron, telling him I couldn't make lunch today, and I lost track of time," she said softly, keeping her gaze low, ashamed to meet her mother's disappointed stare.

Mary scoffed. "Didn't I teach you better than that? You're an adult, Julia. Surely you can manage your time. Anyway, why did you agree to have lunch with Ron? You know your mother needs you at lunchtime." The weight of Mary's frustration hung heavy in the air, and her words, sharp and painful, stabbed into Julia's heart.

"I...I know... It's just that Ron and I... We're not doing so well. He keeps telling me I'm doing too much for you, that you can handle things on your own, and that we need to spend some quality time together where we can find it," Julia said, the words spilling out before she could stop them. It had always been that way; she'd never been able to keep things from her mother. The few times she did, she felt guilty, as if she were betraying their bond.

Mary's lips pursed. She stared at Julia for a long moment, then her face crumpled, and she began to sob. She turned her face away and raised a trembling hand to shield her eyes, her sobs becoming louder, almost theatrical. Julia's heart sank. She knew this move. It happened every time she mentioned Ron and his objections, whenever the truth, and she knew it was the truth, painted Mary in a less-than-flattering light. It was a deflection, a performance designed to make Julia feel cruel for simply being honest. And it worked oh so well. Even knowing the pattern, even recognizing the manipulation, Julia still felt awful.

"I'm sorry, Mother. You know I'll always put you first. I love you so much. Please don't be upset with me," Julia said, her voice trembling as she knelt beside her. Tears blurred her vision as she reached out for Mary's hand, finding it and clasping it in hers. "I'm always here for you."

"P... please don't abandon me, I need you," Mary said, turning toward her, her eyes streaked with tears. This was another thing she could do: cry at a whim and summon actual tears. It hit Julia like a freight train every time.

"I won't. I'd never do that. Ron will just have to put up with it," Julia said quietly, giving Mary a kiss on her forehead and passing her a tissue.

"Put up with me, you mean," Mary murmured, as she dabbed at her eyes, her expression wounded.

Julia sighed, the weight of the moment pressing down on her. "We should go. We'll be late for your appointment."

Mary sniffled and nodded, pointing at the books on the coffee table. "Okay, sweetheart, be a dear and bring those with us, won't you?"

"Sure, Mama, I'll get them right after I get you into the car."

"Good girl. You're such a good girl," Mary said, her smile returning, soft and satisfied as if the drama of the past few minutes had never occurred.

Julia circled the wheelchair and rolled it toward the door, pausing to open it before guiding her mother down the ramp, stopping at the bottom. She engaged the brakes and then reached for the plastic mat roll placed neatly beside the first step. Lying it down over the gravel, she unrolled it until it stretched all the way to her 4WD.

Julia's previous car was a Honda Accord, which she had bought new and kept spotless, but had sold it a few years ago in favour of the 4WD at Mary's insistence because of the use of her wheelchair. The 4WD was better suited to fit it, easier to load and unload, plus, it allowed Mary to see more of the road during their days out. Julia missed that car. The 4WD was just so large and cumbersome, but it was a sacrifice she had to make so she could keep her mother comfortable.

Julia opened the rear hatch, then swung open the passenger door facing the ramp before heading back to Mary, who was watching her. She glanced pointedly at her watch, then back at Julia with a scowl that needed no words as she tapped her feet on the footrest.

Julia met her gaze with a tight grimace. "Sorry, Mother, I promise I'm going as fast as I can."

Mary nodded stiffly and didn't utter a word as Julia disengaged the brake and wheeled her to the 4WD.

"Let me help you, Mama," she said gently, extending her arm. Mary gripped it and pushed herself stiffly to her feet, wobbling dramatically with a wince on her face as she let out an exaggerated groan of effort.

Julia hesitated. "Are you okay, Mama?"

"I'm fine," Mary snapped at her, her voice clipped and harsh. "Where are the steps? You know I can't lift my leg that high," she said, jabbing a finger indignantly at the side-step on the 4WD.

"Oh, I'm sorry, I'll be right back," Julia replied. She rushed to the back of the 4WD, popped the hatch, and grabbed the small step stool.

"Hurry it up will you? I can't stand still like this for long," Mary called out impatiently.

Returning quickly, Julia placed the stool in front of the passenger side door, avoiding the scowl of annoyance on Mary's face as she climbed up with deliberate slowness, each movement emphasised with exaggerated strain.

Julia shut the door when Mary was settled and packed the stool away before circling to the driver's side. Within a few minutes, they were on their way, Julia's grip on the wheel a little tighter than necessary.

Though her mother lived only ten minutes away from the town, the trip was spent in uncomfortable silence broken only by Mary's melodramatic huffs and pointed glances at her watch, each one landing like a jab. Julia kept her eyes on the road, thankful that she had taken her propranolol before she had driven to Mary's house. Without it, she would have been a nervous wreck. Even so, she could feel the tendrils of anxiety fighting to take control of her. No wonder she felt so exhausted at the end of each day. If only Ron could understand how hard it was for her, the effort she spent just to try and stay calm day by day, maybe he wouldn't be on her back so much.

For once, luck was on her side. Arriving at the doctor's office, she spotted a car pulling out of the space directly in front of the building and immediately claimed it as it left, grateful for the small mercy.

She scrambled out of the 4WD, set the wheelchair and step stool in place, and glanced at her watch. Seeing they had five minutes left before the appointment, she exhaled with relief, the tension in her shoulders loosening a little.

With Mary settled in the wheelchair, Julia guided her onto the ramp toward the doctor's office. Dr Elias Hayes had been Mary's physician going on five years now, ever since old Dr Whitemore had hung up his stethoscope and gone into retirement. Mary hadn't taken the news well at first, but when she saw how young, handsome, and charming Dr Elias Hayes was, she changed her tune quickly.

After checking in at the front desk, Julia wheeled Mary into the waiting room and parked her across from the TV mounted high in the corner. A news reporter was mentioning something about a massacre in a nearby town linked to an escaped genetic experiment. Apparently, it was something called a 'Bliss Buddy', a creature that had been bio-engineered to support children who were heavily depressed. Instead, it had gone rogue and killed the family it had been assigned to. It was one of twenty that ended up turning on their families. Most had been contained, but the one they were talking about in particular hadn't.

Mary stared at the TV in fascination while Julia took the opportunity to scroll through her social media feed. She looked on in envy at her friends' posts, thumbing past photos of beach holidays, baby announcements, and dinner parties she hadn't been invited to in years. Most of these people she hadn't spoken to in ages. She'd tried to catch up with them. Multiple times. But each time, she'd had to cancel last minute to help her mother with something. Eventually, they had grown frustrated with her and stopped replying to her messages. She couldn't blame them.

She sighed, and her thoughts began to drift, venturing into a territory they never had before, picturing life without her mother. It was a world where she was happily married to Ron, going away on vacations, spending time on improving their house, visiting friends, going out on dinner dates, to movies, comedy shows, and concerts. A world where anxiety was a thing of the past and life was stress-free.

"Mary? Mary Hinsworth?" Dr Hayes' youthful voice rang out from the corridor, pulling Julia back to reality like a snapped rubber band. An instant tidal wave of shame and guilt crashed into her.

How could she even think something like that? Her mother was her best friend, her confidante, and her biggest support. She deserved better than the ungrateful daughter she felt herself becoming. Fighting off the tears that threatened to take over, she rose and walked over to Mary, gently taking the wheelchair handles in her hands. She wheeled Mary toward the waiting doctor, who offered her a sympathetic smile and gave a cordial nod to Mary before he turned on his heel and strode down the corridor toward his office.

"Alright, what can I help you with today?" Dr Hayes asked, settling into his chair and half-turning to face Mary and Julia, fingers poised over the keyboard.

"Oh, didn't Julia tell you?" Mary snapped, her tone sharp as she shot a glare in Julia's direction. "I'm just here for the prescription for my arthritis," she said in a sudden shift of tone as she turned back to offer Dr Hayes a charming smile.

Dr Hayes glanced between Julia and Mary, noting the tension. His lips pressed into a thin line before he turned back to his computer, the taps of his fingers on the keyboard filling the sudden awkward silence.

He cleared his throat. "Ah, yes, you're taking the... let me see here..." he continued tapping away on the keyboard, bringing up Mary's medical history. "The Hydroxychloroquine, that's right. How is that working out for you?"

Mary shrugged, a shadow of irritation crossing her face. "Okay, I guess. I was hoping it would cure me, but apparently that's not possible." Mary's shoulders relaxed slightly as Dr Hayes chuckled warmly, bringing a small smile to her face.

"No, unfortunately, it's not possible, but at least we can hopefully manage it a bit." He tapped a few more keys on the keyboard, and the printer whirred to life. "Now, I notice here you haven't had a checkup for a while. I'd like to check your blood pressure and heart rate if that's okay?"

Mary nodded reluctantly. "Okay, but I hope it doesn't

take too long. My daughter and I have a lot of things to do today."

"Of course. I won't keep you ladies long," Dr Hayes said with a smile as he wrapped the cuff around Mary's upper arm and secured it with Velcro. With a rhythmic squeeze of the bulb with his practiced fingers, the cuff began to inflate before the hiss of escaping air filled the room as he slowly released the pressure. The monitor beeped softly, and Dr Hayes leaned in to study the digital reading.

A small crease formed between his brows. "128/60," he said. "It's higher than I'd like, but not alarming." He offered Mary a reassuring smile. "Now let's check your heart rate, shall we?"

He lifted the stethoscope from around his neck and placed the diaphragm on Mary's chest, his brow furrowing in concentration as he listened. His frown deepened as he changed positions and paused again.

"Hmmm... Your heart rate is also a bit higher than usual," he murmured with a hint of curiosity in his voice. He withdrew the stethoscope and placed it back over his neck, giving Mary a reassuring nod. "Could be stress, but I'd rather not leave it to guesswork." He sat back down in front of his computer and recorded the results in Mary's patient record before he turned to face them.

"I want to get a better picture of what's happening with your heart rate throughout the day," he said, his voice measured, professional yet warm. "A quick check in the office only gives us a snapshot, but a Holter monitor will allow us to track your heart activity over the next 24 hours."

He turned back to his computer, tapping a few more

keys to re-engage the printer. It whirred to life, and he retrieved the printout, handing it over to Julia, along with the prescription for Mary's arthritis, with a calming smile. "You'll pick it up from the cardiology department at the hospital."

Addressing Mary once again, he said, "It's a compact device—you'll wear it under your clothes, and it'll record everything while you go about your daily routine."

"Is this really necessary? I feel fine!" Mary sputtered, anger and annoyance clouding her features.

Dr. Hayes simply nodded, paying no mind to her dismissive tone. "I know this is out of the blue, but given your readings and your age, I'd like to be thorough. This device will give us the answers we need."

Mary scowled and looked away, crossing her arms over her chest as the doctor continued.

"Now, no showers while wearing it, and be mindful of the wires—it's sensitive to movement. After the test period, you'll return it, and we'll analyze the results to see if there's anything abnormal."

Julia tried to hide the shock she felt as the doctor performed his checks, hiding her worry behind a composed smile each time Mary glanced her way. It did nothing to ease Mary's annoyance, and Julia groaned inwardly, knowing her mother would be even more on edge and trigger-happy than usual for the rest of the day.

"Don't worry, Doctor, I'll make sure she's taken care of," Julia said, placing a gentle hand on Mary's shoulder.

Mary shrugged it off with a sharp huff. "Fine. I don't think we have time to squeeze that in today, so it will have to wait until tomorrow," she said, gesturing curtly toward the door at Julia, indicating she wanted to leave.

"I'd recommend picking it up today if you can," Dr Hayes said gently. "I'd like to get a read on what's happening, just to make sure everything is okay."

"It can wait," Mary said, her voice firm, leaving no room for negotiation. "Come on, Julia, it's time to go."

Julia threw the doctor an apologetic glance before she stepped behind Mary and grasped the wheelchair handles. Not wanting to raise her mother's ire further and say anything, she wheeled her toward the door.

"Before you go, I'd highly recommend that you do some walking around a little without the wheelchair. In fact, it would be very beneficial for you if you did. It can help lower blood pressure and improve heart efficiency..."

"I'll take that under advisement," Mary snapped, cutting him off before he could finish, all pretence of politeness stripped away. "Julia. Let's go. Now!"

Julia swallowed hard and lowered her head as she wheeled past the doctor, her cheeks burning with shame and embarrassment.

After sorting out their account at the front desk, Julia started to wheel Mary back toward the car when Mary yanked on the brakes.

"What do you think you're doing? We have shopping to do."

Julia hesitated. "But, Mama, I really think..."

"No," Mary snapped. "I'm not going to the damn hospital to get that godawful thing. Not today. It can wait until tomorrow."

"Yes, Mother," Julia said quietly, suppressing a sigh.

A heaviness settled in the pit of Julia's gut as she wheeled Mary back around toward the shopping centre, which was just past the strip of shops flanking the medical clinic. Her mother had always been stubborn and unyielding in her opinions and beliefs. Age and distance from her siblings had only sharpened that edge. Dr Hayes hadn't labelled Mary's readings as an emergency, not exactly. But she couldn't shake a growing unease all the same.

CHAPTER FIVE

More than an hour later, the shopping was finally done. Though Julia usually enjoyed shopping with her mother, this time she found her endless umming and aaahing over groceries grating in the face of the bigger picture of her health concerns. Still, she faked the whole trip with a smile and debated the pros and cons of each item with Mary as she usually did. By the time they'd finished and Julia had packed the last of the shopping bags into the back of the 4WD, she was spent. The morning's argument with Ron, arriving at her mother's house late and facing Mary's disappointment, masking her worry about her health—it had all drained her. All Julia wanted to do now was crawl into bed and have a nap. Forget about things for a while.

"Okay, dear, let's go to the library. It should be lunchtime by the time we finish, and I'd love it if we could make some vegetable soup together. Would you like that?" Mary offered Julia a smile of affection, reaching out to give her hand a squeeze.

"Sure, Mama, that sounds great," Julia said, forcing a smile.

The library was just a few short streets away, located opposite a small park that the pair used to walk around before Mary had taken to using the wheelchair.

Julia missed those days. The free-flowing and carefree chatter that used to be theirs was becoming a thing of the past. Since marrying Ron, their chats had become more of a lecture by Mary about how marriages should work, insisting Ron was too demanding and getting in the way of their mother-daughter relationship.

Julia always tried to brush it off, change the subject, but the resentment was building, toward Ron, yes, but also toward her mother. The constant juggling and managing of both relationships was continually gnawing at her, feeding her anxiety relentlessly. This wasn't the life she'd imagined when she married Ron. Lately, she'd even found herself second-guessing everything, including their relationship. The dream of starting a family now felt further away than it had ever been, like something glimpsed through fog.

Julia pushed her thoughts aside as she pulled into the parking lot of the library. It was mid-morning on a weekday, so finding a spot near the entrance was no trouble.

"Don't forget the books, dear," Mary called out as Julia stepped out of the 4WD. She nodded absently, retrieved the wheelchair, and got Mary settled onto it before wheeling her toward the library.

"Julia, the books. What's wrong with you today? Aren't you enjoying your time with your mama?" Mary said sharply, a flicker of hurt and frustration passing over her face.

"Oh, I'm sorry, Mother. I am, of course I am," Julia said, plastering on another smile. "I'll be right back."

She hurried back to the 4WD, retrieved the books, and clutched them awkwardly beneath her chin, their edges pressing into her collarbone as she wheeled Mary up the ramp and into the library.

Inside, Julia released the wheelchair and heaved the books into the return chute with a dull thud. Her arms ached with fatigue, mirroring the mental exhaustion she'd been carrying all morning.

"Take me to the new release section, won't you, dear? I've read about everything else there is worth reading. There has to be something new in by now."

"Yes, Mama," she said flatly, abandoning all attempts at extending the conversation further. She returned to the wheelchair and steered Mary toward the new release section. Thankfully, her mother was too fixed on the display they were approaching to pay any attention to Julia's lack-lustre response.

Julia brought the wheelchair to a halt before the display and let Mary begin her scan of the shelves. She made a half-hearted show of browsing, her eyes skimming titles without registering them. Reading was the last thing on her mind at this point.

Julia absentmindedly grabbed a book at random as Mary shared her thoughts on the books she was browsing, feigning interest in the one in her hands.

"What have you got there that's so interesting?" Mary asked after a few moments, noticing Julia still staring at the book.

"Oh, um, this one looks good," Julia said, holding it out to Mary.

"Oh, Julia, really? A romance book? And not just any romance book, either; it looks like one of those dirty ones. I thought I had raised you better than that," Mary said in disgust. She flicked the book away with a shake of her head, leaving Julia standing there, her cheeks flushed, the sting of shame hitting her in her chest.

"What? No, I'm sorry, I wasn't paying attention to what I was holding. I..."

"Save it, Julia," Mary said coldly. "I'm beginning to wonder who I raised lately; I didn't raise you to be a slut, I..."

Julia froze. The word hit her like a slap. "A slut? Really, Mother? A slut?" Julia yelled out, drawing startled glances from those nearby. A librarian paused mid-shelving, turning toward them with eyes wide.

"Shhhh, Julia, keep it down," Mary hissed, her cheeks flushed. "You're embarrassing your mother."

"Oh, I'm embarrassing you now, too, am I?" Julia's voice rose, trembling with fury. "Well, I'm sorry I'm so distracted by your health issues that you should be looking after rather than being here picking out books. I'm sorry my issues with Ron are affecting you so much. I'm sorry that I picked up a dirty romance book by accident and offended you. Why does everything have to be about you?" The room fell into an awkward silence, broken only by the sound of footsteps as a staff member hurried toward them.

Julia stood there trembling, her breath ragged, before her sobbing took over. Mary sat there open-mouthed and speechless, staring at her in undisguised shock, as if she were seeing her daughter for the first time. Without a word, Mary placed the book she was holding back on the shelf, spun the wheelchair around, and began wheeling herself toward the exit.

"Don't worry, we're done here," she said, snapping at the approaching staff member as she passed by, who looked askance at Julia.

"I'm sorry," Julia managed between choking sobs, trailing behind her mother as they left the library.

The drive back was silent and thick with unspoken words. The tension was so palpable and heavy that it was close to suffocating. Mary stared out the passenger window, arms folded tightly across her chest, her body rigid with fury, whilst Julia's quiet sobs filled the car. The outburst at the library had felt good at the time, but when the anger wore off and she realized what she had done, her stomach had plummeted and knotted in dread, anguish, and guilt. She felt like a monster, like the worst daughter in the world. She wouldn't be surprised if her mother never spoke to her again after this, and she wouldn't blame her.

After arriving back at the house, Mary waited in stony silence for Julia to retrieve and set up the wheelchair before she wheeled herself defiantly into the house. Dejected, Julia followed, only to see her mother disappearing down the hallway into her bedroom.

"Pay my bills and get out," Mary called out over her shoulder, her voice cold and final. "I don't want someone who doesn't appreciate me in this house."

The bedroom door slammed shut. A second later, the

sound of the lock engaging was the final, deadly punctuation to her words—sharp, deliberate, and unforgiving. As if it were the death knell of their relationship.

Julia sank to the floor, her body wracked with sobs, the events of the day crashing down onto her like a ton of bricks. They had never fought like this before.

Julia had always managed her emotions carefully when it came to her mother, knowing how fragile she could be at times, even swallowing her own pain to keep the peace. But today, her cracks had shown. She'd let her frustration out, that which was normally restrained, let loose in the face of the guilt, shame, and exhaustion that had been slowly eroding her defenses. Now, after all had been said and done, she wasn't sure she could forgive herself. If this were the end of their relationship, she'd only have herself to blame.

As Julia's sobs slowly began to ebb, she dragged herself to her feet, straining to hear any sounds that might indicate forgiveness. Footsteps, the twist of a lock, a call of her name. But there was nothing. Silence yawned between them, vast and insurmountable like a chasm she couldn't cross. Julia took a breath that trembled in her chest, blinking hard against the sting behind her eyes.

She approached the kitchen table numbly, barely taking in the few bills that lay there. Bringing up the app on the phone, she paid them without thinking, one after the other. She felt like she was lost in a waking nightmare, adrift in a hazy, indistinct fog from which she couldn't escape. She washed the dishes next, her hands moving without thought, her body running on autopilot. Afterwards, she drew the curtains and blinds across the windows, knowing her mother would likely be in bed for the rest of the day.

Her duties finished, she walked toward the doorway and hesitated there, her entire body begging her to stay. But the words had been said, and there was no path back for her to go. No sentence that could rewind the damage.

So, she left.

CHAPTER SIX

Ron pulled into the driveway and slipped his car into neutral beside Julia's 4WD. His grip on the steering wheel was tight, his knuckles white from the strain. Thoughts of what he was going to say and propose to Julia looped through his mind as they had done all day. He exhaled slowly, then killed the ignition, reaching for his briefcase and the bunch of red roses on the passenger seat he had stopped to buy on his way back home from the florist.

It was stereotypical, he knew. Flowers were the fallback of men who'd run out of words, but he hadn't had time to come up with anything better. Besides the dying hope that Julia might say yes to the holiday, he would bring up once more. Another attempt that he was almost certain would end in failure.

He stepped into the house to an unfamiliar hush. Usually, he would hear a clatter from the kitchen as Julia prepared dinner. Or the soft hum of the television if she was curled up on the couch, waiting for him with a tired smile. Today, there was just stillness.

"Julia, honey, I'm home," he called out as he moved into the kitchen. He set his briefcase on the table before spotting an empty vase on the mantel of the kitchen window. Quickly rinsing it and filling it with fresh water, he removed the rubber band and peeled away the plastic protective covering from the flowers and arranged them inside.

When Julia still hadn't made an appearance, he frowned in concern. "Julia?" he called out, making his way down the hall toward the laundry at the back, taking a peek inside the bathroom and spare room on the way.

She must be upstairs, he thought to himself, the silence all of a sudden taking on a different meaning. Despite himself, he began to feel excitement tighten the front of his pants. Maybe she had decided he was right after all, and she had prepared something for him in the bedroom.

His heart began to pound as he imagined what he might find. Back when they were still dating and living separately, Julia hadn't been shy about surprising him in the bedroom. Lingerie, candles, soft music—all were a part of her sensual advances. She often greeted him with a wicked grin or waited for him to discover her posing playfully behind a half-closed door. Maybe, finally, he had gotten through to her. Maybe it was a sign that she was ready to move forward. That she was ready to make their dream of becoming a family a reality.

Ron grinned to himself, feeling a surge of elation flow through him at the thought. He didn't want Julia to cut her mother out, just to find a better balance. Enough so there was space for their relationship to breathe again. Maybe today was the turning point.

He was barely able to restrain himself from bolting upstairs and sprinting toward the bedroom, but he did. Instead, he let the excitement build with each step, every breath stoking the fire. By the time he reached the landing and neared the closed bedroom door, he had already begun to undo his belt in readiness.

He twisted the doorknob and pushed it gently open. The room lay in shadow, the blackout curtains stifling the last of the dwindling sunlight outside. It took a few moments for his eyes to adjust, and then they fell on the still form beneath the blanket. Julia wasn't waiting for him at all. She was fast asleep.

He let out a quiet sigh, annoyed at himself for getting so worked up, and refastened his belt, the gesture sobering him instantly. "Julia?" he murmured, approaching the bed. He sat on its edge and placed a hand on her shoulder. "Julia? Hey, are you okay?"

She stirred a little beneath the blankets and her eyes fluttered open, blinking in confusion before focusing on him.

Her eyes bore the telltale signs of crying, red and swollen with a hint of moisture still beneath her eyelids.

"Oh, sweetheart, what happened?" he whispered softly, his touch light and soothing as he stroked her hair.

Julia's eyes welled instantly, tears spilling down her cheeks in silence. He felt a sharp pang in his chest as he watched her cry, a desperate need to take her pain away, to take it on himself to spare her from its weight.

He slipped into bed beside her, his arms gently enveloping her as she trembled, her hot tears soaking into his shirt, a testament to her anguish. He held her tighter, not to fix anything, but to let her know she wasn't alone in it.

As time stretched on, Julia's wracking sobs and trembling body slowly stilled. The air was thick with unspoken emotions still clinging to her.

"I... I'm sorry," Julia whispered, her voice muffled against his chest.

"Baby, it's okay. I'm sorry too," he murmured, stroking her back gently. "I didn't mean to get so angry and frustrated on the phone. It's just that things have been so hard lately." He spoke slowly and deliberately, choosing his words carefully in an attempt to soothe without aggravating her.

"I know," she said, her voice cracking with fresh sobs, "but it looks like that might be over now."

"What do you mean? Did something happen with your mother?"

The rising crescendo of her choked weeping was his answer, and his heart lurched. First down with despair, then up on the wings of unexpected hope. He berated himself harshly, the sharp sting of guilt a stark contrast to the gentle touch he offered Julia.

A few moments passed before she spoke again. "We had a massive fight, and she said she doesn't want me in her house again," she said in a torrent of words, anxious to get them out before another wave of crying took hold.

Ron continued to hold her, moving his strokes from her back to her hair. He stayed silent, waiting for her to speak, allowing her to find the words in her own time.

"So, you remember the doctor's appointment she had this morning?"

"Yeah, it was for a prescription, wasn't it?" he said, recalling the conversation they had on the phone.

"Yeah, only the doctor wanted to do a blood pressure and heart rate check while we were there, and he found her blood pressure higher than it should be and her heart rate elevated. He wanted her to get a 24-hour monitor after the appointment to see what was happening, but she refused to pick it up." Julia gave a small, weary laugh. "You know how stubborn she is. She said she had plans and would pick it up tomorrow. From then on, it was all downhill. I was full of worry about her, and she was highly strung. Well, more highly strung than usual," she said, managing another small chuckle. "Then at the library, she saw me picking up a book, some dirty romance type. One I'd just picked up without thinking, and she told me off for being a slut."

"Ummm... Wow," Ron managed, shock almost rendering him speechless.

"Yeah, wow, alright. Anyway, I probably did the worst thing I could possibly do," Julia said, wincing at the memory. "I yelled at her. Answered back so loud that everyone in the library was staring at us."

"Oh shit, baby, I'm so sorry," Ron said, his tone soft. He gave her a tight squeeze, pressing his lips to her temple.

"You can imagine what she was like after that," Julia said, her voice low, defeated. "She didn't want to speak or look at me until we got back to her place, where she told me to pay her bills and get out. She said she didn't want someone who didn't appreciate her in her house."

Ron's jaw fell open in surprise. He'd expected Mary to

be angry, but to say that to Julia? Her own daughter? The one she'd made dependent on her, and who she herself leaned on more than she'd ever admit?

He thought about it for a moment. Actually...Was it really that shocking? Her temper and selfishness had been progressively getting worse since he and Julia had gotten married. It was undeniable that their relationship had changed after that; it had to, and it was obvious to them both that Mary had struggled with that fact. She had never handled change well, especially when it led to losing control over things.

Despite the clear issues between them, he was still concerned to hear of Mary's elevated blood pressure and heart rate. There was still care there, even if it was more for Julia's sake than anything else.

"I'm so, so sorry, sweetheart," he whispered, leaning down to kiss her forehead once more. She lifted her head to look up at him, her expression showing a vulnerability and uncertainty that he had never seen before. He lowered his head, letting his lips brush against hers, and then, with a gentle touch, he wiped her tears away with the pads of his thumbs as if trying to erase the pain that caused them.

Her breath hitched as she choked back a sob. "No, it's... it's okay. When she gets angry, it's best to stay away. Although I've never seen her get quite this bad before."

"Well, hopefully tomorrow she'll be back to her old self and give you a call first thing in the morning as usual," Ron said with a soft smile, one that he tried to imbue with as much hope as he could in lieu of certainty.

"God, I hope so," she breathed, her fingers digging into his shirt as she held him close.

"Do you feel up to eating? I'll go and get us some take-away tonight. My day has been busier than usual, and you need a rest."

She released him and sniffled, nodding with a faint smile. "Maybe some Chinese? For some reason, I'm craving some sweet and sour pork."

"Oh, a craving, is it? Are you sure you're not feeding someone else in there?" Ron teased, giving her stomach a soft poke.

"Ha ha very funny, we'd have to have sex for that to happen," she said with a giggle, the sound brief and brittle before it faded away, leaving a quiet between them.

"I'm sorry, baby. I know we haven't been very active in the bedroom, and I want to change that. Mother has been such an energy drainer that I just don't have any interest besides resting and sleeping after I see her."

"Hey, I know. It's okay."

She shook her head. "No, it's really not. It's not fair on you or me. I'm going to talk to Mother about reducing my time with her. Just maybe not until she calms down. Can you hang on a little longer?"

Ron felt a swell of emotions surge through him, chief among them relief and gratitude, but most of all, he felt seen. This was what he wanted to hear: an acknowledgement of how hard things had been for them both. Until now, Julia had always been firm in her stance about her time with her mother and unwilling to compromise. This was progress, and it gave him hope just when he had begun to lose it completely.

"Of course, sweetheart," he said, kissing her gently. "I'll

be back soon," he said, giving her one last squeeze before he headed to the door.

The rest of the night passed quickly. The pair ate together downstairs, their takeout containers spread across the coffee table, then flicked on the TV, settling on a mind-numbing, trashy reality show. Julia only made it halfway through before she decided to head upstairs for the night, exhausted by the day's events.

He watched her disappear upstairs and felt something stir within him. Something warm, fragile, and almost forgotten. A spark of happiness. Something he hadn't felt since the first heady days of their marriage. Maybe this mess, as horrible as it sounded, was a blessing in disguise for them. The start of a new beginning they so desperately needed.

CHAPTER SEVEN

Mary heard the front door close behind Julia and shot to her feet. She flung open the door and shoved the wheelchair through into the hall before she slammed the door shut behind her, feeling a fury to an extent she had never felt before consume her senses. Her heart thundered in her chest, wild and frantic, as if it were trying to claw its way out from between her ribs.

How dare Julia yell at her? And in the library of all places, right in front of everyone, so they were subject to every pair of eyes and the judgement of all. Mary had never felt so humiliated, disrespected, so furious. All she had been trying to do was talk some sense into Julia, guide her like she always had.

The anger she felt wasn't just directed at Julia. It was for Ron, too. Especially Ron. How dare he get in the way of their relationship, meddling in a bond that had once been unshakable? Before he had come along, Julia had been happier than ever, grounded and vibrant. Since the wedding, Mary had watched Julia fade into a semblance of her former self right before her eyes. No matter how hard Mary tried to steer her back, to coach her as she'd always done, nothing stuck. It was like speaking into a void. It was infuriating. The doctor's appointment only confirmed to her that it was having an effect on her physical health, too. The stress was eating away at her, and there was only one explanation. Them. That marriage. That man.

Her head began to throb in sync with the pounding of her heart, a sudden ache blooming behind her eyes. She pressed her fingers to her temples, massaging absently as if trying to knead the fury out of her skull. A heavy, defeated sigh escaped her lips.

"No more," she muttered to herself, the words laced with finality. "If Julia wants me in her life, she'll have to make a choice. It's either Ron or me," she said.

The words, spoken out loud, felt right, felt like an inevitability. She had thought it would come to this one day. It seemed that day was finally here. She was confident that Julia would make the right choice. After all, what kind of daughter would turn her back on their own mother?

A wave of exhaustion rolled over her, and she walked toward the bed, her eyes drifting to the dresser where a half-cut photo in a dusty frame of her and Julia stood. Julia was ten in that shot, with rosy cheeks and crooked teeth. Back then, Mary was still married to Harold. Once she had caught him cheating, not long after the photo was taken, she had been quick to take the scissors to it. It was her favourite photo. Just her and Julia, frozen at the peak of their happiness.

How had it come to this? The question pressed down

on her, and she felt the weight of all her years bear down on her all of a sudden.

She was just steps away from the bed when the pain struck. Pain so sudden, so savage, it whisked away the breath from her lungs. She clutched at her chest, fingers clawing as if to pry away the invisible grip that had seized her heart in a vice. It was a crushing, unrelenting force, a pain the likes of which she had never felt before. She gasped for air and staggered sideways toward the dresser, her trembling hand reaching but not finding it. The room seemed to tilt, the walls of the bedroom closing in as her vision blurred, transforming into grey static. Her heart thumped frantically, as if it were about to burst out of her chest, each beat a hammer blow sending pain radiating outward through her limbs. She drew in a breath, willing her body to fight back, to resist the heart attack this surely was, but it was no use.

As her legs gave way and she crashed to the floor, her eyes found the photo of her and Julia one last time. Her breath hitched, then ceased entirely, swallowed by the pervasive silence that had blanketed the house ever since her daughter left.

CHAPTER EIGHT

Julia woke up the next morning shaking, nausea roiling in her gut, already feeling like she was in the midst of an anxiety attack. Her skin was clammy, her breath coming in short, sharp bursts, as if there was a physical barrier stopping her from taking in more oxygen.

Luckily, Ron, halfway through getting ready for work, spotted the signs instantly. He rushed to her aid, retrieved her medication for her, and sat beside her, offering her small words of comfort. He didn't touch her; he knew from experience that even the lightest hand could feel like too much. Instead, he stayed close, a steady calming presence she could draw on if she needed to. Slowly, her tremors started to subside. She closed her eyes, concentrating on her breath and releasing the tension in her muscles. Ron let her be and continued to get ready for work.

A few minutes later, she opened her eyes to see Ron gather up his coat and sling it over one arm before he grabbed his briefcase and turned to face her. Julia felt utterly drained and exhausted already, wrung out before the day had even begun. The worst anxiety attacks always left her like this. Her nerves were frayed, her body left with no energy, and her mind on edge, bracing itself for the next attack. Any moment now, she expected the phone to ring. It was her mother's routine, almost ritualistic. But today, the thought of that conversation filled her with dread.

Ron paused, his brow creased with concern, his voice soft. "Are you sure you're okay? I can always take a sick day if you need me. I'm happy to, actually. I'd like a break. Please tell me you need me," he said, almost begging, a twinkle of mischievousness softening the worry in his eyes.

Despite the heaviness in her chest, Julia couldn't help but smile, albeit faintly. "No, I'll be fine. I need to try to fix things with Mama. If I can, that is."

Ron nodded slowly, stepped forward, and gave her a gentle kiss on her forehead. "Ok, baby, please give me a call, though, if you need me or just want to vent."

Julia took a deep breath and nodded. "I will."

Ron opened the door and paused, turning around to blow her a kiss. "I hope it goes well with Mary. And Julia?"

"Yeah?"

"Be kind to yourself today, okay?"

"I'll try," Julia said with a thin smile.

The door closed gently behind Ron. A few moments later, the distant hum of his car faded into the quiet of the morning. That was just it. The morning was too quiet. Julia glanced at her watch and grimaced. If it were any other day, her mother would have called by now.

Ever since Julia had moved in with Ron, Mary had chosen the same time every morning to call, just as Ron was about to leave for work. Julia had never asked her why, but the timing felt deliberate. Thanks to Julia's habit of telling Mary everything, she knew the time when Ron left for work. Her calls felt like they were designed as a dig, as another way she could chip away at Ron. Today, though, the silence was deafening, and somehow, that felt worse.

She paused and scolded herself for a moment, forgetting about Ron's instructions to be kind to herself. She had never thought this way about her mother before. Never questioned her, never doubted her, until yesterday.

The argument had cracked something open, the doubt she had been holding inside spilling forth like floodwater. Now it felt like it couldn't be contained, the dam permanently broken under the weight of a truth she wasn't ready to face.

She got up, brushed her teeth, and got dressed, padding downstairs to make herself a cup of chamomile tea, hoping it might coax her thoughts back in order. It was an exercise in futility. The entire time she was standing in the kitchen waiting for the water to boil and for the tea to settle, she found herself glancing at her watch, checking her phone, and then repeating the pattern over again. By the time she made it into the lounge room with her cup of tea, she was almost bouncing off the walls with nervousness. She took a few sips, but it did nothing to settle her. The silence was unbearable. Finally, she gave in, picking up the phone and bringing up her mother's number on speed dial. Her thumb hovered over the call button, her heart fluttering in her chest like a bird trying to escape its cage. She took a deep, shaky breath to steady herself and pressed the button, lifting the phone to her ear.

The steady pulse of the tone filled her ears, and she

swallowed, every ring pulling at her nerves like a taut string on the verge of snapping. She tried to prepare herself for the outburst she was sure to receive, but it was pointless. She knew how this would go. Mary need only say a few words, and Julia would crumble beneath the weight of guilt and inadequacy.

The phone rang and rang until it cut out. Julia lowered it, stared at the screen in hesitation, then tapped redial. No answer. There was only the repetition of unanswered rings, which alone spoke as loud as any words Mary might have said.

She sighed, lowered the phone again, and fidgeted idly with its case, staring absently at the blank TV screen in front of her. Mary had never seen the need to bother with voicemail. She didn't see the point. Hell, she had barely given out her number at all. When she did, it was with reluctance; the resultant scowl or angry tone made people think twice about using it.

Julia was the only relative who had it. The rest had been cut off years ago, after Mary changed her number and severed ties with what was left of the family. She'd made it clear: no contact, no exceptions. She'd even gone so far as to tell Julia to block her siblings just in case sentimentality got the better of her.

She slumped back into the lounge dejectedly. If Mary wasn't picking up, she must still be pissed off at her. It wasn't Mary's typical behaviour to ignore calls from Julia, but then again, nothing about yesterday had been typical. Her reaction, her words, the cold finality of it all. It felt like something had fundamentally shifted.

She picked up her lukewarm cup of tea and took a sip,

wondering what to do with herself. There was nothing for it; she would need to give Mary some space. For now, she would busy herself by catching up on some much-needed cleaning around the house. If she hadn't heard from Mary by midday, she would try calling again.

She tried to shove the worry aside, bury it beneath the reassurance of routine. She vacuumed room after room, emptied bins, and scrubbed the kitchen bench until the laminate gleamed, anything to keep her hands busy. Her earphones pumped in her favourite blend of ambient music, the kind she normally found soothing. Today, it barely registered.

The time was nearing midday when she stopped to take a break, brewing herself another cup of tea before sitting down in the lounge room. Once again, the silence closed in on her. Her anxiety, dulled by the busyness of her morning, began to stir again. She reached for the remote and flicked on the TV, scrolling through the channels until she landed on a mindless talk show.

Despite the chatter from the TV, Julia still found herself glancing at her watch every few minutes like clock-work. Eventually, she gave up and pulled her phone out of her pocket. She tapped the call button without hesitation, her heart skipping a beat as she pressed it to her ear. She bit her lip nervously. Any second now, Mary would answer; she had to. But the line rang out once more.

"Shit," she said, letting her phone drop on the lounge next to her with a soft thud. She leaned forward with her elbows on her knees, placing her head in her hands. This couldn't be happening. How could she have let it come to this? She was so stupid! She had tried so hard to balance things with Ron and her mother when she should have been prioritizing Mary all along. She should have been firmer with Ron, made it clear where things stood. If only she had listened to her mother, been more like her, then the fight between them would never have happened. Instead, she had let Ron get to her, wear her down.

"This is it," she whispered, the words settling like stone in her chest. "I will not let Ron and his needs get in the way of my relationship with Mother." Her voice grew steadier, more confident with each word, fuelling the decision crystallising inside her. "It's my way or the highway." The phrase was bold, spoken with meaning. A line drawn with clear boundaries. For the first time in what seemed like ages, she felt in control.

All she had to do now was smooth things over with Mary, and things could get back to normal. If Ron decided he didn't like it, then... well, he knew where the door was.

After all, Mary was aging, growing more fragile by the month, and needed her more and more. If worst came to worst and Ron left, she could chase romance later after Mary was gone, may God forgive.

She drained the last of her tea and carried the cup into the kitchen, giving it a quick rinse before placing it in the dishwasher. At the door, she took her car keys off the key hook and stepped outside, locking it behind her. The air felt a little lighter, the sun just that little brighter. Soon she was on the road toward her mother's house, feeling confident in her decisions for the first time in over a year.

CHAPTER NINE

Julia eased into her mother's driveway, the tyres crunching softly over gravel. She parked beside her mother's car and switched the engine off, but didn't move, sitting there for a few moments while she finalized her plan of attack. First, she would apologize and make it clear to her mother that she was priority number one. There would be no more resistance, no more tug-of-war over time and attention. Second, she would see about getting the heart rate monitor organized. She took a deep breath followed by another, her pulse now steady and strong.

She stepped out of the car, the midday sun casting long shadows across the gravel from the trees nearby. As she made her way to the door, a familiar tingle of nerves stirred like an old reflex, like muscle memory. Shrugging it off, she rapped firmly on the door and waited. She checked her watch; it was just after 1 pm. By now, Mary would have had her lunch and settled into her favourite chair with a cup of tea, her nose buried in one of her many library books. Julia knocked again, louder this time. A flicker of unease crept in. Mary never kept her waiting, not as long as this. Maybe she wasn't feeling well? Julia's mind flashed back to the doctor's words from yesterday, and found her unease edging toward something approaching the beginnings of panic.

She fumbled through her handbag for her keys, feeling her heart begin to thud against her ribcage as she retrieved them. Sorting through them quickly, she located the one she needed. Her hand trembled as she slid the key into the lock, twisting it until it gave with a soft click. She opened the door and stepped inside.

"Mother?" she called out, her voice thin and uncertain. She scanned the space slowly, her eyes sweeping over the familiar furniture.

To her right was the living room containing the couch, her mother's favourite chair, a coffee table, and a TV, all steeped in shadow. To the left was a spacious area that housed her mother's bookcases lined with her favourite mysteries and thrillers and a reading chair, which she had abandoned in favour of the one closer to the television. Every curtain and blind was still drawn tight the way she had left them, shrouding the house in a morose darkness. There was no sign of her mother, which immediately set off alarm bells in her mind. She had never seen the house in this state before. Her mother always had the curtains and blinds fully open at this time of the day, letting in the sunlight so she could bathe in its warmth. Not only that, but she should have heard her bustling about somewhere in the house by now, even if she hadn't heard Julia at the door or calling out to her. Beyond the hum of the refrigerator in the kitchen, the house was utterly silent.

"Mother?" Julia called out again, her voice betraying a slight tremor. A heavy feeling of foreboding began to pool in her gut. She set her handbag on the coffee table and moved toward the kitchen, her legs unsteady beneath her. She took a quick peek around the corner and found everything in its place, untouched. Too untouched. There was no sign that there had been any recent activity at all.

Julia's pulse quickened, her foreboding blooming now into full-blown dread. There was only the hallway left and the rooms that branched off it to check. First was the spare room. She opened the door and glanced inside, finding nothing beyond the dust sheet-covered furniture that used to inhabit the reading room. The light trickling from the partially open curtain covering the window highlighted the dust motes floating in the air, disturbed by the sudden airflow. It was clear the room hadn't been touched in months. She closed the door and headed to the open doorway ahead, where the laundry was located. She peeked around the corner and saw nothing out of the ordinary. The washer and dryer lay dormant, the empty clothes basket on top indicating they wouldn't be needed any time soon.

Julia stared down the hallway, its length swallowed in gloom. The shadows clung to the walls, thick and unmoving. Mary's wheelchair sat abandoned against the far wall, barely visible in the dim light. Directly opposite, the master bedroom door stood closed.

Her pulse slowed, inching back to something like normal as she headed for the door, intending to open it just a crack to make sure her mother was sleeping peacefully. She reached for the knob and twisted it gently, frowning when it hit resistance. Mary must have locked it from the inside.

"Shit," she muttered, gnawing at her lip in frustration. "Mother? It's me, Julia. Can you let me in?" she called out, her voice cracking despite her best effort to stay calm. She pressed her ear to the door. Silence greeted her. There were no footsteps, no rustling of sheets. Not even a creak of the mattress.

She hesitated, then turned and rushed back down the hallway, her chest tight once more, each breath becoming a struggle. She snatched her handbag off the coffee table and dug through it with trembling fingers until they found the familiar jingle of the keys. Returning to the bedroom door, she fumbled through them with shaking hands to find the right one.

If Mary were awake, there was no doubt she would have heard Julia by now with the racket she was making, but the room remained silent. Julia finally found the right key, her fingers missing the keyhole completely a couple of times. On the third try, it slid in, and she twisted it, pushing the door open. She immediately froze. There, crumpled at the foot of her bed, lay the unnaturally still form of Mary.

"Mo...Mother?" Julia whispered, her voice was barely audible, strangled by the sudden lump forming in her throat. She stepped through the doorway, her eyes locked onto the unmoving form lying face down on the carpeted flooring. Julia's pulse was a frantic drumbeat in her ears, deafening in the stillness.

"Mother? Mother? Oh God, no!" Julia gasped as she

rushed forward and dropped to her knees on the floor beside the motionless figure. She reached out tentatively, with a shaky arm, and jostled Mary's shoulder, willing her to stir, to groan—anything. But there was nothing. Just silence.

Frantic now, Julia seized Mary by her shoulder and rolled her over onto her back, only to recoil in horror. Mary's face was stiff, frozen in a rictus of terror. Her mouth was agape in a silent scream, her eyes wide and glazed with a milky sheen that dulled her normally sharp gaze. Her skin was pasty white, waxy, and cold beneath Julia's trembling fingers as she felt futilely for a pulse that she knew she wouldn't find and didn't.

Julia scrambled backward on all fours until she bumped against the bedframe. She stayed there, her breath hitching, eyes fixed on Mary's face, which was frozen in a last silent plea for help that Julia couldn't answer. Tears filled the corners of her eyes as a strangled choke clawed its way out of her mouth. Every breath was a struggle against the sudden, large lump lodged in her throat.

She had failed her mother, and this time, there was no repairing the damage done. The words she had left her with back at the library, so full of misplaced anger, filled her mind, piling into her as if they were blows from a heavy-weight boxer she had no defence against.

Her mother had died alone and scared, thinking that her daughter had abandoned her, had chosen Ron over their bond. The lump in Julia's throat surged as if it had expanded to fill her entire airway, making it almost impossible to take a breath. She gasped for air as the room began to tilt and narrow, her panic staking its claim over her body with icy fingers.

Black spots danced across her vision as she clawed herself toward the door. Her scattered mind temporarily regained its focus, fixing only on the meds she had in her handbag in the lounge room. Her heart was pounding a million beats a second, a relentless drumbeat against her ribs as if trying to punch its way out.

She wheezed, her oxygen-starved lungs burning as her limbs gave way beneath her, and she collapsed onto her chest, the rough surface of the carpet she couldn't feel against her cheek. Her eyes fluttered shut, and she surrendered herself gratefully to the darkness closing in and slipped into unconsciousness.

Inside Mary's mouth, a small, wavering, fur-covered limb emerged into the open, tentatively exploring the air before seven others of its ilk followed it. The black, bristling body attached to them, the size of a coin, squeezed free from underneath Mary's swollen tongue. It paused, twitching, then the spider, too, followed the cockroaches, dozens of them, already retreating in a skittering wave beneath the bed, their glossy shells catching faint glints of light before they vanished into the shadows. The room was silent once more, but the quiet was different now, no longer empty. A sliver of darkness lingered, imperceptible except to those who were attuned. It watched, biding its time for a purpose not yet known.

Hours passed. Julia lay collapsed on the carpet, her body curled near the bedframe, one arm flung outward, her breath steady. The spider crept from beneath the bed, legs splayed wide, its movements deliberate, preparing to begin its journey back to its food source. The cockroaches stirred again but remained lingering in the shadows, waiting.

Outside, the sound of car tyres crunching across the gravel broke the silence, followed by the muffled thud of a car door closing.

The spider continued on, undeterred, driven by an unusual hunger and the whispers of the darkness.

CHAPTER TEN

Ron pulled up beside Julia's car and killed the engine, slamming the car door behind him as he made a beeline for the entrance. He knocked on it firmly, resisting the urge to call out in case he raised Mary's temper even further, assuming it could get any worse at this point.

A knot of nervousness began to coil in his gut, and he found himself second-guessing his actions. Was this the right move? If things weren't bad enough now between Julia and Mary, his appearance could quite possibly make things even worse. He hesitated, torn between leaving and knocking again.

After leaving Julia that morning for work, he'd decided to call during his break, just to check in and see how she was holding up. When she hadn't answered, he had left her a message to ring him back when she was free.

The hours passed by without a reply, and his worry had eaten away at him. He'd tried to focus on work, but his mind kept drifting, picturing Julia's grief-stricken face when he'd left her. Eventually, he'd told Carol, his assistant manager, that he wasn't feeling well and left.

After arriving home and seeing Julia's car missing, he changed direction and headed straight for Mary's house. It wasn't like Julia to go this long without returning a call. Given the unusual situation with Mary's health scare and the confrontation, he'd decided that he was justified in checking up on them. Perhaps he was, after all.

He knocked at the door again, firmer this time, and decided to chance calling out.

"Julia? Honey, is everything okay?"

He listened intently for a response or some sign of acknowledgement from inside, but the house remained silent. He leaned in, pressing his ear to the door, straining for the faintest sound. Nothing. Just the cars passing by on the street and the rustle of the wind through the trees.

Ron frowned and reached for the doorknob. Anticipating resistance, he turned it, but the door opened easily, catching him off guard. His stomach dropped. Now he knew there was something wrong. Mary never left the door unlocked, and if Julia had, she'd have copped an earful and rectified her mistake instantly.

Ron stepped inside, his heart fluttering in his chest as he scanned the room, but Julia and her mother were nowhere to be seen. He moved toward the hallway and immediately noticed Mary's bedroom door ajar. Julia's keys were in the lock, glinting in the dim light.

Ron's heartbeat surged as he felt a prickling dread crawl down his back. He raced toward the open doorway and stopped there, frozen in shock.

Julia lay face down, sprawled on the carpet, with the

crumpled form of her mother just behind her. There was a thick, cloying stench in the room, an unmistakable sour-sweet reek of decay which drifted toward him off Mary's body, curling into his nostrils and turning his stomach.

He gagged and yanked his shirt up over his nose as he approached to kneel by Julia's side. Gently, he turned her over, cradling her head with care. Her limbs were limp and unresponsive, her face was pale, but he saw her chest rising and falling in a slow, steady rhythm. Relief surged through him. She was breathing. Thank God. She must have fainted, her system overcome with the shock and grief she must have felt after seeing Mary lying there.

He exhaled, his tension loosening slightly, then looked up and froze, noticing Mary's clouded orbs were staring straight at him, almost as if in accusation.

"What the fuck?" Ron muttered. He eased Julia gently back down on the carpet and rose to his feet, stepping over her to take a closer look.

Mary's body was collapsing in on itself. Her skin had slackened, slipping away from bone, mottled with sickly patches of green and black like deep bruises. Her hands lay curled on the carpet, fingers stiff and claw-like, the nails dulled with a lifeless, greyish tint.

His stomach clenched when he spotted a faint, oily sheen on Mary's forehead, something slick and unnatural, the first signs of skin breaking down. A body shouldn't break down this fast. Not from what little he knew.

Something was very wrong here. Deeply wrong. He reached for his phone, tapped 911, and held it to his ear, his eyes fixed on Mary's body. He caught movement beneath the hem of her dress, a slow, deliberate ripple in the shadows. His breath caught.

"911, what's your emergency?" came the operator's voice, calm and rehearsed. Ron's eyes widened in horror, fixed on the movement.

A small, segmented body, glistening with an unnatural sheen, hauled itself briefly out into the open. It was a millipede, its countless legs moving in eerie synchronization as it began to weave itself over the folds of fabric. It paused, antennae twitching, tasting the tainted air. Then, with patient certainty, it pressed forward, disappearing once more beneath the dress and onto the body below.

"Hello, are you there? Do you need help?"

"Oh, um, sorry, yes. My mother-in-law, she's dead, and my wife, she... she's unconscious on the floor. I found them both just now."

"Okay, I understand. Stay on the line with me. Is your wife breathing?"

"Yes, her breath is steady and strong."

"Okay, good. Is there anyone else in the house?"

"No, just us. My mother-in-law had a heart condition. I think... I think that was the cause of her death."

"Okay, sir, what is your exact location?"

"66 Blackwater Drive, Stockbridge, Massachusetts."

"Very good, sir. I have the address. Help is on the way. Stay on the line with me until they arrive."

"O... okay, thank you," Ron said, lowering himself to the floor beside Julia. He sat close, watching her chest rise and fall, willing it to keep the rhythm going, needing it to.

Ten minutes later, the distant wail of sirens caused Ron's chest to loosen a little. Julia's breathing had remained steady and strong, but his nerves were threadbare, stretched taut by the fear of something going wrong with her.

He informed the 911 operator that help had arrived, then ended the call as the front door opened and a voice called out, "Hello, emergency services, anyone home?"

"In here," Ron responded, his voice tight. He waited as the thud of two heavy sets of boots headed toward him down the hallway, purposeful and fast. Two paramedics, both young men in their twenties, stepped into the dim room, their eyes sweeping the scene with practiced urgency.

Ron gestured toward Julia, and one of the paramedics nodded, motioning him back. "Stand near the doorway, please."

Ron obeyed and shifted anxiously from foot to foot as he watched on, feeling useless.

One of the paramedics knelt beside Julia, his movements brisk and assured. "Her breathing is strong and steady," he noted. He lifted her eyelids and shone a penlight into her eyes. "We've got a response," he said after checking both.

"Sir, what happened?" the other paramedic asked, glancing between Mary and Julia.

"I... I don't know. I found them like this," he stammered, his voice barely above a whisper.

"She's stable, but we need to figure out why she's unresponsive," the first paramedic murmured, reaching for the oxygen mask.

"Is that really necessary?" Ron asked, feeling his anxiety rise.

"Sir, we need to make sure she remains stable on the way to the hospital," the paramedic said before softening his voice to add, "It's just procedure. No need to worry unduly."

Ron nodded, swallowing past the lump in his throat as he watched the paramedics continue to work.

"Ma'am, can you hear me?" Julia remained silent.

Another pair of paramedics entered, an older man and a woman, steering a stretcher into the room between them.

"Okay, let's get her sorted out first, you guys deal with the other one," one of the first paramedics to arrive said, pointing out the body of Mary to the newly arrived duo. Nodding, they approached Mary's body, kneeling down to examine her.

Together, the first team lifted Julia onto the stretcher's hard surface, securing the straps around her with quiet efficiency.

"We're taking her in. You can ride with us," one of them told Ron, his tone reassuring but firm.

Ron nodded, following as they wheeled her through the house and toward the ambulance, the weight of uncertainty pressing against his chest. Just as he hopped in the back of the ambulance, a police cruiser pulled up, its lights strobing across the front of the house. Two officers stepped out with purpose, disappearing inside to deal with Mary. The sirens wailed as the ambulance doors shut. The house vanished from view as it departed, leaving behind a nightmare he would not soon forget.

CHAPTER ELEVEN

Fairview Hospital, Great Barrington, MA

Ron sat at Julia's bedside, the steady beeping of the heart rate monitor pulsing through the sterile quiet of the hospital room. The oxygen hissed softly as it blew a gentle stream through the mask secured to Julia's face. Her eyes flickered beneath its plastic surface, movement beneath her closed eyelids an indication of her imminent wakefulness. Or so Ron hoped.

A gentle knock on the door drew his attention toward it. A man and a woman, both dressed in suits, stood in the doorway, their presence sharp and out of place against the pale walls and quiet machines.

"Good afternoon, sir," the woman said gently, reaching into her jacket and producing a badge. "I'm Detective Millie Armstrong, and this is Detective Sergeant Bob Jordan. We're with the Pittsfield Police Department. May we have a few minutes of your time?"

Ron frowned, uncertain. The word detective landed

with weight. With one last glance at Julia, Ron nodded and followed the officers out into the corridor, trailing the pair toward the waiting room. A nurse passed them on the way, heading into Julia's room. He watched her disappear behind the door just as they entered the waiting room, and the woman spoke again.

"Sir, I'm sorry to pull you away from your wife, but we just have a few questions for you if you don't mind."

Ron turned to face the two who stood before him, their suits crisp, the one speaking to him wearing a smile of reassurance, which softened the tension in his chest.

She looked to be around his age, with brunette hair pulled back into a ponytail and a petite build. She was naturally pretty, with high cheekbones, accentuated by her on-point minimalistic makeup. The man standing beside her was the older of the two, with greying hair and tired eyes. He flipped open a notepad, preparing to take notes, his expression bordering on disinterest.

"You're Ron Mathews, am I correct?"

"Yes, that's correct," Ron replied, trying to focus on the conversation but distracted by the arrival of a doctor speaking with the nurse outside Julia's room.

"We won't keep you long. I know you want to get back to your wife," Millie said, her soft voice gently drawing his attention back. "Okay, let's start with what happened."

Ron gave a short nod and took a deep breath. "I was at work and had been trying to contact Julia since the morning. She'd had an argument with her mother, Mary, the day before, and... well, Julia struggles with anxiety, so I wanted to check in." He rubbed his hands together, his voice tightening. "She wasn't answering, which isn't like her, so I left work early and headed home. I noticed her car wasn't there, so I figured she must have gone to Mary's house. When I got there, I found the door unlocked, which was strange. Mary's obsessive about locking up. I went inside and couldn't see any sign of them."

He paused, swallowing. "Then I saw Julia's keys still hanging from the lock of Mary's bedroom door down the hall. When I entered, I found them both on the floor. Julia was unconscious but breathing. Mary was... gone. Looked like she had been dead for days, which doesn't make sense."

Millie studied him quietly, her expression unreadable. Beside her, the detective sergeant scribbled down his words in his notepad, his face impassive, almost bored.

" What made you think that?"

Ron shifted uncomfortably. "I don't mean to be rude, but it was pretty obvious. There was a foul smell in the room, like something rotting, and her skin was slick and loose, like it was decaying. Her eyes were clouded over, her body was gaunt. Do I need to go on?"

"No, I think you've covered it, thanks," Bob murmured, with an obvious tone of disgust in his voice.

Bob's pen paused mid-air, hovering over his notepad. "Did you touch anything? Move anything?"

Ron's jaw tightened. "I did. Julia was lying on her chest, face down. She was breathing, but I wanted to make sure there was nothing obstructing her airway, so I rolled her over onto her back and checked. I've had first aid training, so I didn't think there would be any harm. Once I made sure everything was okay, that was it. I didn't touch anything else." Ron's tone had a defensive edge now. Unlike Millie, Bob's tone wasn't nearly as warm. He radiated the weary detachment of someone who'd seen too much for too long.

"Was it possible someone else could have gotten in?" Millie asked, shooting a pointed look at Bob, who gave her a gruff, unapologetic smile in return.

"You mean like a break-in? Like someone killed her?" Ron shook his head. "No, I don't think so. Julia had taken Mary to see the doctor the day before, and he'd found some sort of heart condition. The doctor urged her to get a heart rate monitor, but Mary refused, which is why she and Julia had an argument."

"I see," Millie said, exchanging a glance with Bob. Her lips pressed into a thin line as something unspoken passed between them.

"We'll need the doctor's details. Just to double check, of course," Millie said, returning her attention to him with a warm smile.

"Of course," Ron replied. "I'll have to get it from Julia when she wakes, if that's okay?"

"No problem, Mr Mathews. I'll give you my card," Millie said, reaching into her pocket and pulling out a business card with her details on it. "We'll also need to speak with Mrs Mathews once she's stable. We'll coordinate with her doctors to find the right time."

Ron nodded, but a niggling feeling of unease began to creep in as he watched the pair. Something didn't sit right. Why were detectives questioning him? Weren't cases like this usually handled by regular police officers?

"May I ask a question?" Ron said, hanging on to that thought before his limited capacity to think returned to Julia.

"Of course," Millie said.

"Why are detectives involved in this? Isn't this just a case of death by natural causes?"

Millie hesitated. "Well, normally we'd say yes, but the condition of Mary's body raises questions. We're just trying to understand how she got in that state."

"Millie," Bob muttered, his voice laced with warning.

Millie glanced at him with an abashed look on her face.

"Okay, that's enough for now," Bob said, meeting Millie's glance with a look of annoyance as he flipped his notepad closed. "We'll be in touch, Mr Mathews. Just sit tight."

"If you remember anything else, don't hesitate to call. I hope your wife gets better soon," Millie added before the pair turned and walked down the corridor, their footsteps fading into the sterile background noise of the hospital.

Ron stared after them, lost in thought, the business card limp in his hand, his chest weighed down with unease. The image of Mary and the wriggling millipede he'd seen flashed through his mind and sent an icy dread through his veins. He shuddered to think that there might have been other creepy crawlies present besides just the one he saw. Perhaps Mary's house had a bug infestation, but that didn't explain her accelerated decay.

"Mr Mathews?"

Ron blinked and looked up to meet the calm and purposeful eyes of the doctor he had seen before chatting to the nurse at his wife's door.

"We have some good news," he said. "Your wife is awake. She's asking for you."

The words hit him like a release valve, the pressure in

Ron's chest loosening. He hadn't realised how much tension he had been holding in his body until now.

"Thank you, Doc," Ron said, a smile spreading across his face.

"We'd like to keep her for observation and run a few tests over the next twenty-four hours," the doctor replied. "But barring anything unexpected, I can't see any reason why she can't go home tomorrow."

Ron exhaled with a shaky breath. "That's fantastic news, thanks so much, Doc," Ron said, his voice thick with relief.

They exchanged a handshake before Ron turned and strode down the corridor toward Julia's room, his heart lightened with something close to hope.

CHAPTER TWELVE

Julia's eyes opened slowly to the hum of fluorescent lights above, their glare making it difficult for her eyes to adjust as she found her way to consciousness. The world felt wrong, like waking from a dream only to find a nightmare waiting.

She struggled to reconcile where she was as her fingers twitched against the stiff hospital sheets, the fabric coarse and unfamiliar. This didn't feel like home. It wasn't home.

Something was pressed over her face, forcing air into her lungs, and panic began to bloom. Her fingers scrambled over the unfamiliar object and pulled it free, and she gasped in shock, her body struggling to adjust to the sudden change as she choked in air that wasn't being forced on her.

Strange beeping sounds erupted from next to her, and her anxiety skyrocketed as she instinctively pulled away, straining the cords that had been attached to her. A small cry of shock escaped her lips as her hands found the source of the strain and pulled them away, ripping off the cords attached to the patches stuck to her.

Then it hit her. A sharp, suffocating weight crushed her chest, forcing the air she had managed to draw in from her lungs. Her mother. She was gone.

She gasped, feeling the rawness of her throat, her body beginning to tremble as a memory surged forward—the house, the silence, the stillness of her mother's form on the floor.

"No..." she croaked. The word barely escaped, strangled by her grief.

Her mother had been her everything. The center of her world, the voice in her ear, the presence that shaped every thought, every decision. And now she was gone.

Julia's breath came in uneven bursts, her pulse hammering against her ribs. She turned her head, searching, desperate for something familiar, something hers. But the hospital walls were blank, indifferent. She was alone.

"Ron? Ron? Where are you? I need Ron."

A nurse appeared, speaking in soft, measured tones, but Julia barely heard her. The words meant nothing. Nothing mattered. She lay there as the nurse tried to console her, but her mind was fixed on her mother and all that she had lost. Someone appeared before her next to the nurse and said something, but she couldn't hear through the rush of blood in her head, the pounding of her heartbeat. The two departed after a few minutes, appearing in and out of her vision as time and reality blurred, her mind overcome with a loss too great to comprehend.

Finally, someone familiar appeared before her. Ron.

"R...Ron?" she said with a frown, trying to focus her swimming vision on him.

"Yes, honey, it's me," Ron said softly, laying a hand on her arm and squeezing it.

"Excuse me, Mr Mathews, I just need to give Julia here her medicine," a nurse said, appearing from the wavering light behind Ron as if she were a ghost.

Ron nodded as she stepped up beside Julia's bed and offered her the small, familiar capsules. It took her brain a few seconds to realize they were her anxiety meds. The nurse helped her raise the headrest of the bed so she could sit up and adjusted the pillow behind her head. Julia reached out with a trembling hand, her fingers scrambling in the small bowl offered to her by the nurse to find them. She caught one between her fingers and slid it into her mouth, taking a sip of the water from the cup the nurse gave to her in her other hand. She took the other pill and rested back on the pillow, watching the fluorescent light spin lazily above her.

"How are you doing, honey?" Ron asked gently.

She moved her head so she could focus on him, trying to take in his words. She felt curiously numb, as if the weight of her mother's loss was too much to bear and her body had chosen to shut down, now only able to absorb the minimum of external inputs.

"I... I don't know... I..." her voice trailed off, before she felt her tears welling, a pressure building in her head as if it were about to explode. And explode it did, in a torrent of tears as the wall her mind had built up to protect her gave way to raw, unfiltered emotion.

She cried until she felt like there were no tears left to shed, she screamed until her voice was raw, she hit out at Ron, trying to rid herself of the pain, the overwhelming pain that never seemed to stop flowing from an endless well. Reality gave way to a blur of lights, faces, voices, and sound, all converging into a nightmarish blend that she couldn't comprehend as reality dissolved into chaos. The next thing she knew, the world around her faded into merciful darkness.

"Mr Mathews? Just wanted to let you know that visiting hours are over, but we have arranged for you to stay as long as you need. Unfortunately, we can't allow an overnight stay..."

"That's okay, thank you."

The voices drifted through Julia's weary mind, rousing her from sleep. She blinked a few times and was relieved to find her vision steady and the lighting dimmer.

The loss of her mother hit her once more, sharp and fresh, like a reopened wound. Tears welled again, unbidden.

"Ron?" Julia whispered; her throat felt swollen, her voice frayed from the screaming she barely remembered.

"Julia, hey baby, I'm here. Oh, sweetheart," he said as he immediately rose from his chair, leaned over, and wrapped his arms around her in an awkward hug, doing his best to avoid the tangle of cables and the IV line that had been reattached during her lapse into unconsciousness.

She buried her face in his shirt, drinking in his scent and the familiar warmth of his arms around her. Tears flowed down her cheeks as sobs began to wrack her body, and he held her to him tighter, rocking her gently back and forth.

"It's okay... It's okay... everything will be okay," he whispered.

She clutched at him, digging her fingernails into him as if trying her hardest to meld with him so he could take some of the pain and loss she was feeling away. She desperately wanted to believe him, but she didn't know how things could ever be okay again.

"I don't think it will," she choked out. "It can't be. My mother's gone, and I'm nothing without her. Nothing." Her body shook, every motion fragile as if she could break at any moment.

He pressed his cheek against her temple. "Hey, we'll get through this together, okay? You're not alone. You'll never be alone. I'll always be here for you, always."

Julia nodded automatically. She so desperately wanted to believe him. She needed to. She held onto that hope as she continued to sob until her body gave out and exhaustion pulled her under. Sleep took her, the deep and dreamless kind, as she was still cradled in Ron's arms.

CHAPTER THIRTEEN

24 hours later
Massachusetts Office of the Chief Medical Examiner,
Boston, MA

Dr Samuel Knox stood over the transport table, fingers curled around the zipper of the body bag. As he drew it open, a wave of stench hit him—wet, sour, and far too strong. He reeled back in disgust and gagged, one hand instinctively rising to cover his mouth. This was wrong.

The decomposition was too advanced for a woman who had been dead for less than two days. According to the preliminary report performed by Dr Williams, Knox's designee, the patient, Mary Hinsworth, had been found roughly eighteen hours after she passed away from a suspected heart attack. She had been kept in cold storage ever since she arrived. Yet the smell told a different story.

He snatched his mask from the hook, fitted it over his face, and immediately breathed easier, the air filtration system doing its job and buffering against the lingering stench.

Knox frowned in confusion, his eyes narrowing behind the fogged lenses of his glasses beneath the mask as he stepped back up to the transport table. His gloved hands hovered just above the body, reluctant to touch what lay before him, wary of contaminants despite his protection.

He drew a slow breath and exhaled, adjusting his mask as he leaned in and reached into the bag to begin the careful process of lifting the body out. Stringy flesh clung to the lining, pulling away like melted wax. He grimaced, adjusting his grip to minimize damage. Once the body was fully transferred to the examination table, he stepped back and stared.

The body was in bad shape; the skin had begun to slip and peel away from places where it should have remained intact. The bloating was excessive, distending the abdomen unnaturally, and the discolouration was far beyond what he would expect at this stage.

"This doesn't make sense," he murmured, more to himself than for the recorder blinking quietly beside him.

He had just stepped back in to adjust the limbs for external examination when something caught his eye. There were strange markings along the inside of Mary's arm. He lifted it gently with the underside of his scalpel and recoiled. There were bite marks and pieces of rotten flesh missing. He spotted something flat and brown a little further underneath. Reaching for his tweezers, he pulled it out and lifted it before his glasses. His eyes widened in disbelief. It was a cockroach, covered in the slimy flesh it had been embedded in.

He set the bug down into a nearby dish and turned the body onto its side, inspecting the back. The skin there was ravaged, gnawed, hollowed, and crawling with evidence of infestation. His heart thudding, he lowered her back onto the examination table.

His stomach was roiling with nausea, but still, protocol demanded he continue. Taking another deep breath to steady himself, he cleared his throat and spoke for the recorder's benefit.

"Beginning internal examination. Will run tox screens to rule out environmental accelerants. Signs of unexplainable advanced decomposition."

He reached for his scalpel, pressing the blade against the abdomen. The tissue gave way too easily, like wet paper, revealing something Knox wasn't prepared for. The organs were liquefying. His breath caught in his throat. This wasn't normal decomposition. This was something else.

Knox had seen death in all its forms—violent, peaceful, slow, sudden. But this? This was different. Unnatural. And he wasn't sure he wanted to know why.

He took a moment to calm his racing heart. He still had to investigate the heart for signs of myocardial infarction.

Knox's brow furrowed as he exposed the organ and began to examine it. Like the other organs, it too had begun to liquefy, but he was able to trace the path of what remained of the coronary arteries to a blockage. A telltale sign of myocardial infarction. The heart had seized, starved of oxygen, shutting down in a final, irreversible moment.

"There it is," he muttered, before he said in a louder, steadier, clinical voice, "Initial findings confirm the preliminary report. Cause of death: cardiac arrest due to myocardial infarction."

He clicked off the recorder and stood motionless, staring down at the body. The air felt heavier now, pressing against his chest despite the mask. The smell, the skin slippage, the insect damage, the liquefied organs—none of it aligned with the timeline. None of it made sense.

His hands trembled slightly as he peeled off his gloves. He couldn't shake the feeling that he was missing something. Something big. The kind of thing that didn't belong in a morgue, or maybe didn't belong anywhere.

He stared at the cockroach still lying in its dish, half-submerged in tissue. His stomach turned again.

It was time to call his boss. This sort of shit was way above his pay grade.

CHAPTER FOURTEEN

Pittsfield Police Department, Pittsfield, MA – 14 miles north of Stockbridge

Detective Millie Armstrong stared at the incomplete incident report from the Mathews case on her monitor and rubbed her forehead with a weary sigh. At twenty-six years old, with a year of detective work under her belt, the job had lost none of its ability to surprise her. More often than not, her instincts had proven reliable, honed by years of meticulous fieldwork and sharp intuition. But this case... There was something about it that unsettled her. A quiet, persistent feeling that continued to gnaw at the edges of her thoughts.

It wasn't like her to second-guess herself. Her rise through the ranks had been swift. She had graduated from Northeastern University in Boston with a 3.9 GPA in criminal justice, then entered the Boston Police Academy, where her acceptance had been nearly instantaneous. After just over three years in the field, she had earned a reputation for her thorough investigative work, catching details others often overlooked. That reputation hadn't gone unnoticed —her promotion to detective had come earlier than most, fast-tracked by a string of commendations and the quiet endorsement of senior brass.

Despite her youth, she had become one of Pittsfield's fastest-rising stars, landing a partnership with Detective Sergeant Bob Jordan, the most seasoned investigator on the force. His experience was unmatched, his instincts razor-sharp. And yet, even with his guidance, this case felt different.

Bob had assured her that despite the condition of the mother's body, all signs pointed to her suffering from a heart attack. Given the appointment she had the day before, he'd called it a near certainty. It didn't explain the early stages of decomposition visible on her body, but he was certain the autopsy would offer a reasonable explanation.

Normally, she would have taken his word for it, filed the statements, closed the folder, and moved on, but after seeing the scene for herself, she was not nearly so certain of Bob's instincts this time. Something felt off, and she wasn't ready to let it go.

There had been something that had raised the hairs on the back of her neck like static as soon as she had entered that bedroom. A heavy, almost tangible gloom had filled it, and she was sure she had felt a shift of air in the atmosphere around her when she stepped in, as if the room itself had inhaled. It had fairly crackled with a quiet, seething anger and malevolence, directed at her from the lingering shadows in the corners like something sentient, watching her every move. It had coiled around her stomach, sour and unrelenting, leaving her nauseous before she had even laid eyes on Mary.

Luckily, after a brief examination of the body and its surroundings, Bob had called it quickly and let the paramedics wrap things up. Millie had barely registered his words, so focused was she on the room itself. Something was wrong in there, and as soon as she left, the oppressive feeling had lifted as if whatever had been watching her had simply… let go.

When she described the unsettling feelings she'd experienced and asked Bob if he'd noticed anything strange, he'd just shrugged it off. No big surprise there. Bob was a straight shooter, a no-nonsense type of operator, believing in the power of science and facts. Millie was open to the belief that some things existed that couldn't be explained. In fact, she had grown up in a household where her grandmother had openly believed in the spiritual, the supernatural. As a kid, she had loved the thrill of her grandmother's spooky stories, her hair-raising tales told in hushed tones around a crackling fireplace. But she hadn't experienced anything in her life to believe like her grandmother had. Until yesterday.

"You know you actually have to type something for words to appear on the screen, right?" Bob's baritone voice broke through her reverie as he approached her cubicle, a big grin on his face.

"Ha ha, very funny," she replied, rolling her eyes. "I was just thinking about the case. Everything points to it being an open and shut one, but that body…"

"Yeah. Speaking of." Bob leaned against the desk. "I just got a call from the medical examiner. His preliminary findings point to a heart attack, like I figured, but there are some... oddities about the body he's looking into. He's going to do a toxicology screen to work out the cause of the decomposition. But there was something else he found, too."

Millie waited for him to continue as he waved to someone passing by, gave them a nod, and then proceeded to stare off into the corner of the office. *Lost in that big old full head of his,* Millie thought fondly to herself.

"Well?"

"Oh, um... yes... Sorry, I'm getting old and get distracted easily. You know, when I'm not in the field. Just five years away from retirement now, and it can't come quick enough."

Millie folded her arms and stared at him, tapping her fingers and checking her watch in a show of exaggerated impatience.

"Well, sorry, Ms. Impatient. Just wait until you get to my age, you'll be dying for retirement too."

"I doubt I'll live that long. What are you, like one hundred and thirty?"

"You're a cheeky one, I'll give you that," Bob said, chuckling. "Anyway, they found about a dozen cockroaches inside the old lady. They'd been feeding off her, which is highly unusual, to say the least. The medical examiner says he might need some tests done of the room she was found in, just in case something triggered her condition."

"Triggered? You think she could have had some help in dying?" Millie asked, her eyebrows raised in surprise.

"It didn't strike me that way, but who knows? Humans never fail to amaze me."

"Okay, so how long will the report take?"

"The doc has gotten the go-ahead to get the testing fast-tracked, so two to three days for preliminary results. Maybe two weeks or longer for the full. The coroner will keep her on ice until then."

"That's going to make Mr and Mrs Mathews happy, I bet. Normally, she would be released within seventy-two hours. This delay's going to raise questions, maybe even tempers," she muttered, shaking her head.

Bob gave her a dry smile. "Well, who knows, it could still be that one of them is responsible for her death. We still need to question Mrs Mathews." He checked his watch and frowned. "According to the doc at the hospital, she should have been released and back home by now. We should go question her."

Millie blinked. "What? Like right now? Don't we want to let her get settled first? Remember, she suffers from a bad case of anxiety disorder..."

Bob snorted. "Yeah, yeah, okay, you softy. I'll organize someone to take a look at Mrs Hinsworth's house to see if she has an insect problem. Tomorrow, we'll go and interview Mrs Mathews. Until then, have fun staring at your screen. Make sure you use your fingers to type. Telepathy doesn't work so well on computers."

Millie laughed. "You're a riot, Bob."

She turned back toward the screen, shaking her head with a wry smile. She typed in the newest information Bob had given her and read through it again. There was one missing gap where Mrs Mathews' interview would go, below that of her husband, Ron.

Some people get all the luck, she thought to herself,

thinking about Ron. He'd caught her attention as soon as they'd begun the questioning in the waiting room at the hospital, and she had instantly felt herself drawn to him. Sure, he was handsome, just a few years older than her, and seemed to have his life together, but she could also see how caring, loving, and attentive he was when it came to Julia.

She sighed, thinking of her own failed romantic life. Perhaps she shouldn't be so quick to judge based on one meeting. After all, her judgement in her personal life was far different from that in her professional. Here, she was in her element. Outside of it, not so much. She'd always seemed to fall for the guys who had major red flags, which she somehow didn't see until it was too late, and she found herself in a relationship. Now here she was, pining over a man who was married. What was wrong with her?

"You need to get laid," Millie muttered, realizing too late she'd said it out loud.

A snicker drifted toward her from the cubicle opposite, where Detective Maggie Wilson sat. She leaned forward with a sly grin.

"Oh, honey, don't we all," she whispered, giving her a wink.

"Oh, um... I didn't mean to say that out loud," Millie said, turning a bright shade of crimson.

Maggie laughed and gave her a mischievous grin. "Don't you worry. I remember what it's like to be young."

"Oh God," Millie groaned, her face burning, placing her arms on the table and burying her face between them, wishing the desk would swallow her whole.

CHAPTER FIFTEEN

R on stood in the doorway, staring at their bed where Julia lay curled up beneath the covers, finally at rest after hours of tears and uncontrollable sobbing. Her stillness felt fragile, like a temporary calm between storms. He chewed at his fingernails absently as he considered what to do to help her, worry pulsing through his veins. He'd so far been lucky with his own parents, both of whom were still alive to this day, still calling on Sundays. He had no reference for dealing with a loss of this magnitude, no blueprint to follow to help with the kind of pain Julia was drowning in. Not to mention the guilt Julia must be experiencing.

Since he had brought her home a few hours earlier from the hospital, Julia had swung between raw, unrelenting grief and self-loathing. At times, she had pushed Ron away from her in anger, furious, blaming, and inconsolable. At others, she had clasped him to her as if he were the last person on earth in a world that had come undone.

Eventually, the storm of emotion had ebbed as Julia exhausted herself into a near-catatonic state. She had moved like a sleepwalker, devoid of anything but mechanical motion as he had guided her up the stairs. After tucking her into bed, he'd sat beside her, holding her hand in both of his. Her tears still came, slow and silent, and he wiped them away with care, hoping that his presence would do something, anything to make her feel less alone. She'd just lain there, eyes open and unfocused, until sleep had finally claimed her.

His heart broke for her, but there was nothing he could say to make it better. All he could do was be there next to her. Be whatever she needed him to be. Words and actions would not heal or soften the pain. Unfortunately, only time would do that. Time, and maybe therapy, but that would come later after she'd had a chance to grieve.

Ron took one last glance at Julia before he pulled the door closed behind him quietly and padded downstairs to make himself an instant coffee. Sitting down at the kitchen table, he stared out the rain-slicked kitchen window and let the comforting sound of the drops drumming against the roof soothe him for a few minutes as he drank. Before he realized it, the coffee was gone, and he was upending an empty cup.

He set the cup aside and pulled out his phone, typing out a quick email to Carol and his boss, Mike, to let them know he would be off work for a couple of days to be with Julia and make funeral arrangements.

After hitting send, he leaned back in his chair, then decided to make another coffee, this time using the machine. He'd need it if he was going to look into funeral arrangements, and he needed to be ready at a moment's notice if Julia woke.

He checked his watch; 4:30 pm. Still early enough for a coffee without sabotaging sleep. Although he wasn't sure how much sleep he would get anyway.

As Ron rose from the table, he noticed how dim the kitchen had become. The rain clouds outside were blocking the late afternoon sun that usually poured through the windows at this hour of the day.

He switched on the lights, and they buzzed dimly overhead, casting a tired glow that matched Ron's exhaustion and the mood that clung to the house. Shuffling toward the coffee machine, his shoulders sagging under the weight of the day, he fumbled with the bag of coffee beans and tipped them into the grinder. The familiar scent of them was like the presence of a best friend, comforting and soothing.

He selected a double-shot espresso, and the machine whirred to life, its mechanical hum blending with the patter of rain against the window. Ron leaned against the counter, blinking slowly, watching the slow drip of dark liquid filling the cup below.

He must have spaced out for a few seconds, as the next thing he knew, the cup was filled, steam rising from its surface and curling upward, vanishing in the air. He picked it up and revelled in its warmth as he took it to the couch and set it on the coffee table.

Pulling his phone from his pocket, he began his search for local funeral homes. Whether it was from the rhythmic sound of rain, the warmth and comfort of the couch, or the monotony of scrolling through countless listings, he soon found himself in a battle against his eyelids to stay awake. He switched on the TV for distraction, took a sip of his coffee, and continued his search.

In the gathering darkness of the living room, the glow of the television flitted across Ron's tired face, casting restless shadows that stretched and shrank with each shifting frame. His phone sat heavy in his hand, the screen illuminating name after name of funeral homes and their ratings. He scrolled aimlessly, the words blurring together, their meaning pressing down like a weight against his chest as he thought about what was to come and how devastated Julia would be.

Outside, the rain increased its intensity, lashing against the window, its sound and rhythm soothing to Ron's tired ears. After draining the last of his coffee, he leaned back on the couch, making himself more comfortable. The soft cushions enveloped him like a lover's embrace, coaxing him deeper into their hold. His eyelids fluttered, each blink lasting longer than the last, and he forced his eyes open each time but found himself losing the battle. He should keep going. He needed to focus. But the murmuring of the voices on the TV, the lull of the rain, and the warmth of the couch were all conspiring against him.

Without realizing it, sleep pulled him under.

He opened his eyes to silence, his gaze drawn toward the TV where static now ruled. The room was drenched in darkness except for the luminescent, steady glow of the screen. A thin, high-pitched whine began to ring in his ears, directing itself from the TV toward him before thunder cracked, its boom reverberating through the room, sending picture frames crashing to the floor to a chorus of breaking glass. Ron pushed himself back onto the safety of the couch and covered his eyes as shards flew in every direction. The room shuddered before a loud ripping sound drew his attention to the shadows of the ceiling where an ever-widening crack tore through the plaster, sending plumes of dust downward to coat the floor below.

"What... what the fuck is happening?" Ron shouted, confusion and panic flooding his system. He knew it must be a dream, yet the vivid sights and sounds were all too terrifyingly real.

As if in answer to his cries, the ceiling above parted with a loud snap, creating a gap that the rain gladly filled, and sending plumes of smoke erupting from the TV as it found its way into its electronic components.

Ron shifted, trying to get off the couch and run for the stairs to get Julia so they could get the hell out of there, but it was no longer soft beneath him; it had transformed instead into something rigid. Its arms were now restraints that snaked around him and pinned him in place. He struggled, straining against the bonds that seemed to hold impossibly tight, as the sound of footsteps, slow and deliberate, reached his ears. All other sounds, including his own grunts and cries, were suddenly muted as if someone had hit a button on a remote, but the footsteps, they continued, and they were coming ever closer.

Ron stiffened as something took shape in the flickering light—a shadow, its edges undefined, its presence suffocating.

He tried to move, tried to scream, but his body remained heavy and silent, pinned in place. He urged himself to wake, put all of his effort into doing so, but it was futile. He was trapped between the world he had left and whatever waited in the dark.

The shape continued to thicken as the darkness in the

room drew towards it, surrounding it like starving beasts, feeding, shaping it, creating something that shouldn't be, couldn't be. The air crackled with a wrongness that crawled up Ron's spine, pressing against his ribs like a hand gripping too tightly.

A whisper of laughter reached Ron's ears, distorting into a parody of itself before it turned into a harsh, cackling laugh. A laugh that spoke of rot, of age, of something far older than any physical presence had a right to be. It was familiar, yet unspeakably wrong.

And then a face emerged, and Ron screamed.

Ron sat bolt upright with a start, a shriek caught in his throat, the memory of his last one still lingering in his ears, refusing to let go. He was covered in sweat, and the couch cushions now held the warm, salty smell of his perspiration. Everything was back to what it had been.

Except the scream hadn't stopped. It was different, raw, panicked. It came from above.

Julia. It was Julia.

The realization struck with cold finality, slicing through the last remnants of sleep like a blade. He shoved himself off the couch, his limbs sluggish, his heartbeat thundering, the terror from his dream bleeding into waking life as he ran for the stairs.

CHAPTER SIXTEEN

Julia thrashed on the mattress, the sweaty bedsheets tangled around her body as she opened her eyes and screamed from her already ragged throat. Immediately curling into a ball, she hugged her knees to her chest and cried, trying to forget the horrific scene of her discovery of her mother that replayed itself over and over in her mind, whether she was asleep or awake. She couldn't seem to escape it. If she did, it wasn't for long. It was relentless. When she wasn't consumed by her memory that was burned into her like a brand, she was tortured by her own thoughts. A cycle of self-blame, hatred, shame, guilt, and anger that repeated over and over again. There was no relief. How could she keep going like this, and did she want to? What was life without her mother? Until Ron, Mary's love was all she'd ever known.

Ron. The thought of him twisted her stomach in tight knots as white-hot spikes of anger shot down her spine. He did this. He had caused the strain between her and her mother. Why did she choose him over her? His constant complaints, his obvious hatred of her. How could she have put up with it for so long? Her anger seethed and boiled within her gut, coiling within like a viper ready to strike. She wanted to hurt him. Hurt him like he'd hurt her. He was so lucky to have everything: a dream job, both parents alive and well, a house, money, her. Why couldn't something bad happen to him? The golden child, the one who always got what he wanted. It sickened her. She wanted him to suffer. Wanted him to...

Ron burst through the door and ran to the bed, climbing in next to her and clasping her to him, ignoring the sweaty mess they were both now lying in.

"Hey... Hey, sweetheart, it's okay. I'm here. Let it out, let it all out. I'll always be here for you," he whispered into her ear. His body was a warm and steady presence pressed against hers.

Julia's resistance crumbled as her anger faltered, replaced by shame and guilt over the feelings she never should have had. Her mind was a whirlwind of chaotic thoughts and misplaced emotions, and she knew it. Her meds. She needed her meds.

"Ron, can you get my meds for me? I'm a mess, I can't handle this... I can't handle..." She couldn't continue through the lump in her throat as her swollen eyes filled with tears once more, something her body seemed to have a never-ending supply of.

Ron sat up slowly, brushing a damp strand of hair from her forehead. "Shhh... sure, honey, I'll be right back, okay?" He rolled off the bed, gave her a kiss on the forehead, and headed for the bathroom, where the familiar sound of the cabinet door opening reached her ears.

A few moments later, Ron returned and handed her a couple of pills and a glass of water, and she washed them down quickly, desperate for the mess in her head to quiet. She sat back, closed her eyes, and breathed deeply as she waited for the pills to kick in. Her heart was fluttering in her chest to the point where it was almost painful. She felt Ron's hand fall on top of hers, warm and steady. He gave it a gentle squeeze and, slowly, breath by breath, the chaos receded, and she began to return to something resembling calm.

She opened her eyes to the concerned gaze of Ron. He smiled at her tentatively as if he were unsure which version of her he was facing this time. She couldn't blame him. One minute she was lashing out at him, and the next she was clinging to him like a lifeline. The whiplash of grief and her anxiety made for an unpredictable combination. She knew she had to give herself grace; she'd lost her mom after all, but still, her treatment of him had been terrible.

She managed a fragile smile before her face crumpled, and tears overtook her once more. She looked at Ron, wanting to be saved, wanting him to make the pain go away, but knowing there was nothing he could do. This was grief, pure and human, a road she had to travel alone.

"Oh, Ron, how am I going to do this?" she whispered, her voice quivering. "I was asleep, and the scene of me finding Mom replayed over and over in my mind, just like it does when I'm awake. It's like there's no escape from it, whatever I do. I just want it to stop. I want to remember her how she was, not as I found her." She burst into a torrent of tears, sobs tearing through her as Ron pulled her into his arms. He held her close, his hand stroking her hair with a tenderness that only made it worse.

This was what her mother used to do when she was little, when her nightmares were simpler and could be soothed away. Her sobs turned to gasps, her throat tightening as if grief itself had reached inside and gripped her lungs. She clung to him, choking on memory.

Gradually, she lost herself in Ron's arms, drawing on his strength and presence to ground her. It was part of what had attracted her to him from the beginning. It was the same steadiness she'd leaned on with her mother, a strong anchor in a storm. She pulled away and looked earnestly into Ron's eyes, his face softening as his eyes met hers.

"You... you won't leave me, will you? You're all I have left. I don't know what I'd do..."

Ron cupped her cheek gently. "I'll never leave you, baby. I promise. I'm here for you always."

Julia nodded, reassured by his words, and buried her head in his chest, drawing strength from the steady beat of his heart for what she had to ask next. She pulled herself away from Ron once more and leaned back against the headrest of the bed, her breath coming in shallow waves.

"What about... What about Mom's funeral? I don't know how these things work. Do we need to start organizing it now?"

"I'm looking into it now, actually," Ron said, his voice gentle and careful. "I think we have to wait for the police to contact us when Mary has been released before we can book in a date, though."

Julia's stomach clenched at the word release, but she said nothing.

He paused for a moment, with an uneasy look on his face. "The detectives... they want to ask you a few questions about... about what happened. Just part of the procedure, you know." He smiled wanly at Julia, reaching out and giving her hand a squeeze.

"Ye... Yeah, of course," Julia murmured, nodding, as fresh tears welled again.

"I'll be there with you if you need me, okay?" Ron said softly. "They're going to contact us about a time, but I think they might leave it until tomorrow. You need to settle in first."

Julia nodded again, feeling weariness press down on her like wet sand. The meds had well and truly kicked in now, and she felt bone-tired. She yawned and slid back down beneath the bedcovers, fumbling to pull them into place before Ron took over and repositioned them, tucking them in securely.

"I'm going to get some rest. Wake me if the police ring, okay?"

"Sure, honey," Ron said, leaning over to give her a kiss on the forehead as she closed her eyes.

"Oh, before I go, what was the name of the doctor you saw with Mary?"

"Dr Elias Hayes," Julia mumbled, already beginning to drift off.

"Thanks, sweetheart, sleep well."

She barely registered the sound of his footsteps as he left the room. Darkness enveloped her like the flick of a switch, and the soothing balm of sleep pulled her temporarily away from reality.

CHAPTER SEVENTEEN

The next day

Ron paced the hallway outside the bedroom, his footsteps muffled against the worn carpet. Through the door, he could hear the low, gravelly voice of the male detective... Bob was it? And the lighter, more expressive tone of the attractive one, Millie.

Attractive? Where the hell did that come from? He hadn't even given her a second thought since they'd met her. But still... there was something about her...

Jesus, Ron. What the fuck?

His wife was in there, retracing her steps of the most horrific day of her life, and here he was entertaining thoughts of another woman he didn't even know. He swore at himself and refocused on the voices just barely audible through the door, just in case Julia called out for him.

He stifled a yawn. The night before had been hell. Julia had tossed and turned all night, jolted awake by nightmares, and that, combined with the lingering horror of his own that he had woken from on the couch earlier, had made him fearful of closing his eyes. What paltry amount of sleep he had managed to get was hardly enough to keep the tiredness at bay.

He was thankful he'd let his work know he wouldn't be in the next few days, though if things continued like this, he would likely need to take the entire week off. Maybe more.

He sighed and checked his watch. The detectives had been in there for thirty minutes or so now. Surely, they had to be close to wrapping up. As if summoned by that thought, the bedroom door opened, and the detectives stepped out. Millie gave him a warm smile as Bob turned to close the door gently behind him.

"May we speak to you for a moment?" Millie asked.

"Ah sure, is... is she okay?"

"She said she wanted to be left alone for a bit. Can't blame her, what that woman has been through..." Bob said, shaking his head in sympathy.

Millie gave a quiet nod in agreement. "C'mon, let's go downstairs, give her some space."

"Right," Ron said, leading the way. "Do you guys want anything? Tea? Coffee?"

"Coffee would be great," Bob said. "I noticed your coffee machine when I came in. The latest model is it?"

"Bob!" Millie hissed, shooting him a glare.

"No, no, it's fine," Ron said with a chuckle. "It *was* the latest. That was before they announced a new one, which comes out next month."

"Ha, of course. Companies, hey? Always chasing the next upgrade. Release something shiny, rake in the cash. Problem is people fall for it and keep buying them, so they keep doing it. Not that I'm saying *you're* one of those people, of course," Bob grinned as Millie elbowed him in his side in annoyance.

"Forgive Bob, he has no damn filter."

"Hey, honesty goes a long way in law enforcement."

"Yeah, so does basic courtesy," Millie muttered, giving him a shove.

Ron laughed as he showed the pair to the lounge room. "You guys are definitely far more relaxed than the stiffs I thought you'd be," Ron said.

"Hey, I might be old, but I can still be stiff when I need to be," Bob joked, causing Ron to burst into laughter as Millie's face turned crimson.

After noting their preferences for sugar and creamer, Ron disappeared into the kitchen. A few minutes later, he returned with three steaming mugs and placed them carefully on the coffee table.

"So, um... what happens now?" Ron asked as he settled into the armchair opposite the detectives.

Millie took a sip of her coffee before answering. "Well, now that we have Julia's statement, we just need to wait for the autopsy results."

Ron nodded, then hesitated. "How long is that likely to take?"

Bob picked up his mug and took a sip, leaning back on the couch. "Well, you see, that's where things take a strange turn," he answered carefully, his eyes intensely focused on Ron.

Ron squirmed in his chair, the muscles in his jaw tightening as he took in Bob's words and his gaze. "What... what do you mean? Is it something to do with the bugs? The condition of her body?"

Millie's eyes widened as Bob set down his mug, grabbing his notebook and pen from his pocket.

"How do you know about the bugs?" Bob asked, a subtle tightening around his mouth betraying nothing of what he was thinking.

Ron's cheeks flushed. "Sorry, I should have said something in the interview, but I was so worried about Julia, you know?"

"It's okay," Millie said, offering a thin smile. "Please go ahead."

"Well, after I saw Mary, I called 911, and while I was on the phone, I saw a... a millipede, I think it was, crawl out from beneath Mary's dress. It disappeared back underneath shortly after, but man, it was weird."

"I see," Bob said with a nod. He scribbled something down in his notebook before he set it aside and leaned forward, a furrow creasing his brow, his face taking on an expression of scepticism. "See, the funny thing is, it *is* weird. The type of bugs the medical examiner found aren't usually drawn to dead bodies. We've already checked with a pest inspector, and he said there are no signs of an insect infestation." He stared accusingly at Ron, his gaze intense. "So, the question is, how did such a concentration and variety of insects get there?"

Ron stiffened. "Are... are you accusing me of something?"

"No, just asking a question. Hoping you might have the answer." The friendly warmth in Bob's eyes was gone, replaced by a cold, smug smile.

"Look, I don't know what they were doing there, and I don't know how Mary got that way so fast, but I *do* know neither myself nor Julia is at fault here," Ron said angrily, his cheeks flushed and his eyes flashing in annoyance.

Bob's eyes scanned Ron, his lips pursed, before the tension in his face released, and he gave a short nod. Picking up his mug from the table, he drained its remains in one gulp and stood up.

"Time for us to go, Millie," Bob announced, tilting his head toward the door. He turned back to Ron, extending a hand to him.

"Thanks for your hospitality, Mr Mathews. We'll be in touch if we need anything else."

Their handshake was strained, with Ron's lingering anger hanging heavy in the atmosphere.

Millie rose from the couch, casting a wistful glance at her mug, which was still a quarter full. She offered Ron a brief, apologetic smile and followed Bob to the door.

"Wait," Ron said, his voice edged with urgency. "When will Mary's body be released? You know... for the funeral."

Bob paused, hand resting on the doorknob of the front door. He turned halfway, his expression unreadable. "Yeah, about that," he said, glancing at Millie. "Millie, do you want to do the honors? You're better at this type of stuff than I am." Bob gave Ron a faint smile and a nod and turned the doorknob, disappearing through the door.

Millie sighed, watching him go before turning back to face Ron with a softened expression. "I'm so sorry about Bob. He can be a bit Jekyll and Hyde when he's in detective mode."

"Yeah, I can see that," Ron said with a tight, humorless smile. "Is there something wrong?"

"The ME is concerned. Mary's condition raised some red flags. He's pushing for a tox screen, expedited, thankfully, but even with strings pulled, it'll take two to six weeks." Millie hesitated, a sad smile tugging at the corners of her lips. "Until then... we'll have to hold Mrs Hinsworth's body. I know that's not what you wanted to hear."

Ron's thoughts instantly turned to Julia and how the news would affect her. He felt sick to his stomach. This wasn't what either of them had expected. Julia was already unravelling and barely holding herself together. How would she cope with this? With her mother's body suspended in limbo? Without the closure she desperately needed?

"Oh, shit," Ron muttered, sighing deeply. "Is there any way to get her released before then? It's just with Julia's anxiety and all, I don't know how she's going to cope with a delay like that."

Millie shook her head, a look of genuine sympathy on her face. "I'm really sorry, Mr Mathews. Two to six weeks is rushing it already. Trust me, I would push it if I could. I lost my father a few years back. Grief's brutal even without anxiety riding shotgun." She stepped forward, taking his hand in hers and giving it a squeeze. "Just take care of her, okay? It's obvious how much you love her. Be there for her, be her rock, and she'll pull through."

She looked down at her hand on Ron's and quickly released it, her eyes darting away from his. "I have to go. Good luck with everything, Mr Mathews. We'll be in touch if we need anything else. Remember, you also have my card if you need to pass along any information that you think might be important." She gave him a brief smile, her cheeks flushed slightly, and opened the door, heading toward the running Chevrolet Impala parked in the driveway.

Ron lingered for a moment after waving them off, then shut the door behind him and leaned against it, closing his eyes.

Mary's funeral was on hold now for weeks at least. Julia would be gutted. She needed closure. If not that, then a firm date for when she could expect it, but she had neither. And then there was the other thing. The way Bob had suddenly gone all bad cop on him. Were they suspects? Was that what this was? The tox screen would clear things up, but an investigation was the last thing he'd expected to be tangled in. And Millie... what was with the hand-holding thing, the softness in her voice? What was that? Sympathy? Something else? It was all too much to deal with right now. He needed some time to let things settle, to sort through the noise and figure out what to say to Julia without making things worse, if that were even possible.

CHAPTER EIGHTEEN

One week later

R on rolled his Lexus ES up the driveway, the crunching of gravel accompanying each revolution of its tyres. He pulled to a stop next to Mary's dusty car and cut the engine, his eyes fixed on the house before him.

A week had gone by, but it had felt like months to Ron. Each day had dragged like wet laundry, his worry for Julia deepening with every passing one. She hadn't left the bed since coming home from the hospital, apart from trips to the bathroom and back. She'd barely eaten, every meal largely untouched. Talking was a rare commodity. A few short, sharp words on occasion were all that she managed before collapsing back into bed. He had taken to sleeping on the couch a few days ago. Her constant glares and grunts of annoyance had made it clear he was doing more harm than good by being there by her side at night. Even checking in and asking if she needed anything earned him the same cold response. It was like she'd built a wall around herself, and all he could do was pace the perimeter, hoping to find a crack.

He loved Julia, but the strain this was taking on their already frayed relationship was unraveling their fragile connection. Grief had a way of warping everything. It and her anxiety problems were a formidable combination that he could only hope would shift once Mary's body was released and they could finally have the funeral. Until then, he needed to hold on, to have faith.

He'd wracked his brain for days, trying to work out what he could do for her, but so far, nothing he had tried had landed. Every attempt had been met with either anger, withdrawal, or indifference.

To make matters worse, his boss had been on his back about returning to work, and so he had, with no small amount of reluctance and guilt, a few days earlier. Now here he was on his latest attempt at reaching Julia, parked outside Mary's house on his way back from work. He wanted desperately for her to know that he was still here. That he still cared.

He tightened his grip on the steering wheel, his knuckles a pale white against the leather, dreading what he was about to do. He had passed by the house several times over the last week, waiting for the day when the police tape would be removed. Now that it had, and he was here, all he wanted to do was turn around and go home.

He blew out a breath and stepped out into the late afternoon gloom to face the house. It loomed before him, cloaked in the long shadows cast by the surrounding gums and elms. The wind rustled their branches, sending curled-up brown leaves drifting down to the ground, joining a carpet of them already littering the driveway.

Fall still had a few weeks left in it, but the yard already looked halfway abandoned. Ron could only imagine what it would look like by season's end, overgrown and choked with weeds and leaves. Mary would be rolling in her grave at the sight if she knew. That is, if she had a grave; maybe rolling in the freezer?

Ron grimaced a little with guilt at the hint of amusement he got from the thought. Mary had always been one to make sure appearances were as perfect as she could make them. Hedges were trimmed to regulation height, leaves swept away before they had a chance to settle, every weed pulled almost as soon as they'd sprouted. Her gardener, who came twice a week, used to take care of all of that. Now, nature had free rein.

There was a heaviness about the place, as if the very atmosphere of the house had been affected by Mary's presence and matched her energy. Ron shook the thought off. Melodramatic nonsense. Sure, Mary had been horrible—controlling, cold, a master of passive aggression—but this was just his imagination running riot. He was tired. Overstimulated. He just needed to get in there, get what he needed, and get out.

Approaching the door, he fished for Julia's set of keys, searching through each until he found the one with the chipped blue plastic. He slipped it into the lock, and it gave with a reluctant click. He pushed the door open to a protesting groan as dust bunnies scattered like startled insects, caught in the shaft of light spilling across the carpet from the doorway.

The blinds and curtains were still drawn, just as they were the day he found Julia and Mary, amplifying the house's sombre mood. There was a faint sour, musky stench to the air, the kind that soaked deep into carpet fibres and refused to leave, no matter how hard they were scrubbed. He knew the source. Mary's body had leaked, its juices soaked deep into the carpet, leaving behind a part of her that could never be erased in a final, grotesque imprint. Ron's stomach turned, his throat tightening as he fought to keep the bile down.

He quickly turned towards the curtains overlooking the driveway and yanked them open, then slid the window across to let in some light and air. Pausing there to let the welcome breeze of the autumn air drift into the room, he gulped in its freshness gratefully. Turning around, he surveyed his surroundings. Despite the welcoming glow and warmth that flooded the room, there was still a chill in the house, and not the kind that could be fixed with a heater. This was the kind that seeped into bones. One that went beyond the physical.

He paused, collecting his thoughts. Where would Mary have kept her photo album? His first guess was the bookshelves. He entered the lounge room and scanned them, but found nothing beyond Mary's beloved thriller books that filled every inch of their shelf space.

He recalled the time Julia had described the pictures her mother had when she had opened up to him about her family early in their relationship. Unless Mary had tossed them out, they must be in the house somewhere. Then again, he wouldn't put it past her to do that, given how she had cut off her family. He hadn't been to the house often enough to be familiar with where Mary kept things, but it was small, and Mary was methodical. There couldn't be many places to look.

Aside from the bedroom, the storeroom was the other logical place to keep the photos, so that's where he headed next. He stepped into the hallway, greeted by its gloom. Pockets of darkness swallowed the edges of the walls on both sides, leaving only the faint outline of the carpet ahead of him. Here, the chill seemed more intense, and it wrapped around him in tandem with the shadows and the growing scent of decay. Then, near the storeroom door, he spotted a flicker of movement. It was just at the edge of his vision, a shift of the shadows that darted toward the storeroom door. He stopped with a sharp intake of breath, straining to see what it could have been.

"Hello?" he called out tentatively. He wasn't sure what he'd seen, but it hadn't felt like a trick of the light. Was there someone in here with him?

He took another step forward. "Hello, is anyone here?" There was no answer, just a stillness stretching out around him in the darkness like something waiting.

He shivered involuntarily, rubbing his arms over the jacket that should have kept him warm but seemed to have lost its ability against the cold that had seeped into the hallway. He paused and gave himself a shake, letting out a strained chuckle. He was letting his imagination get the better of him. Nothing but memories lingered here now.

He neared the storeroom door and came to a halt, his pulse quickening. He was certain the door had been closed when he'd left the day he had found Mary and Julia. Now it stood ajar. The darkness seemed to deepen as he stood there, thickening and cloying, as though something was waiting inside. Watching.

"C'mon, Ron, get it together," he whispered. No doubt the cops had been through the house, checking things out, and had left it open.

Despite the rational explanation, he couldn't help but feel a tinge of apprehension as he stepped up and pushed the door open, his chest tightening. As he had expected, nothing leapt out. There was no movement, no sound.

He felt the tension ease from his shoulders as he reached for the light switch and flicked it on. A faint buzz emanated from the light fixture above as it struggled to accommodate the flow of energy through its aged wiring before it came to life, flooding the room with welcoming artificial light. He surveyed the room, sweeping his gaze across the old furniture draped in drop cloths. The room was stacked tall with them, from Mary's old couch that she had replaced with the new one to old rickety kitchen chairs, their legs barely visible beneath the cloths. Judging by the layer of dust on the coverings, nothing had been disturbed since they'd been placed here.

He was just about to turn around to leave when he heard a whisper, soft and weightless, barely more than a breath against his ear.

"Roooooonnnnn."

His heart instantly began to pound. He froze in place, his body tense, rational thought telling him it was nothing. A trick of the mind. But there was no mistaking what he'd heard.

A wave of air washed over and past him, curling around the dust cloth-laden furniture like unseen fingers tracing forgotten memories. Long undisturbed dust flew into the air, filling it with the scent of age, wilted flowers, and remnants of perfume as the dust cloths rippled with a wind that sprang from an unseen source. No draft from a broken window, no whisper through a cracked door could have moved the way it did, with deliberate intent.

Above Ron, the light stuttered, its glow waning with each hesitant flicker as the globe emitted a faint 'tick' sound followed by a soft hum as it struggled to maintain its intensity against something it was in an unseen war against. Then came a sharp buzz, erratic and desperate, before a final snap, and the room fell into near complete darkness.

The heavy curtains against the window fluttered as if something unseen had brushed past them. Beneath the cloths, old newspapers, yellow and brittle from the passage of time, trembled and crackled, rustling like murmured voices disturbed from their rest.

The wind seemed to speak of intent, of a presence that was trying to pull his attention to something as it threaded its way through the stagnant air. That something was a cardboard storage box, partially hidden beneath a cloth that fell away to reveal it in the dim light available before the wind stopped, sending the room into stillness once more.

Ron stood there stunned, his body shaking, afraid to move lest whatever had swept through the room return, and this time with ill intent. His eyes fell on the box that was now exposed, and he scanned the room warily. It was layered in darkness, but remained still, the movement now replaced by a pregnant silence as if whatever had revealed the box waited for his next move.

He shivered, fingers of ice shooting down his spine as he

glanced nervously around him before he finally found the courage to move again. His gut screamed at him to get out of the house, but he had come this far. Perhaps what he was searching for was in that box. Without thinking, he grabbed it and followed his instincts, getting the hell out of there.

CHAPTER NINETEEN

R on pulled into the driveway with a long, exhausted sigh. The quiet comfort of the suburban street was a jarring contrast to the oppressive atmosphere he'd left behind at Mary's house. He eyed the box next to him with apprehension.

He had no idea what was in it, only that whatever it was had seemingly wanted him to take it. Now that he was back home, the whole thing just seemed ridiculous. It was clearly his overactive imagination playing tricks on him, freaked out by returning to a house where he had found Mary in a state of rapid decomposition.

He chuckled, shaking his head as he grabbed the box and climbed out of the car. A few minutes later, he was on the couch with the cardboard box perched on the coffee table as if it were a guest waiting to be acknowledged. Normally, he'd head straight up to see how Julia was doing, but he wanted to check out the box in case it did contain the photo album he was looking for. Maybe he could surprise her with it and help lift her out of the funk she was in.

He flipped open the box and was presented with some crumpled sheets of yellowed newspaper packed inside, intended to protect the remnants of the past it contained. Nestled at the top was an old music box, its paint faded and chipped. The lid was slightly ajar, waiting for someone to wind it so it could finish its cycle. A faint puff of fragrance emanated from its surface, a ghost of the past lingering from where it once had been placed, most likely on a desk near perfume and makeup.

Next was an antique porcelain doll, its glassy eyes wide and vacant, staring at nothing and everything. Ron recoiled instinctively and shivered in disgust. He knew that was the style of dolls back in the past, but he'd always found them creepy. His mother had kept a few on a shelf in the hallway when he was a kid. Their prim little figures with frozen smiles and dead eyes had haunted his dreams until she finally packed them away. He picked this one up with a grimace, holding it at arm's length, half-expecting it to spring to life. He set it beside the music box and wiped his hand on his shirt with a shudder.

Underneath the next layer of newspaper lay a stack of old handwritten letters, bound tightly with twine, their parchment curled at the edges. The ink on the topmost letter had bled downward, staining the next few beneath. They felt brittle, thinned with age, their words little more than whispers and echoes of emotions of the past trapped in paper. He felt an urge to undo the twine and scroll through them. To see if they held the answers to the mystery of what had made Mary the horrid person she had become, but he resisted. He set them down on the coffee table before turning his attention back to the box's remaining contents.

He brushed aside the last of the newspaper, and his fingers met something firm and leather-bound. He lifted it out, and a surge of relief washed over him. This was exactly what he had been searching for, something he hoped might offer Julia something other than grief. The photo album. Its edges were worn and softened, its cover embossed with an ornate design of time-dulled gold and silver. He opened it just long enough to verify the photos within were of Mary and her family, and quickly closed it. The less he saw of Mary, the better. At least he could give Julia something more than the pixelated memories on her phone. Something to hold, a tangible bit of history from a past she treasured.

He gathered up the photo album and placed the letters, doll, and music box back in the box, placing the lid back on it before he headed upstairs. The bedroom door was closed, a familiar sight that he had grown used to over the past week. He gave an obligatory knock on the door before he entered.

Julia was curled up on the bed, her swollen eyes blinking in confusion at his intrusion.

"Hey, sweetheart," he said, moving toward the bed and perching on the side of it, giving her a soft smile. Julia blinked a few more times before her eyes settled on the leather-bound album clasped to Ron's chest. Her eyes widened in recognition.

"Is... Is that Mom's old photo album?"

Ron nodded. "It sure is. You told me about this album

when we first started dating, and it clearly meant a lot to you. I figured it was worth tracking down."

Julia sat up, her face softening and a faint smile tugging at her lips as she reached for it. Ron's heart leapt at the sight. Maybe, just maybe, he'd gotten this right.

He passed it over to her with care. She pressed it to her chest, her eyes closing as a few tears slipped free.

"Thank you," she whispered, her voice barely above a breath.

Ron pulled a tissue free from the box on the nightstand and dabbed gently at her cheeks before he leaned over and placed a kiss on her forehead. "Do you want me to stay for a little bit?"

She hesitated, then shook her head slowly. "No, it's okay. I'd like to be alone while I go through it."

Ron nodded, keeping his tone of voice light. "Sure, honey. Can I get you anything? Something to eat? A drink?"

"No, it's okay. I had something a little earlier."

"Okay, are you sure? I didn't see any signs of..."

"Ron, please just leave it, will you? I'll eat when I feel up to it. I don't need you constantly badgering me about it."

"Okay, okay, I'm sorry. I just worry about you, you know?"

"Well, don't. I can look after myself," she snapped, turning her back on him, the photo album still firmly pressed to her chest.

Ron lingered a moment, then stepped out, closing the door with care. He rested his forehead against its cool, smooth surface and silently cursed his own stupidity. Idiot.

All that effort gone to waste in the space of a few words. He should have known better, given how she had been behaving. "Stupid, stupid, stupid," he muttered, pulling away and heading downstairs. He had barely touched alcohol in the past year, but tonight was going to be an exception.

After a meagre and bland microwave TV dinner that tasted more like cardboard than anything else, he moved into the lounge room. He pulled open the cabinet door near the TV unit and was greeted by a bottle of whiskey, its amber depths catching the glow of the light above, hinting at the comfort and numbness it offered.

He grabbed it, fetched a glass from the kitchen, and returned to the couch. The remote clicked in his hand, and the television blinked to life. He flicked through the channels, settling on a current affairs show providing just enough noise to keep the silence from swallowing him whole.

The liquid swirled in the glass as he poured in a generous measure. Setting the bottle down, he lifted the glass to his lips and took a deep pull, grimacing as the harsh taste burned his tongue but feeling the heat slowly spread through his chest. The second sip came easier, the third even more so.

He pushed himself further back onto the couch and pressed the cool rim of the glass to his temple for a moment before taking another sip. Before he knew it, the bottle was half-empty and the edges of the world had softened, the memory of the argument still there, still aching but softened beneath the whiskey's haze.

CHAPTER TWENTY

The next day

It had been just over one week. Over one week of pain. Over one week of suffering. Over one week of putting up with someone she was beginning to despise more and more. Ron was trying, she knew he was. He'd even brought back Mary's photos yesterday, providing a small mercy in a sea of grief. But it wasn't enough. She couldn't stop herself from putting more and more blame on him with every hour that passed. At first, she had fought against it. Knew that her emotions were off base and clouding her judgement, but now she no longer cared. Her mind had screamed for the need for someone to take the blame, and besides her, Ron was the only other one involved in the chain of events leading to Mary's death. The love she felt for him was hanging on by a tenuous thread, and it was constantly under assault from her own mind.

Sleep, too, had brought no relief. Every time she had closed her eyes, she heard whispers—soft, sibilant, insidious. They had slithered through her dreams, wrapping around visions of Mary's face as it twisted, warped, and decayed into something unrecognizable, a grotesque echo of her, bloated with fury and grief. It had tortured her, this thing that wasn't Mary but wore her face. Both with words and with accusatory silence, with eyes that burned with hurt and betrayal. But lately, she hadn't been the target. Its anger had shifted, directed now toward Ron. The whispers now placed Ron in their crosshairs, insisting he was to blame. They had worn her down, and she was beginning to believe them. Not because it made sense, but because it made the pain easier to carry.

The last few days, while Ron had been away at work, had brought her something she hadn't felt since before Mary had passed. Peace. With him gone, the air felt lighter. Her thoughts were clearer. She had even managed to get some sleep without the horrific dreams. But the moment Ron returned, so did the nightmares. They crept back in like mould under wallpaper—quiet, invasive, inevitable. Each time it happened, the connection grew clearer. It no longer felt like a coincidence. It was him. His presence stirred something dark inside her, and she didn't know if she could shift it away with him being in the same house with her anymore.

Today, though, today had been different. After Ron had left, she had slipped into a thankful sleep, but this time she had dreamed. What it was about, she couldn't remember, but something had stirred in her. She had awoken with a need, a purpose, a sense of direction. As if the dream had handed her a map she couldn't read but somehow knew how to follow.

She picked up her phone. The screen lit up with notification after notification, meaningless noise she already knew wasn't what she needed. But one notification in particular caught her eye—a social media reminder of a shared memory with her mother from a year ago. She was hesitant to view it. Her eyes were already raw, inflamed, and sore from crying over the photo album. The thought of more tears felt unbearable. Still, she tapped on it, perhaps because of curiosity or perhaps because of something deeper.

The image appeared instantly. It was Mary and Julia standing in front of a building housing her mother's favourite opera show. Her mother was so happy that night, so radiant. It was one of the rare times Julia had managed to get to smile like that in the past year. Tears blurred the screen as her eyes fixed on her mother's face, studying every detail, every line as if just by doing so, she could bring her to life right in front of her. If even just for a moment. Just long enough to say everything she hadn't.

She remembered how hard it had been to get the tickets to that show. She had missed out on the initial announcement, so by the time she had logged onto the website, all the best seats were gone. No matter how many times she checked over the weeks, waiting and hoping for more shows to be announced, none were. Eventually, she had stumbled on some through a reseller's website and snagged them, paying more than double the original price. Still, it was worth it, just to see her mother smile like that. Ron, of course, had arced up about it, complaining about how much she'd spent on them. That memory cut through her grief like a cold wind and brought an end to her tears. She had almost forgotten. How many times had he done that—picked apart her choices, her joy, her efforts? It felt like it was all that he'd done since they got married and moved in together. She felt the familiar seething anger return, and she scrolled past the memory, trying to quell it by distracting herself.

Post after post of happy snaps and statuses of her friends living their best lives presented themselves to her. That was the problem with social media. It was always showing the façade of happiness, like the negative side didn't exist. Like grief and mess didn't exist. Everyone competing against each other for the most likes, either giving them a boost to their self-esteem or a quick dopamine hit, trading validation for vulnerability. She scrolled on, numbed by the sameness of it all. Then, a video stopped her thumb mid-swipe. She sat up quickly and tapped it, upping the volume on her phone.

A pure black screen with the words, "Where the departed linger, and the impossible becomes possible," was displayed in white lettering before it was replaced by a lady in her early 40s sliding into view. She was standing before a decorated table, with gold and black lettering that Julia assumed was Latin. The backdrop displayed shelving with various occult paraphernalia. Dressed in crimson and black, the lady's long black hair cascaded over her shoulders, framing a face with porcelain skin and dark, gothic makeup that sharpened her every expression. Her eyes captured Julia's attention, piercing blue that seemed to hold an unsettling wisdom and the promise of answers to mysteries. Her entire presence was magnetic, and Julia found herself invested before she even spoke a word.

She smiled and spoke. Her voice was velvet, slow and deliberate.

"Hi, I'm Lilith Darkmoon, proprietor of 'Beyond the Veil'. Loss does not mean silence. The ones who have passed still linger, waiting—watching. You do not have to bear the weight of suffering." Pictures of people standing at funerals, a photo of the person recently passed, appeared on screen one after the other, emphasizing her point. *"I can help you ease your burden. Bring closure. Connect you to the ones who left too soon and mend what is broken."* She leaned forward, the light catching the shimmer of silver rings on her fingers as she performed a flourish with her hands, a phone number appearing underneath. *"Send me a message on this number, and we can begin the process of healing."*

The video lingered for just a moment longer, her gaze locking onto the camera and through it into Julia's eyes, as if she could see her and was talking directly to her. Then the screen faded to black.

Julia saved the phone number and set her phone down on the mattress, leaning her head against the bedrest and feeling the beginnings of hope stirring in her chest. Could this be what she was meant to see? Meant to do? She had never believed in the occult, mind readers, fortune tellers, or new age medicine, but this felt different. Like the ad had been waiting for her. Like her mother had placed it there, nudging her from the other side. Perhaps it meant there was a chance to mend what was broken. To say goodbye properly. That thought alone was worth exploring. After all, what could it hurt to give it a try? Anything was better than the suffering she was going through right now.

She picked up her phone, her hand shaking as she

tapped out a message and hit send. Her heart pounded madly as she waited for a return text. She didn't have to wait long.

'166 Ashen Way, 2 pm. I can help you with what you seek. Bring a photo of your cherished one with you.'

A smile unfurled on her lips, tentative but real, breaking the heavy shadow that had settled in her chest. Thanks to Ron, she also had the picture she needed. The world, for just this fleeting moment, felt full of possibilities again. It was enough to get her out of bed, into the shower, and dressed.

Feeling somewhat human again, she perched on the edge of the bed and opened the photo album, thumbing through its pages in search of one to take with her. Before she had a chance to choose, a photo slipped loose and fluttered to the floor. She reached down and picked it up. It was one of the more recent photos of her mother in the album, even though it had been taken fifteen years ago. Yet, it felt like fate, as if that particular photo falling out, Ron's retrieving the album, and her seeing the ad were all meant to be. A predetermined destiny, like someone was guiding her through the paths she needed to take to mend things with her mother.

Tears pricked at the corners of her eyes, but she got up quickly. There would be plenty of time for tears later. She carried the photo downstairs and slipped it into her handbag with care before making a quick breakfast of strawberry jam on toast. The rich aroma of coffee filled the kitchen as she prepared a mug for herself, placing it and the toast on the kitchen table as she sat down.

The meal satisfied her hunger, but the frantic flutter in

her chest intensified as the minutes ticked by agonizingly slowly, counting down the time until she needed to leave. Finally, the moment arrived, and with a rush of adrenaline, she snatched her handbag and her keys and burst out the door.

CHAPTER TWENTY-ONE

Julia felt butterflies in her gut as she followed the GPS past Main Street toward the streets leading out of town. Here, the roads were patchy and uneven, speaking to the fact that few people traveled down them. Still on the outskirts, there were a few shops here, mainly general stores and antique dealers with faded signage and cluttered windows. Places that didn't fit in with the mainstream polished shopfronts back in town. She took the next left turn off at the roundabout, tyres crunching over loose gravel that had spilled onto the road from its edges. According to the GPS, the next turnoff was Ashen Way.

The signs of civilization were sparse here, giving way to the increasingly dense presence of trees, their twisted branches stretching like skeletal fingers toward the sky. A few farmsteads came into view, their paddocks filled with wandering livestock. Cows gazed at her passing car in fascination while the bleating of sheep filled the air and drifted through the partially open driver's side window. She passed a failed housing estate. The few houses that made it through to development now lay abandoned, standing in defiance against the years. Their shutters hung askew, sent swinging by the wind in this area that never seemed to fully die. Windows—opaque with dust and age—watched her as she passed, as if they were hollow-eyed sentinels guarding whatever lingered within.

Before the turnoff came into view, she passed an ancient, overgrown cemetery on the corner that had been reclaimed by nature. Headstones, heavy with disrepair and covered in vines and twisted roots, stood at wild angles, their once clear inscriptions now faded like memories too fragile to hold.

Flipping on her indicator, she turned onto Ashen Way. The road here seemed curiously maintained. The trees she passed were all trimmed, as if an arborist had taken particular care of this road in favour over the others. Beyond the trees in the overgrown cemetery, houses came into view, their neatly manicured lawns and tended gardens a stark contrast to the overrun older ones she had passed. Children ran and played, chasing each other and playing on swings and trampolines, some giving her a wave and a smile as she passed. She smiled and waved back as she took in the sight in amazement. It was like she had entered into another world, a secret part of Stockbridge she hadn't known existed. She passed a well-maintained general store complete with a café, where people sat at window seats chatting, holding mugs of coffee or tea. She felt an involuntary shiver run through her. Something felt strange about this place. She'd lived in Stockbridge all her life and had never heard of this area. Though she had to admit, she hadn't been out of town for many years, so focused had she been on her mother.

Up ahead, she could see a park area, complete with a wooden bridge that crossed a small river leading to a path through the trees. Opposite the road, nestled between some trees, was Beyond the Veil, the shop she was looking for. There were a few empty spaces for cars there, and she used one, pulling in and switching off the ignition as she stared through the front windshield at the store. Its sign flickered weakly in sunlight that seemed to shine directly onto the store, its dark-tinted windows doing their job keeping its secrets closely guarded and hidden from view.

A nervous energy flowed through her as she sat there, trying to work up enough courage to get out and walk in. Now that she was here, she couldn't help but question whether she was doing the right thing. What if she had worked herself up for nothing? What if this was just a giant hoax, a marketing ploy that preyed on people like her to fleece them of their money? She closed her eyes to try to still her racing thoughts. Even if it was a hoax, at least she had tried. Luckily for her, money wasn't a problem, so if it came to that, it wouldn't be the worst thing in the world. She nodded, releasing her grip on the steering wheel, grabbed her handbag containing the photo, and exited her car, arching her back for a stretch. After so many days in bed, her muscles had stiffened. If nothing else, this entire experience had at least gotten her out of the house and into the sun. That at least felt like a minor victory.

She approached the door, its glass pane bearing no reflection as though refusing to acknowledge the sunlight that bore down on it.

Julia hesitated and then reached for the handle, its surface oddly cool against her fingertips. The door opened with a hushed sigh, and the sunlight behind her faltered, swallowed whole by the shop's heavy atmosphere.

Inside, the air was thick with incense and candle wax, wrapping around her like something sentient, something watchful. Shelves lining the walls and aisles in the middle were bowed under the weight of ancient tomes and weathered artifacts. Glass cases glistened with polished crystals, silver talismans, and ritual tools resting in the dim candlelight, which flickered in unseen breezes, their flames bending in slow, deliberate motion, casting shifting shadows that seemed to breathe.

Ahead of her, tucked in the back, was the counter, the wall behind it laden with twisting symbols and an ancient, gilded mirror. Beside it, a heavy velvet curtain, deep crimson, concealed a room, its secrets hidden within. Of Lilith, there was no sign.

Julia stepped forward, the wooden floor creaking beneath her weight, and the moment she did, the door behind her clicked shut—not with force, but with finality, as if announcing there was no going back now. The velvet curtain rustled in response, parting to let through the welcoming smile of Lilith Darkmoon. Surprisingly, she was dressed exactly as she had been in the video. Perhaps she had filmed it just this morning, and Julia had been one of the first to see it. Julia felt an instant connection with her, a warmth that eased her anxieties and filled her with a sense of trust.

"Welcome. Julia, I take it?"

Julia nodded and paused before asking. "How did you know my name?"

"Your mother, Mary, told me," Lilith said gently.

Julia suddenly felt weak at the knees, and she stumbled backwards, rescued from crashing into the shelves behind her by Lilith's hands grasping for her own.

"I... how... how is this possible?" Julia managed, trying to steady herself with the aid of Lilith.

"The spirit world is a place that defies logic as we know it. It is a wild place, full of magic and miracles. Few can make sense of its chaos. Fewer still can navigate its complexities and make contact with those who reside there. But for one so open such as I, and practiced in unravelling its mysteries, it is not so difficult. As soon as I received your message, I felt your mother's hand in its sending. Contacting her took some effort, but it helps when the spirit is willing. Come."

Lilith pointed toward the velvet curtain beside the counter and smiled. "Your mother awaits you."

Julia felt her heart racing a million miles per hour as she stumbled toward the curtain, her legs still unsteady beneath her. She pushed through, taking a step to the side to wait for Lilith, who entered behind her. She managed a quick look around the room before Lilith guided her to a small, rounded table in the middle, draped in an opulent velvet and gold tablecloth.

As in the room outside, the walls were lined with shelving, these looking to be made of ancient oak. Archaic-looking tomes lined one bookshelf, while another was filled with aged tarot decks and crystals of all shapes and sizes. Yet another had glass vials and containers filled with herbs, roots, and other substances she couldn't identify from the brief look she got. The room was bare of a light fixture, the light instead provided by a multitude of burning candles placed strategically throughout. A faint haze of incense curled through the air, turning the space into something between reality and a dream.

Julia felt her vision begin to swim as the scents of the room filled her senses, and a feeling of comfort washed over her. She knew it was likely whatever was in the incense was influencing her, but she didn't resist. She was here to talk with her mother; there was nothing she wouldn't do for that to happen one more time.

Lilith pulled out a seat for Julia, and she sat gratefully as Lilith took hers on the other side of the small table. Placed in the middle was an ornate silver box, its filigree catching the candlelight. Its appearance was simultaneously antique and modern, as if it were constructed yesterday.

"Before we begin, I need to let you know the cost. Unfortunately for a service such as I provide, it is not cheap, you understand," Lilith said, a tinge of regret in her voice. "What I do takes a lot out of me, and I can only do these services once per day."

Julia nodded. "Of course. I'll pay anything you want," she said quickly.

"Great," Lilith said with a smile. "Now comes the matter of what type of service you would like." Across from her, Lilith hesitated, her piercing blue eyes staring deeply into Julia's as they caught the flicker of the nearest candle, reflecting something deeper, something unreadable. "You loved her so much. That type of bond doesn't fade. It can never," she murmured, her voice soft and persuasive yet sharp in its delivery.

Julia swallowed, feeling the weight of Lilith's words press against the hollow ache in her chest. "I just... I need to talk to her again. To explain..."

Lilith studied her as if in consideration. Her hands wrapped around the silver box, her long fingers tracing lazy circles over its patterns.

"It doesn't have to be just talk," she said. "You could have her back whole. As if she never left."

Julia's breath caught in her throat. "That's not..." she managed in a strangled choke, not able to finish the sentence. It was impossible. It had to be.

"Possible? For a bond such as yours, it is. For a year." Lilith gazed at her, her smile slow and deliberate. "Time enough to mend wounds, to say what wasn't said." She leaned forward, her eyes gleaming. "For five thousand dollars, I can give this gift to you."

Julia's vision blurred at the edges, the world spiralling in a haze of smoke and candlelight. A small part of Julia, the rational part, screamed at her. This couldn't be real, shouldn't be real. A bigger part, the grieving, desperate part, made her lean forward in eagerness.

"How?" she asked, her voice barely above a whisper.

"That's not something you need to concern yourself with," Lilith said, her eyes darkening, her fingers drifting toward the clasp on the box.

The air visibly shifted in the room, thickening as if in response to Lilith's words. Julia suddenly felt like they were no longer alone. It felt like something unseen was watching her.

"All you need to know is that if you agree, if you place the photo of your mother in this box," Lilith said, her fingernails clicking loudly on the box, "in two days' time, she will return to you."

"It's that simple?" Julia said, her voice ringing with a desperate hope.

"It is for you. For me, it is another matter," she smiled, the warmth in her eyes returning as she leaned back in her chair. "Be that as it may, it is nothing when compared to the life I can give back."

Julia nodded slowly, still trying to comprehend Lilith's words and scarcely believing them. What did she have to lose? Money wasn't a problem, and although Ron would initially complain, Mary's return in a few days would quickly quieten him.

"Then yes. I want to do it. Please, bring her back to me," she whispered, tears forming at the corner of her eyes.

Lilith gave Julia's hand a reassuring squeeze, her eyes softening in understanding as she nodded, and then released her grip.

"I will. Please, if you will place your mother's photo in the box," she said, flicking open the clasp and lifting the lid carefully, swivelling it to face Julia with reverence.

Julia retrieved the photo of her mother from her handbag and studied the box in fascination. The interior was lined with deep midnight velvet, the fabric flawless and strangely undisturbed as if it had never held anything before or had swallowed whatever had been placed inside long ago. At the center of the fabric was an inlaid sigil, its intricate design etched in darkened silver that glittered in the candlelight. Julia felt a shiver run through her body at the sight of it. It was strangely unsettling, its curling script unfamiliar and alien, a harshness to its design that felt almost other-worldly.

She hesitated, glancing between it and her mother's photo, a hint of uncertainty clouding her decision.

"It feels strange, I know, but magic such as the likes the box contains is powerful and can give off a certain... aura. It is the nature of such things. But please do not worry. It is necessary," Lilith said reassuringly.

Julia's apprehension vanished the moment she looked at her. A strange certainty washed over her; she knew, some-how, that Lilith was trustworthy, and her instructions were to be heeded. She had to follow them.

Julia smiled at her and nodded, placing the photo on top of the sigil. It could have been a trick of the candles surrounding them, but she could have sworn she saw a sudden burst of light the moment the photo touched its surface. Lilith smiled and rotated the box back toward her, closing the lid and hasping the clasp in reverence.

"Your part in this is now done. Shall we retreat to the counter to complete our transaction?"

Julia nodded, and Lilith rose to her feet, giving a final pat to the box before heading to the curtain, holding it open for Julia.

As Julia walked through, she felt an instant shift in atmosphere, and a wave of dizziness washed over her. She blinked in confusion. The air was lighter in here and contained a different scent that she could now notice after exiting the small room.

"Come," Lilith said, brushing past her on her way to the counter. She pulled the credit card reader from a shelf underneath and tapped in some numbers as Julia made her way around the front of the counter on unsteady feet. Her head was thick and cloudy. It felt almost like she was in the aftermath of a drug-induced haze, likened to the ones she used to have occasionally back in her college days. She rummaged in her handbag, her clumsy fingers making several attempts to grasp her wallet. With it finally in her hands, she pulled it open and grabbed the credit card, tapping it on the screen that Lilith held outstretched to her. With a beep and an entry of her PIN, the transaction was done. No matter what happened from here, whether her mom did come back or not, she had tried her best. She could rest a little easier tonight knowing that.

"It is done. In two days, you will be reunited with your mother." Lilith smiled, her eyes alight with a curious, satisfied glint.

"Thank you so much. You don't know what this means to me," Julia gushed, already feeling the rush of anticipation and excitement at the thought of seeing her mother again.

"Believe me, it is my pleasure. Have a good day," Lilith said as she turned and disappeared back into the storeroom.

Julia headed toward the front door and paused there in confusion. It sounded like there were hushed voices drifting from the back room, Lilith and someone else... She shrugged it off. She was probably on the phone, arranging an appointment with another customer.

Exiting the shop, she emerged into the darkened sky of the fading afternoon light. She frowned. She hadn't been in the shop that long, had she? A glance down at her watch confirmed that she had. Shit. Ron would likely be home by the time she got back. She would have some explaining to do. She sighed and began mentally preparing herself for the conversation she didn't want to have.

CHAPTER TWENTY-TWO

Ron sat on the couch, his third glass of whiskey in hand, and picked up his phone for what felt like the hundredth time. He stared at the blank screen as if willing the display to show something more than it did.

When he had returned from work an hour ago to see Julia's car gone, he had been filled with dread. The anger and disdain in her eyes from the previous week, coupled with yesterday's fight, had left him with the crushing certainty that she was gone. He had raced upstairs, panic fuelling his steps, but the sight of her untouched possessions instantly brought a wave of relief, washing away that fear.

Since then, he had sent off a quick message to make sure she was okay and asked when she would be back, but had heard nothing. At first, he had shrugged it off. It could just be that she was catching up with friends and was caught up in the moment. Or maybe she was still pissed at him. Either way, he had felt his anxiety building as time went on. He knew it was a bad idea, but he had turned to the half-drunk whiskey bottle from the day before to ease his nerves.

The familiar sound of a key turning in the front door lock had him standing up in a rush, a portion of the whiskey in the glass he had forgotten he was holding spilling onto the carpet.

"Shit," he muttered, placing the glass on the coffee table with a clink, and fumbling for the tissues, putting a line of them on the carpet to absorb some of the spill.

He'd just placed the last one and was heading toward the kitchen to get a cloth and disinfectant when Julia walked in. She stared at him before her eyes drifted to the whiskey bottle and glass on the table and the tissues on the carpet behind him, her eyes narrowing with a look of disgust.

"Are you drinking?" she said accusingly, with a tone of incredulity in her voice.

"No, of course not," Ron answered quickly, wincing as he noticed the heavy scent of whiskey spilling from his mouth, contradicting him.

Julia's lips curled upward in revulsion, a streak of irritation clear in her eyes.

"I mean, I've only just had one, so I'm not technically drinking, drinking, you know?" he stumbled, trying to get himself out of the hole he knew he had dug himself into.

Julia's face twisted with anger, and she turned away from him. "How could you?" she said softly, her tone filled with hurt and anger, a quiet fury he had never heard from her before, which sent his stomach plummeting.

"Here I am, dealing with losing my mother, the person who mattered most to me in the entire world, and you're down here drinking as if it doesn't matter. As if I don't matter."

"Nnno... that's not it at all, sweetheart. I love you, you know that. It's just... I don't know how to help you. I try, but it's like you don't want my help, like I just annoy you rather than anything else."

"Whatever," she muttered before adding under her breath, "in a few days you won't have to worry about me, anyway."

A block of ice instantly formed in the pit of Ron's stomach. "What... what do you mean? Are you leaving me?"

"It depends on what mother thinks is best," Julia said, turning to face him with a strange, almost smug smile.

"Mary? What do you mean? Are you okay?"

"Oh, I'm better than okay," Julia said, her eyes flashing with a wild glint. "You see, in two days, mother will return. Oh yes, she will."

Ron felt lost for words as he stared at her. Her expression was unsettling, bordering on maniacal. He took a step toward her, and an overpowering smell of incense and herbs hit him, drifting toward him from her clothes.

"Honey, what have you done? What are you talking about?"

"I went and saw someone. Someone who can bring back my mother. It only cost five thousand dollars and a photo of her. Now, in two days' time, she'll come back to me," Julia said in a strange, somewhat singsong voice. Her eyes, though fixed on him, held a distant, almost reverent gaze, as if she saw something beyond him.

She focused once more on him and smiled coldly before

she turned and headed for the stairs, leaving Ron to stare after her in confusion.

His eyes remained fixed on her disappearing form as his mind struggled to grasp what she had said. "What the fuck? Julia, what did you do?" he whispered. The alcoholic haze made it more difficult to think than it should have, and he stumbled back toward the couch, sitting there with his head in his hands as he struggled to process what he'd just seen and heard.

It was obvious that someone had used Julia's fragile emotional and mental state to their advantage, whispering promises and exploiting her grief to push her into an irrational decision. The question was who? In today's world of complex scamming operations, it was easier now more than ever to fool people out of their money. Had someone cold-called her and claimed they could help?

He picked up his phone and logged into the Crescent Capital Bank app, scanning the transactions. There. Sure enough, there was the five-thousand-dollar payment. He tapped the screen, expecting to see the recipient's name, only to see an error message.

This record could not be retrieved. Contact support if the issue persists.

"C'mon, not now," he muttered. He exited the screen and tried again, but the same error message stared back at him. "What the fuck?"

He tried closing the app completely and opening it again. He even tried restarting his phone and trying again but no matter what he did or what he attempted to do, the same error message appeared.

Irritated, he looked up the number for internal support

and dialled it, trying to rein in his frustration before someone answered.

"Hello, Crescent Capital Bank, Sophie speaking. How can I help?"

"Hi Sophie, this is Ron Mathews, manager of the Stockbridge branch. I'm having trouble accessing a particular transaction on my account. Can you please look into it for me? It's one made today for five thousand dollars."

"Of course, Mr. Mathews. Before I proceed, I'll need to verify your identity. Can you confirm your employee ID and the last four digits of your internal access code?"

Ron sighed and rattled off the numbers, his voice clipped but controlled.

"Thank you," Sophie said after a pause. "Just a moment while I pull up your account."

Ron fidgeted, listening to the keyboard tapping through the phone, his impatience building with every clack of the keys.

"Hmmm..." Sophie said, her confusion obvious even over the phone line. "I found the transaction, but it seems like there are some technical difficulties accessing it. I'll have to contact tech support to get it fixed up for you."

Ron sighed as he slumped back onto the couch in frustration. "Yeah, okay. Can you get them to contact me once they've fixed the issue?"

"Of course, sir, I can do that. I'll raise the ticket now, and you should hear back from them in the next few days."

"Few days? This is kind of an emergency, can't it be looked at as a priority?"

"Unfortunately, sir, as you may know, the upgrade to the system is due in a few days, and most of our resources are concentrated on that. But I can assure you, your ticket will be one of the first looked at after it's done."

Ron swore silently, his jaw clenched tight, his knuckles bone white as he gripped the phone, his voice rigid. "Fine, that will have to do. Thanks for your help." He jabbed at the end-call button and threw the phone onto the couch.

"Yeah, thanks for nothing," he spat, his voice thick with anger.

His eyes caught the sparkle of the remaining amber fluid in the glass on the coffee table.

"Fuck it," he muttered. "It's not like Julia will talk to me the rest of the night, anyway." He shrugged, picking up the glass and tipping its contents down his throat. Its warmth as he swallowed was as satisfying as it was comforting.

He poured himself another and switched on the TV, settling himself in for a night of mind-numbing programs and alcohol. Hopefully, by tomorrow, Julia would be in a more approachable mood, but he doubted it. It felt like the gap between them was now too large to bridge.

CHAPTER TWENTY-THREE

Two days later

Today was the day. At least that was according to Lilith, though doubt had begun to eat away at the edges of Julia's hope. After the argument with Ron when she'd returned, she'd gone straight to bed. She'd found herself suddenly exhausted with a headache, most likely brought on by the heavy concentration of scents in Beyond the Veil. She had awoken with a feeling of unreality, as if it had all been a dream, and she'd felt terrible about the way she'd treated Ron. The two had avoided each other since. It felt as if they were simply sharing a house instead of being married, such was the distance between them.

Now, as she sat upright in bed, she fidgeted nervously, glancing at the alarm clock on the nightstand. 11:36 am. So far, there had been no sign of her mom returning, no phone call, no door knock, nothing. She sighed, catching herself glancing once more at the clock. She couldn't sit here all day feeling like a nervous wreck. Reaching for her bottle of meds on the nightstand, she downed one, hoping to put a stop to the anxiety before it built. Whilst she waited for it to kick in, she brushed her teeth and had a quick shower before going downstairs for her daily fix of strawberry jam on toast. Today called for a special touch, so she swirled a dollop of thickened cream on top. Afterwards, she made her way to the lounge room, wrinkling her nose in disgust at the smell of alcohol and BO that had started to gather in the room.

What would her mother think if she came and saw the state of the room? She began cleaning, stripping the layers off the crumpled makeshift bedding that stank of stale sweat and whiskey and throwing it into the wash. Next, she gathered up the empty glasses that had begun to build up on the coffee table and stopped, her eyes widening in shock when she saw the two empty bottles of whiskey abandoned on the floor, a third one almost empty on its side. She knew Ron had been drinking, but she hadn't realized how much. Had she really been so difficult to deal with that she had led Ron down the path of alcoholism?

She sat on the edge of the couch, her eyes fixed on the bottles, recalling the interactions they'd had since her mother had passed, and she realized she had been. She had barely said a nice word to him since she'd come back from the hospital. Every time she saw him, it made her defensive, an unfair weight of blame directed at him. Not only that, but she had done her best to push him away from her so she wouldn't have to hurt so much. So she didn't have to talk about her mother's death and how it made her feel, so she could begin to heal. She didn't want to heal. She didn't want to move on. Tears once more filled her eyes, but this time from shame and guilt. Ron hadn't deserved what she'd been doing to him. It was time to put a stop to things before it was too late to save their marriage. That was if it wasn't too late already. She made a decision. When Ron came back from work today, she would apologize and hopefully start on the path to mending things.

She stood up, dirty glasses in hand, and put them in the dishwasher before returning to grab the empty bottles and put them into the recycling bin. Next, she sprayed the carpet where Ron had left the tissues after the alcohol spill and scrubbed it until the smell of alcohol was gone. It wasn't until she was done that she realized the rest of the house needed a good clean too. It had been well over a week since it had been tended to. Her mother would be disgusted, being the clean freak she was.

Hours later, she sat down at the kitchen table with a warm mug of tea, satisfied with her day. The act of cleaning the house and the satisfying sight of order emerging from chaos proved therapeutic, as it always did, this time perhaps more so, given her mental state the past week. She checked her watch, seeing it tick just over the 5:30 pm mark. Ron would be home any minute now. She sighed, thinking about the monumental hill they had ahead of them if they were to come through this with their marriage intact.

She could see Ron was barely hanging on by a thread, could tell by the way he looked at her—cautious, worn, afraid to say the wrong thing. His unravelling hadn't started with Mary's death. It had begun long before, quietly fraying at the edges while her mother was still alive. And she knew that much of it was her fault. Her relationship with her mother was unhealthy. Ron, his sister, and her friends had all said that, and a part of her knew that was true. But the bigger part, the one that had always ruled her life—anxiety accompanied by attachment issues—always won out. It was little wonder her friends had dropped away from her, and her marriage was on the rocks. Maybe Ron was right. A baby could be the tether, the thing that might pull them back toward each other, back to what they once were. Forming a family with Ron had always been on her mind from the moment they talked about the possibility. Perhaps tonight was the night. A night for new beginnings.

The familiar sound of the Lexus pulling up the driveway broke her away from her thoughts, and she smiled, feeling excited, finally, by something beyond the impending arrival of her mother back in her life. She got up from the table and approached the door, feeling anticipation curling in her stomach.

The lock clicked softly, and the door swung open, revealing Ron, dressed impeccably in his suit the way he always was, his eyes ringed with darkness, his face weary and heavy from the weight of the day. His aftershave drifted to her, and she took it in, her heart heavy and aching at how drained he looked. He stared at her in surprise, his face guarded, before she stepped into him, her arms wrapping around his frame, pressing her head against his chest. Surprised, he swung the door closed behind him and dropped his suitcase to the floor, returning her hug.

She raised her head from his chest and pressed her lips to his—soft at first, tentative, but then deeper, urgent as she pulled him toward her and pressed herself against him. His hands found her waist and began to trace the line of her curves, and suddenly they were moving, their bodies against the wall, their hands and mouths eager to explore. Silence gave way to moans, and soon a trail of clothes littered the way up the stairs and into the bedroom, where the distance between them melted away.

CHAPTER TWENTY-FOUR

Julia took in a gasp of breath as she woke, greeted by the soft glow of the time on the clock on the nightstand—7:34 pm. She blinked, attempting to clear the remnants of sleep from her vision. The room was dim, the haze of twilight pressing against the curtains barely enough to illuminate more than objects draped in shadows. Beside her, Ron lay sprawled beneath the sheets, the warmth of his skin still lingering against hers, his breath slow and peaceful.

She stayed there for a moment, revelling in the love she felt as she gazed at him. A love that had been too far hidden beneath the pressures of life. She made a promise to herself right there and then that it would never be buried like that again. But then, she heard something drift through the open door. A sound. Something muted. Something that felt ancient and intrinsically wrong to her ears. A rustling, like dry leaves skittering across wood, followed by a deep, guttural moan that instantly raised goosebumps up and down her bare arms before she realized what it must be. Her mother. Her mother had come back. She must've come through the front door and left it open.

Then came the voice. Low. Drawn. Like breath scraped over stone.

"Julia."

She sucked in a sharp breath, her pulse thrumming against her ribs. The voice was off, but it was definitely her mother.

She eased off the bed, moving slowly so as not to disturb Ron. She could wake him later after she and her mother had spent some time together first. She slipped on her robe and cinched the belt tightly around her. The carpet was cool beneath her feet as she stepped into the hallway, toward the staircase. Shadows stretched long and jagged ahead of her, the walls seeming to inhale, as if eager to see the culmination of her and her mother's reunion.

"Mother?"

Reaching the bottom of the stairs, Julia glanced around for any sign of her. The house sat curiously silent, and she shivered, pulling the edges of her robe together. It was far colder downstairs than upstairs, and unusually so for the time of the year. Before her, the living room sat in murky half-light as if reluctant to reveal its secrets. Then her eyes caught a faint movement. There, on the far side of the couch. A shape indeterminate from her vantage point.

She moved closer slowly and cautiously. Despite her eagerness, if the door had been opened, there was every chance it could be someone else. Her heart felt like it was going to burst out of her chest, but then it stopped along with her breath. There, with her back to Julia, was a woman sitting stiff and motionless on the couch.

The hair—gray, curled, and long, reaching down to her shoulder blades. The posture rigid, the way she'd always sat in quiet contemplation. Her mother.

"Julia, my dear, are you just going to stand there? Come and give your mother a hug."

Her voice. Just like she remembered it. Just as it had always been.

"Mother!" Julia yelled out, feeling joy course through her veins as she ran into the living room and into the outstretched arms of her now standing mother. Her perfume. Her soft, gentle caresses. The steady breath on the top of her head. Everything was perfect. Everything was how it should be. Her mother was back. Tears poured freely from her eyes, and she clasped Mary to her as if she never wanted to let go. She never wanted to forget this moment. This was everything she'd dreamed of, everything she'd thought she'd lost, now become reality once again.

"Oh, Mother, I've missed you so much."

Her mother stiffened at her words, as if displeased by them.

"Mother?" Julia pulled back and squinted at Mary, trying to determine what had upset her. Her face was stiff, her eyes staring off into the distance.

"Mother, are you okay?"

There was no answer.

Concerned now, Julia separated from her mother and reached toward the lamp, switching it on.

"Mother, I..." she stopped, her eyes widening in horror.

Before her, the face of her mother, now revealed in the light, began to melt away. Her skin dropped away from her bones, slapping the floor with a sickening splat. Only pieces remained, the previously smooth, moisturized skin peeling away to reveal patches of rot. Her eyes bulged from their sockets, pushed outward by the bright blue glow of something beneath until they popped out, hanging by the threads of their optic nerves before they dropped to the floor. The body of what was once her mother hunched over and shook from the transformation that was taking place. The flesh that had sloughed off her now decrepit body steamed, bubbled, and melted on the carpet below. A horrible, sickening stench radiated from her, a cloying, thick smell of rot and decay and fermented body fluids.

Julia screamed and backed away, staring at the thing's face that used to be her mother's, but now wasn't. Patches of skin clung stubbornly to its skull, slick with something that gleamed in the dim light. Her once vibrant hair was now long and stringy, hanging in damp, rotting strands. But worst of all were the eyes—now two immense orbs of glowing blue, burning like drowned stars, too large, too knowing. They pulsed with awareness and were locked onto her, seeing past skin, time, and thought, unravelling her from within.

And below them, the tongue. Thick, grotesque, coated in something viscous, sliding between exposed teeth with an obscene deliberation. It twitched, curling slightly, as if tasting the air. As if tasting her.

"What's wrong, dear? Don't you want to give your poor mother a kiss?" the thing hissed, its voice soft and serpentine. Inhuman. Yet a tiny bit of her mother's voice remained in its tone.

The thing stepped toward her, and Julia could only stare, her body trembling, held under the gaze of the creature that had her in its grip. It took another step forward, and all Julia wanted to do was run, to cry out and scream for Ron, but though she tried, she couldn't. It was as if the creature had her under its spell.

Now just a few centimetres from its face, Julia could smell the foulness emanating from its body. It smelled of rot, of something ancient and forgotten, a sourness with a hint of sulphur as if it had been dragged from the depths of hell itself.

It drew itself up, uncurling itself from its hunched-over form to rise above Julia. Towering above her, it loomed, an unnatural silhouette against the dim light. Julia couldn't move, couldn't speak, could only stare at it, her eyes drawn to its face or what passed for one. The thing extended its hands, its fingernails long, sharp, and pointed, attached to dirty, purple, swollen fingers, and gently cupped her face.

The touch emanated evil. Julia's skin tingled with it under the creature's vile hands. The body of her mother's this may have been, but what had claimed it was dark and demonic, her spirit twisted and transformed into something ruinous. The hate it radiated was suffocating, thick in the air like the charge before a storm, and she instinctively knew with every ounce of her being it was here not to be with her, but to take its wrath out on her. No, not just on her. On all those her mother had ever cursed in bitter silence, for every alleged grievance they had caused, every wound left unhealed. This thing had not forgotten. And now, it had the power to make them all pay.

Slimy clumps of thick goo dropped down onto Julia's chest from the creature's foul chin as it stared deep into her eyes, enjoying every ounce of her terror. It grinned at her with malevolence, its tongue sliding across its teeth before it began to exert pressure on both sides of her head, its bulbous palms pressing inward with slow and deliberate force.

Julia's breath hitched as she stood in the thing's grasp helplessly, her eyes watering, desperate to look away, to break the hold it had over her. Her vision burst with flashes of red as the force increased. She could hear her skull creak as the thing leaned closer, its twisted smile stretching, delighting in her pain and helplessness.

A scream bubbled in her throat, stuck there, unable to get out as her skull began to give way. A first crack. A fracture split through her skull like lightning. Then another.

"Julia!" Ron's faint cry cut into Julia's panicked awareness, and her heart cried out for him to save her, doing what her voice no longer could.

The demon broke its gaze and looked toward the source of the sound before it turned its malevolent gaze back on her. A scream finally erupted from Julia's throat before it cut off as the creature gave one final unrelenting squeeze. Her head burst in a wet detonation of bone and flesh. Fragments of skull and brain matter flew, a grisly spray that tainted the TV screen in streaks of deep crimson and globules and painted the velvet-covered couch. The coffee table beside them took the worst of it. Large chunks of splintered bone skittered across its surface, smearing the polished wood with viscera.

The thing straightened, admiring its work before it turned its attention to the screaming Ron, who was barrelling toward it. Its smile directed at him was one filled with promise, speaking of a similar fate to Julia, before it began to fade away into the ether, back into the darkness from whence it came.

Ron rounded the couch and fell to his knees on the blood-soaked carpet, every last bit of energy he had sapped at the sight of his wife's decimated body. He reached out toward her as if he could put all the broken pieces of her back together before dropping his arms uselessly, hanging his head as hot tears and huge body-wracking sobs consumed him.

Upstairs, Mary's photo album sat abandoned on the floor, having been tossed aside during the intense love-making session between Ron and Julia. A soft wind caught the edges of its pages, touching nothing else in the room, intensifying until they turned with a sound like brittle leaves, stopping on a page filled with but one photo. In it, a younger Mary stood between her brother and sister. Her hair was darker, her expression distant, guarded. Her brother was grinning with unbridled joy, her sister gripping Mary's hand tightly, her eyes reflecting a deep love.

Soft, slithering whispers laced the corners of the room, barely audible at first before they grew in volume, insistent, increasingly angry, layering on top of one another until they sounded like Mary calling one name over and over. Bryan. The curtains lifted, even though the window was closed. The page twitched.

And in the photo, Mary's younger self turned her head a fraction towards the frozen figure of her brother, her eyes aglow with sinister intent and a twisted smile to match.

CHAPTER TWENTY-FIVE

Pittsfield Police Department, Pittsfield, MA – 14 miles north of Stockbridge – 5:36 pm

Millie pushed through the heavy glass door of the office, grateful for the respite from the deluge outside. Shrugging off her coat, she hung it up on the coat rack, grimacing at the ever-increasing puddle beneath it. The cleaner was going to hate them all after they left. She took in the usual musk of coffee and stale body odor, a stark contrast from the comparative freshness of the rain outside. At least it was warmer in here. There were always pros and cons.

She had just returned from a job. A tedious one—tracking down a runaway teenager whose parents were convinced she'd been kidnapped. In reality, the girl had holed up in a friend's basement, escaping a home life that suffocated more than protected. No crime, just teenage desperation.

She headed toward her cubicle, spotting Bob seated at

his desk, cell phone pressed against his ear. His expression was a dark one, darkening ever further with each passing second. Whatever he was hearing, it wasn't good.

She settled in her cubicle opposite, setting down her bag and watching on with curiosity.

"Say that again?" he muttered, rubbing his temple. "No sign of forced entry? No disturbances? Just... gone?"

Millie frowned. Bob rarely looked rattled.

"Alright, Doc, we'll check it out. Be there soon."

He hung up, leaned back in his chair, and exhaled sharply, tossing his phone onto the desk before finally meeting her gaze.

"That was the medical examiner," he said. "A body's missing from the morgue. Mary Hinsworth—remember her? One with the bugs? Been in cold storage awaiting the full tox results. Until today."

Millie felt a slow chill creep over her skin. That case had already given her the willies, and now this. How was this possible? Cold storage meant security. It meant procedure. Bodies didn't just disappear.

"So where the hell did she go?" she murmured, already reaching for her notepad.

Bob shook his head. "That's what we're about to find out." He stood up, grabbing his jacket from the back of his chair, and slipping into it with practiced ease. He looked at her and hesitated. "Sorry, kid, I know you just came back from a job and were looking to get your nightly fix of reality TV in."

"Oh yeah, because after I come back from a long day of dealing with people and their issues, I just love watching more of them on TV."

Bob laughed, grabbing his car keys and jingling them in his hand. "Don't mind if I drive, do you?"

"Only if you don't drive like you normally do."

"What? You mean cool, calm, and collected?"

"Yeah, the opposite of that. Obeying the speed limit would be a good start."

Bob stuck his tongue out at her and grinned as he headed toward the glass door of the exit.

"Oh, very mature, Mr. Senior Detective," she said, shaking her head in amusement. With a sigh, she grabbed her still-dripping coat off the rack and ventured back out into the rain to follow Bob.

An hour later, Bob pulled his car into the almost completely vacant parking lot at the Office of the Chief Medical Examiner. Only one other car was there at this hour, everyone else doing the sensible thing and heading home on time. Millie could only dream of that happening. Ever since she had started in law enforcement, she had almost never had a normal eight-hour workday. There was always something to keep her either in the office or out in the field.

Bob led the way toward the back door and knocked on it, the door opening to the haggard face of Dr Samuel Knox. Dark circles ringed his eyes, his pallid face looking even more so in the glow of the security light above the door.

"Detectives, please come in," he said simply, skipping pleasantries as he stepped aside to let them pass.

Bob gave him a nod and walked through, Millie on his heels. A narrow corridor stretched before them, its walls lined with smooth, pale tiles that reflected the clinical glare of fluorescent lights overhead. The air was colder than the already chilly air outside and laced with the faint metallic tang of disinfectant and something more elusive.

Dr Knox closed the door behind them and secured it before leading the way down the hall, his boots barely making a sound against the polished linoleum. Millie fell into step behind Bob, her eyes sweeping across the corridor, noting the bulletin board pinned with notices and procedural reminders. A cart sat tucked against the wall a few metres ahead, stacked with sealed containers labelled with scientific names even Google wouldn't likely help with. Ahead of them, Dr Knox headed toward a slightly ajar door near the end, the glow beyond softer, more diffused.

He pushed through it, leading them into a room that was lit with rows of fluorescent lights positioned directly above meticulously clean stainless steel tables, each fitted with a deep sink and drainage pipes darkened with use and time. A surgical tool table covered with an array of scalpels, forceps, bone saws, and other tools was positioned near one of the tables in the middle, awaiting the arrival of its newest victim. The air was thick with chemical sterility, antiseptic the prevailing scent, but there were hints of something else, something that no amount of chemical could erase. Millie shuddered. No matter how many morgues she'd visited over the years, there was no avoiding the lingering smell of death and body fluids, no matter how much they were scrubbed. This one was no exception.

"Over here, detectives." Dr Knox stood by the refriger-ator units, their proximity to him making him rub his hands together, trying to keep them warm. To his right was a single metal door labelled simply as "Long Term Storage."

Dr Knox pushed the door open, and the trio entered a room lined with reinforced freezers that appeared more ominous than the ones outside. The lighting here was dimmer, the cold more absolute, designed to press pause on time's toll. One compartment on the bottom left stood open, its steel door ajar, its latch unhooked. A tag hung loosely from its slot, fluttering slightly in the artificial current of air.

"After you, detective," Bob said, giving Millie a smile, gesturing toward the compartment with a flourish of his hand.

"Why me?" Millie said as she swept past him.

"Because I said so," Bob replied, his voice filled with exaggerated seriousness. "And also because my body doesn't do so well crouching down anymore, especially when it's minus one hundred."

"Well, actually, it's more like minus ten," Dr Knox corrected as he glanced at his watch.

"You're a laugh a minute, Doc," Bob muttered.

Millie knelt down next to the vacant compartment, snapping on a pair of disposable rubber gloves before pinching the spinning tag in her finger and peering at it. The name was unmistakable. Mary Hinsworth. She frowned as she let the tag go.

"Dr Knox, when was the last time these units were checked?"

Dr Knox ran a hand through his greying hair, his gaze flicking toward the vacant compartment. "Three days ago. All were secure."

Millie nodded, exchanging a look with Bob. "Were there any signs of forced entry in the morgue at all when you found her missing?"

"As I mentioned on the phone to Detective Jordan here, no, there were none. The door here is kept unlocked, and so is the entry to the morgue itself. The back door you came in through was also still locked, as was the front door. Neither of them showed signs of tampering."

"It screams to me of an inside job," Bob said, eying the doctor in the way that Millie knew meant he was on the lookout for any indication of a suspicious response.

"I highly doubt it. Everyone in this office has worked here for years, and we haven't had any cases like this happen since the time I started here nine years ago," Dr Knox said, nonplussed by Bob's attempt at intimidation.

"What about the footage from the security camera? Has that been checked?" Millie asked as she pulled out the steel unit and examined it.

Dr Knox sighed and rubbed his forehead, drawing a sharp look from the two detectives. "Yes, but there's a problem," he said, his eyes glancing nervously between Millie and the vacant compartment.

"What problem might that be, Doc?" Bob asked, his eyebrows raised.

"There's a gap in the timestamp of the footage. From the time Mary's body was still present until afterwards, when the storage unit was open."

"What about the other cameras?" Bob asked in surprise.

"They all have similar gaps but of varying lengths."

Millie gave one last look at the unit and stood up with a groan, her muscles stiff from the cold. "We should try to get someone to dust this room for prints. Doubt they'll find anything, but it's worth a shot," Millie said to Bob, who nodded in response before he turned his attention to Dr Knox.

"Let's take a look at that footage, shall we?" Bob said, gesturing for the doctor to lead the way.

The security station was crammed into a narrow room next to Dr Knox's office, tucked further down the hall from the morgue. He sat down on the creaky swivel chair, bringing up the grainy footage onto a small monitor that looked like it hadn't been updated since the 90s. Bob ran a hand through his hair and squinted at the screen.

"Ever consider investing in something post-1995?" he asked in irritation.

"We don't generally have a need to review the footage here, so it's not worth spending the money," Dr Knox said drily, returning Bob's irritated glance with one of his own.

"I'd say you have a need now," Bob muttered, shooting Dr Knox a look of disapproval.

"Be that as it may, here is the footage," Dr Knox said, ignoring the look and pushing a button to initiate the recording.

The quiet, sterile room of the long-term storage facility came into view on the screen, the timestamp on the corner showing 3:44 pm. Seconds passed without anything happening before the feed suddenly flickered and the time-stamp jumped.

Millie leaned forward, arms folded, scrutinizing the screen. "Rewind that."

Dr Knox complied, the grainy footage rewinding in jerky increments until the moment the screen glitched. The timestamp jumped—first by a second, then by five full minutes.

"Let me show you the feed from the other cameras." He tapped on the keyboard, bringing up the recording from the morgue outside long-term storage.

The footage played, showing a vacant room, before the screen glitched once again and the timestamp jumped from 3:50 pm to 3:54 pm. It resumed, capturing a final sliver of movement of the door swinging shut, as if someone or something had just slipped through. He followed it up by playing the footage from outside the back door, and another glitch occurred, this time from 3:54 pm to 3:57 pm.

Millie and Bob straightened up, exchanging concerned glances with each other.

"Do you have any backups of this footage?" Millie asked.

"Yes, we do, but the same thing happens in that, too."

Bob cut in, his voice low. "Then someone wanted it gone. Where were you at the time the body went missing, Doc?"

Dr Knox swivelled in his chair to face the two detectives before answering. "I was in my office dealing with the paperwork for the day." He noted the narrowed eyebrows of Bob before he added, "The security footage will verify that." Bob hesitated, then nodded in acknowledgment.

Millie jumped in, her tone measured. "So now we know when the body disappeared, but we don't know *how* it disappeared."

Dr Knox turned back to face the screen, his fingers tapping idly on the bottom of the keyboard, as if willing an answer to appear on the screen. "No," he admitted.

Bob narrowed his eyes at the blank space where the

missing footage should have been, instead showing nothing more than a frame of white static. "Which means we have a problem." He straightened and swivelled his torso from side to side to stretch, wincing with each protesting crack of his spine. "Okay, I'll organize to get forensics and the tech team down here ASAP. Doc, do you have any idea why someone would want Mary Hinsworth's body?"

"None at all. I was still awaiting the results from the tox screen. Other than that, no one else showed any interest in her."

Bob grunted in response. "Okay, thanks, Doc. I'm sure we'll have more questions for you later."

The pair stepped out of the security station and walked toward the hallway door. Bob pulled out his phone and began punching in the number for the forensics department. "I'll get the party started. You're okay to do the paperwork, yeah?"

"Of course, you know how much I love doing it."

Bob smirked at her as she rolled her eyes at him before he pressed the call button.

By the time they walked out of the exit to Bob's car, it was almost 8:00 pm, the sky a bruised, purple-black.

"Is it just me, or is this Hinsworth case getting weirder?" Millie asked. Since seeing the missing footage, the same quiet, persistent itch that something was off about the case had come back tenfold. What should have been a cut-and-dry death by natural causes case was now veering into territory that felt anything but. Unsettling didn't begin to cover it.

Bob looked at her sharply and shook his head. "It's strange, alright, but don't go chalking it up to ghosts and ghouls. We've got avenues to explore here. In fact, if anything, this mess is pointing more and more to either Mr or Mrs Mathews being involved."

Millie nodded, still unconvinced as Bob unlocked the car and the pair climbed in.

"Let's call this a night and let the experts do their job. Hopefully, they'll find something and we can wrap this case up tomorrow nice and easy," Bob said, with a snap of his fingers to emphasize his point.

"Yeah, that would be nice," Millie muttered, her mind still racing with thoughts of the strange case.

Bob's hand was just hovering over the key in the ignition when his phone let out its familiar muffled jazz ringtone. He fished it from his pocket and groaned when he saw the screen glowing in the dim cabin light: Pittsfield Police Department.

"Goddamn it. When it rains, it pours," Bob muttered, tapping on the accept button and moving the phone up to his ear. "Hello, this is Detective Sergeant Bob Jordan."

Millie's heartbeat quickened as she watched Bob's face drain of colour. He held the phone tightly against his ear, his grip tense, his expression frozen in something between disbelief and unease. Whatever the caller had just said, it wasn't good.

"What time did this happen?" he asked, shooting a worried glance at Millie. He listened carefully, his brow furrowed as he took in the information being fed to him.

"Uh-huh, right. Hold tight, we're on our way."

He lowered the phone, staring at the screen thoughtfully as it went dark. He looked up toward Millie, his expression haunted. "You're not going to believe this..."

CHAPTER TWENTY-SIX

Julia Mathews was dead. As Bob pulled the car to the curb outside the Mathews' house, Millie's mind was still spinning.

There wasn't much to go on, but what little information Bob had provided her with sent her thoughts down avenues that weren't procedurally sound. Bob was adamant that there was a rational explanation, that what Mr Mathews was saying was a straight-up lie. Either that or he was laying the groundwork for an insanity plea to dodge the brutal reality of his wife's murder.

Millie wasn't so sure. Her analytical mind urged caution, procedure, facts. But something deeper was stirring beneath the surface. A quiet tug from the part of her that believed in things logic couldn't touch. She knew she had to approach this by the book, but nothing about this case felt like it belonged in one.

The flashing blue and red of the two police cars just before them cast shadows that jittered and danced as if darkness itself was celebrating in victory. As Millie exited the vehicle, she immediately felt a strong sense of wrongness. She paused in confusion, her eyes darting around the scene before her, trying to make sense of what she was feeling, then she saw it. It was quick, a flicker at the edge of her vision, vanishing the instant she turned her head.

Bob walked by her, giving her a curious glance as he did so, and approached the two officers standing outside the front of the house.

Something was watching her; she could feel it.

She turned, sweeping her gaze over the crowd gathered beyond the police tape, where two officers stood guard. It looked like the whole street had turned up, a surprisingly large turnout considering the number of houses. Faces blurred together as she looked over them quickly. Nothing stood out. But still her pulse was hammering, her skin prickling in unease as if there was a danger she wasn't seeing.

Then she did see it. The darkness parted at the back of the crowd. It wasn't sudden, or a dramatic shift, but rather a slow, inevitable unveiling, as if whatever was revealing itself there wanted her to feel the full brunt of the terror it knew it was making her feel. It drew back like a stage curtain, revealing a pale face—too pale. A familiar one that should've been impossible to be there, yet was.

Millie's breath caught in her throat, her muscles stiffening and locking her in place. The face of Mary Hinsworth stared at Millie, her mouth stretching impossibly wide in a rictus grin. Her skin was waxen, stretched too tightly over bones that no longer held the weight of life. But that wasn't the worst of it. Her eyes were wrong. They were not the eyes of the dead or the living, but rather something else.

Something not from this earth. They were large. Too large, and radiated a malevolent pure blue. They stared at her in awareness, a promise of something only it knew, but Millie could guess. This thing that was Mary but no longer was evil. Pure evil.

The crowd didn't react. No one flinched, no one turned around. It was as if they didn't see what Millie was seeing at all.

Millie managed a strangled gasp through the tightness of her throat before she felt the weight of a hand on her shoulder, jolting her out of the temporary paralysis she had entered into.

"Millie? You okay?" Bob's concerned voice drifted over her shoulder. Her focus broken, she turned to face him, her face almost as pale as that of the living corpse she had just seen.

"Bob, do you see that?" Millie asked, her voice strained. She turned back to face the crowd and lifted her hand to point, but halted mid-raise. Mary was gone. Darkness had swallowed the space behind the crowd again. A few curious onlookers stared at the two detectives, the only ones paying attention to them. It was as if Mary had never been there at all.

Bob was watching her now, with a deep frown on his face. "See what?"

Millie swallowed hard, glancing between him and the space where Mary had been. She *had* seen her. She *knew* she had. She could still see those gleaming, depthless eyes staring at her as if they could see beyond the flesh to her soul. Her fingers curled into her palm, feeling her fingernails digging into her flesh. She forced herself to steady her breathing, trying to bring her heartbeat back under control.

"...Nothing," she murmured, though they both knew it was a lie.

"Listen, it's been a long day. How about you head home? I can take care of this," Bob said gently, his face softening.

"No, it's okay. I want to keep going. Weren't you going to talk to the officers?" she asked, giving him a brief smile as she brushed past him, taking the lead.

She approached the officers and knew something was desperately wrong when she got closer. Both of their faces were drained of colour, the pair of them breaking free from staring inside the house to greet her and Bob.

Millie noticed a puddle of congealed vomit next to the doorframe and grimaced. She could feel her already frayed nerves fray further, and she knew that whatever awaited them inside was far from the normal crime scene.

"Officers," Millie said, giving them a nod as Bob pulled up alongside her. He was straight to business as usual.

"Which one of you called it in?" His voice was steady. Strong as it usually was, but tonight there was a faint undertone. Something tight.

"That'd be me, Officer Myers," the more solidly built of the two officers said as he stepped forward. He looked to be in his mid-thirties, his accent suggesting he was previously from Brooklyn. His eyes darted nervously between them as he continued. "I got a call from dispatch at 7:46 pm asking me to respond to a possible homicide at this location. Met a man at the door who said he was the husband of the victim, the victim being his wife."

Bob nodded. "Alright. Walk me through it. What did you find?"

Officer Myers hesitated, rubbing the back of his neck. "The guy could hardly talk; it was hard enough getting that detail from him. He walked me into the lounge room where the victim was. I've never seen anything like it. Never want to again. Her body was lying next to the couch. Head crushed. Whatever did it..." He swallowed. "There was no intact part of it left. Blood, bone... everything was everywhere."

A heavy silence settled over the group. Behind the trio, the other officer dry retched, the recollection of Officer Myers triggering his own.

Bob rubbed his temples, forcing his voice to stay even. "Weapon?"

Officer Myers shook his head. "If there was one, we didn't find it."

Millie glanced at Bob, and for the first time that day, he met her gaze with something close to apprehension. First, there was the bizarre condition of Mary's body, and now this. Her daughter dead in extraordinary circumstances. Even Bob had to admit something wasn't right. And they were about to discover just how much.

"Alright, thanks, officer. We'll take a look," Bob said, adjusting his tie nervously as Millie pulled her notebook from her pocket, the pen in her hand trembling slightly. Officer Myers gave them a grim nod and stepped aside.

Bob opened the door, and the scent hit them before they even took a step inside. The air was heavy with the smell of blood, with a hint of something else that Millie recognized as sulphur, coming from the direction of the living room to their right. They stepped through the hallway and stopped. As soon as she transitioned into the room, she felt a deep, creeping feeling of wrongness, the same feeling she had gotten from Mary's bedroom. The room felt suffocating, the air thick with a sense of foreboding, as if the walls themselves were holding the weight of the horror they had witnessed. Then Millie's breath stuck in her throat when she caught sight of the horrific scene in front of her. Blood was everywhere, covering the wall above the TV in a wide arc along with thicker chunks of organic matter. Streaks of the thick crimson liquid lined the walls on either side.

Millie gulped down the gorge rising in her throat and stepped carefully toward the couch, avoiding bloody chunks of bone that had travelled nearly the full length of the room. On the floor in front of the couch, a large stain bloomed outward from where Julia's body lay. Her skull had been eviscerated, collapsed inward, as though gripped in an impossible vice. Bone fragments on the couch and coffee table glittered like glass in the light from the chandelier above.

Millie swallowed hard. "Compression trauma?" she whispered, more to herself than to Bob as she scribbled in her notebook.

"From both sides," Bob murmured, kneeling beside the body. "But no tool marks. And there's no way... no way human hands could've done this."

Millie's gaze drifted to a family portrait on the TV unit, which had miraculously avoided the mess that covered most of the room. Julia smiled from the frame, her arm wrapped stiffly around a familiar, stern-looking older woman. Her mother. The resemblance between her and the... thing she had seen outside was uncanny... and unsettling.

A low retching groan drew both Bob and Millie's attention towards the kitchen. They approached slowly, mindful of the mess on the floor they had to avoid with every step. Just inside the entrance, a uniformed officer stood silently, arms crossed, watching Ron with a guarded expression, part suspicion, part sympathy. He gave them a brief nod of acknowledgement as they passed through.

Ron was slumped by the sink, the front of his shirt soaked with sweat and vomit, his face colourless and his eyes hollowed by grief and a haunted, desperate disbelief. His hands trembled in his lap, flecked with blood that was not his own. He didn't look up; his body language spoke of defeat, of grief, of a deep, heavy loss that was beyond his ability to handle.

"I saw her..." he mumbled as he twisted his wedding ring with shaky fingers.

Bob gave Millie a flick of his head toward Ron, indicating she should approach.

Bob always left the handling of emotional witnesses to her. People skills were not his forte, so Millie almost always got the role of comforter. It was a bit like the stereotypical good cop, bad cop that way, but it often worked.

Millie handed over her notepad and pen to Bob and moved toward Ron, crouching down before him. "Saw who?" Millie asked, her tone gentle and comforting.

Ron was silent as he continued to spin the wedding band on his finger before his body began to tremble and he broke into deep, heavy sobs. "I... saw..." he tried between hacking coughs as he struggled to breathe between the tremors wracking his body. "I... saw... Mary. It was her... but it wasn't. She was... She was demonic. Like something... something had possessed her... warped her... She... She killed Julia... she..." He stopped as his grief consumed him. Tears streamed down his face as he drew his knees up and placed his head between them. Millie knew she wouldn't get anything further from him for a while.

"I'm going to get someone to look after you, okay? Do you have someone you can stay with? A relative? A friend?"

Ron managed a weak nod between sobs, and Millie reached out a hand and placed it on his shoulder, giving it a comforting squeeze before she stood up. She gave Bob a haunted look that said more than words ever could.

The pair left the house, and Millie drew a long, satisfying breath, the crisp air washing away the lingering odor of blood and death.

"Okay," Bob sighed, blowing out a breath. "I'll get forensics down here. They should hopefully have finished up by now at the medical examiner's office. You go and get one of the paramedics to look after Ron." He hesitated for a moment, a look of calculated suspicion on his face. "That's two deaths surrounding him now, which makes him the prime suspect. We'll need to question him tomorrow."

"What about... about what he said? That he saw Mary..."

Bob barked out a short, harsh laugh. "Listen, I know you believe in the 'supernatural'," he said, pointing his fingers in a gesture to imitate a quotation mark, "but there's no way a corpse just decided to up and leave its freezer, travelled down the road sixty miles, and killed someone."

"I saw her, Bob," Millie blurted out, her face immediately turning crimson. She hadn't intended to speak of her sighting, but Ron's words made it feel impossible to keep to herself.

Bob frowned and shook his head with a sigh. "What do you mean you saw her?"

"Outside the house, before we spoke to Officer Myers. I saw her at the back of the crowd, staring at me."

"Oh, so that was what you were trying to show me. There was nothing there, Millie." He approached her, placing both hands on her shoulders, staring into her eyes. "Listen, I know this case is strange, but how many times have we run into something supernatural in other cases?"

"None," Millie admitted.

"Exactly. And how many cases have there been where there were things that seemed unexplainable, only to end up having a logical explanation?"

"All of them. Yeah, okay, I get it," Millie responded with a sigh, rubbing her forehead wearily.

"The most important thing for you to do right now is to think logically. I need your brain grounded here, in reality, okay?" He released his hands and pulled out his phone. "Now, go and get the EMTs to look after Ron and get one of the officers to drive you back to the office. Then go home and get some rest. We're going to need an early start tomorrow to go through all that's happened today."

Millie nodded. "Will do, and Bob... thank you," she said with a smile.

Bob nodded and turned back to the house, his phone already halfway raised as he made his first phone call.

After informing the waiting EMTs about Ron, she approached one of the officers who was standing guard at the temporary barricade. Soon she was sitting in the back of a patrol car on her way back to the office.

The engine hummed softly, a sound too normal for the thoughts spiralling in Millie's mind. She stared straight ahead, past the driver's headrest, past the dashboard's steady glow. Bob was right. She needed to rely on rational thinking and what the evidence told her. But she couldn't get Ron's words and the twisted, inhuman face of Mary out of her head.

Outside, the world smeared past in streaks of light and angular shadow, reflecting fractured shapes against the glass. Before she knew it, the precinct loomed ahead, its lights casting a sterile and familiar glow that promised order. But the dread she'd had about this whole case sat coiled behind her ribs like something with teeth. Bob wanted to rely on evidence. Facts. Millie wasn't sure any of that would matter if what she felt was right.

CHAPTER TWENTY-SEVEN

Bryan Holloway stood at his easel with his brush held high. His eyes narrowed in concentration behind his glasses before he lowered it, touching a smear of ochre to the earth beneath the solitary tree on the canvas. The painting was taking shape achingly slowly, but Bryan was patient, as he always was, knowing it would be worth it in the end. His paintings, though rarely prize winners, never failed to fetch a good price at the local art gallery. He could already tell this would be one of his better ones. He took a step back, admiring his work. He'd named it "A Piece of Nature." A large tree, symbolizing the last of its kind, sat alone in a field covered by shimmering wheat. Beneath the tree sat a small, lone figure still in progress, sitting cross-legged with a book in their lap.

He breathed in slowly as he closed his eyes, enjoying the smell of linseed, cedarwood, and the potent scent of paint. This was what he lived for.

Symphonic music drifted from the old radio on the partially open windowsill. He had chosen Beethoven tonight, the sweeping strings and airy notes of the wood-wind wrapping the attic in its comforting embrace. Shadows danced to it on the floor as the gentle breeze from outside shifted the curtains.

"Bryan!" Silvia's voice floated up from downstairs through the open door, muffled but clear. "I'm off to bed, love. Don't you dare paint till dawn again!"

He smiled, dipping his brush into titanium white. "Just finishing the sky," he called down, though he doubted she heard. She often said he had the radio up too loud, but he knew she didn't really mind all the same. It was a sign of his presence, a comforting sound that spoke of contentment and dreams coming true.

He felt a sudden gust of wind brush across the back of his neck.

Bryan paused, puzzled. The skylight was latched shut, and the attic's only window was on the opposite side of the room. Perhaps it was Sylvia, who sometimes liked to surprise him when he was lost in his work. He turned, expecting to see her smiling face, but there was nothing there.

He frowned and approached the window, sliding it shut. The room was starting to get a chill to it, anyway. He gave the space one last scan, eyeing the shadows behind the rows of paintings lining both sides of the room, and shrugged, returning to his easel. Maybe Silvia had left a window open downstairs.

Picking up his brush, he studied the painting and debated his next move.

Then he heard something he couldn't explain. A moan, low, deep, and wet, like someone struggling for breath under water. He froze. The sound seemed to curl around him, dripping with malice and ill intention. And then, behind him, he heard something move.

It was the sound of slow, measured, bare feet slapping across the old pine floorboards, and these were definitely not Silvia's.

Trembling, he turned around.

He gasped inadvertently in horror, his eyes widening as he took in what stood before him. "Mary?" he choked out.

Mary, or rather what wore her shape, stared at him with a macabre grin. Her skin, what little remained of it, clung to her skull, thin and stretched in places and hanging off like old wallpaper in others. There was a slickness to her face. It glistened beneath the attic light like oil on water. Her hair hung in long, damp ropes, matted and stringy, with a mix of silver colour and something dark that seeped rather than dripped.

Her eyes captured his gaze, unravelling his thoughts as if they were made of string. Impossibly blue, too large for the sockets they'd laid claim to, they glowed with the luminescence of drowned lanterns. They pulsed faintly, as if they had peered into his soul and found him wanting.

Beneath them, a tongue, thick and swollen, the colour of spoiled meat, slid sluggishly between her rotted teeth, shining with a slick, slimy film that gleamed in the light. She moved purposefully. With desire and need. She smiled, the muscles left in her face straining with the effort of holding together.

He took a step backwards. "You... you're not—"

She moved toward him, her limbs cracking and creaking with every movement she made, resulting in a grotesque, stop-motion imitation of a puppet with no one pulling her strings. Her face was filled with anticipation, with dark, undeniable intent.

He took another step backward, and his back met the easel, feeling it tilt behind him. "Whatever you are..." he whispered, "you're not my sister."

Her smile stretched wide, and she lunged, tearing into him before he had a chance to ward her off, her talon-like fingers carving into his chest with ease. He fell back first onto the floor with a heavy thud, managing to raise his hands in a weak defence, as she pounced on top of him with unnatural agility. His hands found her shoulders, and he strained to hold her at bay with every bit of strength he had left. He managed a desperate scream as she gnashed her rotten teeth at him, her tongue whipping around her mouth in a frenzy. Drool dripped onto his face, blurring his vision as she pushed down against his weakening grip. It was then that he knew. He knew she was toying with him. She could have ended him with a few more swipes of her fingertips, overpowered him easily, but she wanted him to suffer. Just like the echo of her final words amplified a hundred-fold. "You've done nothing but pick me apart, my choices, my actions, my lifestyle, like you are some kind of saint. You silenced me for years, Bryan. So here's my silence, forever. I hope you carry it with you until the day you die, alone, up in that attic of yours."

"I'm... I'm... sorry," he said, tears spilling from his eyes. "I only wanted to make you see what type of person you were becoming. So bitter... So angry... It didn't need to end that way. It didn't..."

With a snarl, Mary's body surged downward, her

mouth yawning unnaturally wide before clamping onto his throat, slowly, agonizingly digging her rotten teeth into his flesh. Blood spurted from his wounds, flying upward to coat the canvas of his final, precious artwork as the pressure of her teeth on his throat grew. They found their way through muscle and fibre before they severed his vocal cords and finally pulled free, taking half of his throat with them.

In a final, desperate attempt at forgiveness as he choked and gurgled, Bryan's pleading gaze locked onto her luminous blue eyes before they dimmed into unseeing darkness, his appeal lost to the thing that Mary had become.

"Bryan?" Silvia's worried, trembling voice from downstairs drifted through the open attic door, as Mary faded back into the darkness. With a final gust of wind, the last traces of her were carried away, leaving behind Bryan's lifeless body and the fulfillment of Mary's final words.

CHAPTER TWENTY-EIGHT

Millie brushed her teeth, staring at her exhausted reflection in the bathroom mirror. With makeup stripped away, the full toll of her long day stared back at her. Sunken eyes and prominent dark bags told of the sleep her body craved but could not find. Her mind was both her best and worst asset. It made her sharp, efficient, and relentless in pursuit of truth, but it never shut off. Though she made sure to go to bed early, it often took hours before her stubborn brain decided to give in to the calls for sleep. Today, after everything, she doubted she'd sleep at all. Finishing up, she turned on the faucet and leaned down to get a mouthful of water, washing out the minty granules left over from her brushing and leaving her with the aftermath of fresh breath. Rinsing off her toothbrush, she placed it back into its holder and sighed, mournfully staring once again at her reflection. If she kept this up, she would age quickly.

"There goes my chance at love," she muttered, thinking of the potential consequences.

A groan escaped her as the familiar, insistent ringing of her phone shattered the silence. "Aaaaaaannnd there goes my chances at sleep," she added as she headed toward her phone on the nightstand.

She picked it up, tapped the accept button, and raised it to her ear. "Hello, Detective Millie Armstrong speaking. How can I help?"

"Millie, it's Bob. Don't you check your caller ID?"

Millie grimaced. "Sorry, Bob, I guess I'm more cooked than I thought."

"Well, get yourself an energy drink and slap your face because we've got another dead body." Bob's words hit her like a knife to the stomach, and an icy dread seeped into her bones.

"Shit, it's not Ron, is it?" she blurted out, her heart suddenly kicking into gear.

Bob paused before replying. "No, it's not. Why do you ask?" There was a hint of something akin to playful suspicion in his tone.

"No reason," she replied too fast, her cheeks flushing. *What the hell, Millie? What's wrong with you? Get a grip.* "Who was it?" she asked, trying to regain some semblance of composure.

"Bryan Holloway."

"Who's that?" Millie asked in confusion, her brain struggling to place the name.

"Well, here's where things get interesting," Bob said, with a strange hint of excitement in his voice. "Bryan Holloway is the brother of one Mary Hinsworth."

Millie sat on the edge of the bed, trying to take in Bob's words, glancing at the time on her alarm clock on the nightstand. 10:39 pm, almost 3 hours after the death of Julia Mathews, Mary's daughter.

"Oh shit," Millie said simply, as she started searching for some jeans.

"Yep. Meet me here at 39 Mooncrescent Way ASAP."

"On my way," Millie said, tapping the end call button.

She emerged from the house five minutes later, an emergency energy drink from her refrigerator clutched in her hand like a talisman. Under the cloak of a quiet weekday night, the empty roads allowed for a quick twenty-minute drive to the scene.

The strobing blue and red lights of the parked EMT and police vehicles greeted her as she pulled up to the scene. She drained the last mouthful of the blueberry blast energy drink and tossed it onto the floor of the passenger-side seat. She eyed it with a hint of shame, noticing the dust buildup on the dashboard and various wrappers from protein bars abandoned in drink holders. She'd have to devote some time this weekend to give her car a good cleaning. That was if she wasn't working. At this rate, chances are she would be. She climbed out of the car, closing the door behind her with a thunk, and turned to face the house.

Nestled at the end of a cul-de-sac, the house itself looked typical of 1980s New England suburbia, complete with clapboard siding and a pair of eagle plaques above the garage. Between the splashes of red and blue from the police cruisers parked outside, she could just make out the cream and blue trim of the house colour. A few wind chimes dangled from the eaves, chiming once faintly as if in response to her arrival, though Millie couldn't feel any wind. What little lawn they had was freshly mowed, the hedges lining the path to the door clipped with care. The porch light was on, casting a gentle glow, and a warm light spilled from behind the curtains overlooking the street. Above, she could see a similar glow of light behind the attic curtains, and a chill ran down her spine. She didn't know why, but she knew there was something off about what was waiting beyond it.

"So, are you just going to stand there all night or…" Bob's familiar voice called out. She lowered her eyes and saw him leaning against the side of the front door, grinning at her.

"You're the one that's always on about making sure I observe the scene of a crime from every angle," she retorted, a faint smirk on her lips.

"Okay, well, wake me up when you're done," Bob said, proceeding to close his eyes and pretending to nod off.

The chatter of radios from the cluster of parked cruisers accompanied her to the front door. She could see shadows of figures moving inside through the window and the muffled murmur of conversations. There were no signs of forced entry that she could see. Whoever the killer was must've either been given entry by someone inside or come in through the back.

"Before you ask, no, there's no sign of forced entry in the back either," Bob said with a knowing look in his eyes.

"Clearly, I've been working with you for too long," Millie retorted, grinning half-heartedly, her senses prickling with unease the closer she got to the open doorway.

"Brace yourself. What's upstairs isn't pretty," Bob said, clearly noticing her growing anxiety.

"Can't be much worse than what we saw earlier," Millie

said with a grimace, a flash of the horrific scene a few hours before crossing her mind.

Bob snickered as he moved past and ahead of her, leading the way inside. He turned the corner toward the staircase, giving the gathered officers and EMTs in the kitchen a nod as he passed.

"I'm glad you found that funny," Millie muttered, her stomach already beginning to churn with dread.

"Hey, in times like these, you gotta try and find a bit of humor. Helps balance out the mind so you can think a bit more clearly," he said, throwing a smile over his shoulder at her as he climbed the stairs.

While Millie knew he was right, at least about the balancing of the mind part, she found it hard to get past her instincts, which were screaming at her that what they were facing here was something beyond both of their understanding. Still, she concentrated on her breathing as she continued to follow Bob, trying to calm her rapid heart rate and racing mind.

The stairs led to a landing on the second floor. A hallway lay in front of them, along with several open doorways branching off it to further bedrooms, only one of them used as intended, the others used for storage, judging by the quick glances she cast through them as the pair passed. At the end of the hallway, another set of stairs curved upward, leading to the attic.

Bob continued without pause, each heavy footstep echoing off the polished wooden steps. He stopped halfway, noticing she wasn't behind him. "Millie?" he called, looking down at her.

Millie was still at the foot of the stairs staring upwards.

The closer she got to the door, the more the air around her seemed to thicken, as if there was something up there waiting in anticipation of her arrival specifically. Her jaw clenched. Despite how deeply she tried to draw breath, it didn't quite seem to reach her lungs. The door upstairs was open, spilling yellow light onto the staircase, but it felt almost too inviting.

"It's been here," Millie whispered.

Bob either didn't hear or didn't care, shrugging as he pressed forward. The light from the attic fell across his shoulders as he reached the top step, casting his shadow down the staircase. It stretched toward Millie as if it were reaching for her before it slid away as Bob entered through the open door.

Millie shivered, taking one last breath before following him upstairs. Each thud of her footsteps synced with her heartbeat until they seemed like one and the same.

She entered through the doorway to find a scene of terrifying contradiction. Beautiful, dreamlike paintings lined the walls, a few layers deep. Those most detailed took centre stage. Painting supplies sat on a table near the back wall adjacent to the attic's lone window facing the street. The window she had seen from outside. The middle of the room was host to a scene of brutality and savagery, matching that of the Mathews' house just a few hours ago. A half-finished canvas on an easel displayed a scene of vivid detail, but it was ruined by bloodstains and dotted with spots of blood, the killer's contribution to a previously beautiful painting that would remain unfinished. Below the painting lay the body of Bryan, his body coated with blood, his face contorted with terror at what he had seen and gone through in the last moments of his life. Half of his throat had been torn out, leaving behind severed strands of muscle, arteries, and what looked like his vocal cords, the ridges of the cervical spine visible beneath the gore. His dress shirt, still half-tucked into his slacks, was torn open, exposing his chest, where deep slashes and gash marks could be seen underneath the coagulated blood that had pooled there.

His eyes were open and unseeing, his expression one of open-mouthed pure horror. Nothing natural had caused this.

"Jesus," she breathed, taking it all in. There was a feeling in the air. A lingering sense of fading energy that could only be described as malevolent. Spite and hate had reigned supreme here.

She approached Bryan's body, avoiding the blood spatters on the floor, and crouched down next to it, her training and instincts taking over despite the horrific scene. Something had caught her eye about the wound in his throat, and now that she was closer, she could see clearly what it was.

"Is it just me, or does it look like his throat has been torn out with just one giant bite?" She took out her pen and pushed back some flaps of torn skin, noting the uneven serrated edges. "From a mouth with broken or missing teeth, it seems," she added.

"You're not wrong," Bob said. "It does look like that, but it would have to be someone with a hell of a large head. Either that or some sort of animal. Both seem unlikely."

"The chest wounds do look like something an animal could be capable of," Millie admitted, noting the claw-like scratches trailing the edges of the gashes. Despite saying that, her mind kept circling back to Mary or the thing she had become. Millie hadn't seen her hands in that fleeting glimpse she had of her, and Ron hadn't mentioned them either, but she couldn't shake the feeling that Mary was responsible for this murder, too.

She stood up, taking in the room once more, but nothing else caught her attention. "Okay, fill me in," she said, returning to the entrance where Bob stood with folded arms, waiting.

"Nothing much to tell, really. I got a call just as I was wrapping things up at the Mathews' house. The wife, Silvia, had just turned in for the night when she heard the sounds of struggling and Bryan screaming. When she went upstairs, she found Bryan like this with no signs of an intruder. Whoever it was had gotten in, done the job, and gotten out fast."

"Silvia didn't hear anything suspicious at all before the attack?"

"Not a thing. No signs of forced entry from either the back or the front of the house. Windows and doors were locked and secure. The attic window was shut and is too high for anyone to get in that way, besides."

"Did you find anything before I arrived?"

As Bob shook his head, Millie was struck by the way fatigue had sunk into him, the hollows beneath his eyes, and his sagging face showing the toll of the day. Even Bob, usually unfazed, was feeling the strain of this bizarre case. "Nothing more than you have."

He looked at Bryan's body and sighed heavily. "This case makes no goddamn sense. If it weren't for the condition of Bryan and Julia's bodies, I'd say Ron was behind it. Hell, it still could be him or someone associated with him, but it's a stretch."

Millie nodded slowly, her intuition telling her otherwise. "Where was Ron when this was called in?"

"According to the officers I had posted at the motel he was put up in, still there in his room."

She hesitated, a frown on her face. "Hotel room?"

Bob shrugged. "Yeah, he opted to get one instead of calling his relatives."

"Probably wanted to be alone to process things, poor guy," Millie said.

Bob looked at her with a faint knowing smirk on his lips.

Millie's cheeks flushed red. "Well, I guess we just have to wait for the crime scene guys to do their thing and get back to us. Hopefully, there'll be a clear trail to follow," she said diplomatically, trying to hide her doubt and get the conversation back on track.

Bob eyed her and nodded slowly. "Speaking of, here they come now."

The familiar faces of Elliot and Cillian, the forensic investigators, appeared at the door. They halted, taking in the scene, and shook their heads.

"Jesus, Bob, you're keeping us busy tonight, that's for sure," Cillian said as he snapped on a pair of rubber gloves.

"Well, how about you guys find us something so we can make future nights quieter, hey?" Bob replied, his usual jovial tone gone.

"Workin' on it, boss," Elliot said before the pair began to case the scene.

Bob and Millie left the room and halted at the foot of the stairs, glancing at the bedroom where the sobbing figure of Silvia was just visible, sitting on the corner of the bed.

"She's all yours," Bob said as he pulled out his pen and gave it to Millie, eyeing the bloody one she still held in her hand.

"Oh, uh, yeah, thanks," Millie said, grimacing at the blood-smeared pen. She reached into her pocket, pulled out a tissue, and carefully wrapped it inside before handing it over, exchanging it with the fresh one.

She took a deep breath, preparing herself for what lay ahead. If there was one part of the job that tore at her, it was talking to victims at their most vulnerable, right when they were at the height of their emotions. Normally, she'd use it as motivation to bring those responsible to justice. This time, she wasn't at all sure that would be possible.

CHAPTER TWENTY-NINE

The next day

"No, it's okay, I'll see you there at 2 pm." The phone slipped from Ron's trembling fingers as the call ended. With a soft thud, it landed on his lap, the glow of the screen fading to black as his gaze remained fixed on it, unseeing.

The phone had rung for what felt like forever before he'd found the will to answer. It was as if every ring carried the weight of his grief and the wreckage of a sleepless night in that sterile hotel room. Now, he had to find some reserve of strength to face the detectives' questions on a heart running on fumes.

Tears resumed their well-worn path down his face as they escaped from his swollen eyes, a shudder once more running through his grief-stricken body. It felt like he hadn't stopped crying since he had first seen what remained of Julia after that... thing had ended her. Had he even slept? He couldn't remember. He glanced at the bed in dazed curiosity. It looked unslept in, the sheets still firmly tucked beneath the mattress, only the topmost layer looking ruffled. Looked like he hadn't then, though he supposed he could have just lain down on top. He had no memory of doing so, however.

He let out a sharp chuckle at the sheer stupidity of his own thoughts before they transformed and tumbled out of him. A laugh too long, too loud, tinged at the edges with a hint of something broken. Who could blame him? He was clearly losing his mind. Hell, maybe he already had. How else could he explain what he'd seen?

Because really, what made more sense? That something not-Mary, a terrifying caricature of her, had burst Julia's head like a melon? Or that when he saw what remained of Julia lying there on the floor, his mind had snapped, and filled the spaces with hallucinated horror?

He leaned forward, resting his head in his hands, the onset of a throbbing headache making its presence felt. He was pretty sure he hadn't drunk anything all night and was probably dehydrated, so it was no surprise. Standing up gingerly, he headed to the kitchenette. Lucky for him, this particular hotel room had one. He retrieved a glass from the cupboard underneath the sink and filled it with water, downing it in one gulp, the water spilling down his lips onto his already damp shirt. He noticed with disgust that it was from a mix of tears and sweat, a casualty of his body trying to cope with trauma. He leaned back against the counter and sighed, his eyes catching the old-fashioned wall-mounted analogue clock above the entry to the bedroom. It was 11 am. In a few hours, he would need to be on his way to the detectives' office.

He ached to collapse onto the bed, just curl into a ball and sink into his own misery, but he needed to look at least vaguely human for the interview. He considered calling a taxi to head back to the house for clothes, but the thought barely formed before he shoved it aside. The place would be sealed off for the investigation. And going back there, to where Julia had died, wasn't something he could stomach. Not yet.

Wait... hadn't he come into the room carrying something? A suitcase? He did. A recollection vaguely floated through his mind of an EMT handing him one with some spare clothes they had gathered for him. He had another vague memory of his carrying it into the room with him. He had carried it in, hadn't he?

He moved back into the room and scanned it. There it was, lying abandoned on its side next to the bed. Relief rushed through him. It was something. A small semblance of control. At least now, he could walk into that interview looking presentable, even if inside, he was in pieces.

He took a shower, enjoying the steam enveloping him, wishing it would take him away as it vanished. Away from reality and the enduring pain of a life without his wife. Tears once more cascaded from ducts that seemed to have an endless supply. Her smile, her laugh, the future they had planned together were nothing more than whispers of a life that would no longer contain them. In a world full of struggle, of uncertainty and instability, she had been his rock. A constant in his life that radiated goodness and love.

He honestly didn't know how he was going to get through this interview, but he had to try. He was sure he was a suspect, at the very least in Bob's eyes. Millie, he wasn't sure about. She had treated him with care the few times they had interacted, but he didn't know if that was just her nature or if she didn't harbor the same suspicions Bob did.

He sniffled, dragging in a breath of the moisture-laden air, trying to enjoy the last few minutes of the shower before he had to emerge out into the unforgiving world once again.

A few moments later, he was towelling himself dry, his thoughts turning toward the upcoming interview when an errant thought flew through his mind. The charge on the bank account that mysteriously wouldn't show. Had it been fixed yet? If it had, maybe he could pay a visit to the place or person Julia had been to see. At the very least, he could tell the detectives so they could follow up on it.

Quickly pulling on a shirt and slacks, he perched himself on the edge of the bed and pulled out his phone. Scrolling through his apps, he clicked on the logo of Crescent Capital and waited for it to load. Once it did, he tapped on his account and scrolled through the transactions until he reached the one that Julia had made.

"Here we go," he muttered to himself and tapped on it. His hopes soared as a small loading icon, a tiny spinning animation, briefly flickered on the screen, only to be cruelly replaced by the harsh, red-lettered error message he had come to know so well:

This record could not be retrieved. Please contact support if the issue persists.

"Fuuuuuuuuck!" With a roar of anger, he flung the phone onto the bed.

"Useless fucking support. Should've been fixed by

now," he growled as he absentmindedly rubbed at his temple. His headache had returned with a vengeance, and he didn't have any painkillers. He glanced at the time; almost 12 pm. Fortunately for him, there was a general store just a short walk away on a strip that contained a few shops opposite the hotel. He should be able to get some there and grab a bite to eat at the same time. Not that he wanted any food; in fact, his stomach began to roil at the thought, but he'd need the energy for what lay ahead.

A few minutes later, he stepped out onto the landing of the second floor, where his room was located. He looked around for the officers that had been stationed outside to keep an eye on him but he couldn't see them. He shrugged and after a brief stretch, he headed downstairs and squinted toward the strip of shops opposite that consisted of a tired-looking general store, a squat little cafe with fogged-up windows, and a laundromat that looked like it had been there since the beginning of time.

The parking lot stretched ahead in a wash of faded lines, old oil stains, and the occasional car. He walked across it toward the general store, pushing through the door and grimacing as it squealed in protestation. Inside, it was dimly lit and cool, with a strong odor of damp mould and bleach. He wrinkled his nose as he walked down the aisles, easily finding the painkillers on the second shelf, beside the sunblock and travel shampoo. He paid for them quickly, with a nod and a tight half-smile to the bored teenager behind the till.

Leaving the shop, he hesitated outside, eyeing the cafe next door, trying to work up the will to go inside. His hunger was nonexistent, his stomach on the verge of being brittle, a knot of nerves taking its place, but he figured he should eat.

He stepped inside and was greeted by low hums of country radio and the clatter of cutlery. A woman in her fifties, her greying hair tightened into a neat knot, stood behind the counter and gave him a smile and a nod as he made his way to a booth near the window. He studied the menu, his eyes skimming the words but not taking anything in.

"What can I get you, son?" the lady asked, having approached the booth without him noticing. She stood there with a notepad in hand. The nametag displayed her name, Layla, prominently on her chest.

"Toast," he said finally. "Just dry toast. And maybe a banana, if you have one." The safest bet. Something bland enough to trick his body into cooperation.

Layla nodded and poured him coffee without asking before she left to get his order ready. Ron reached for a cup and the decanter of water on the table and poured himself enough to wash down a few of the painkillers. Leaning back on the cracked vinyl seating, he stared out the window and watched the parking lot shimmer in the sun like it had somewhere else to be.

His thoughts turned once more to Julia and the mysterious person she had visited. Stockbridge wasn't exactly a large town, so odds were there weren't many people who could offer mystical services. He pulled out his phone and navigated to the search engine, tapping out 'Psychic near Stockbridge MA.' It brought up a few hits, but none were useful—a tasseomancer who read tea leaves out in Pittsfield and a few tarot readers who posted inspirational quotes but hadn't updated their sites since 2018.

He tried again: 'Spiritualist, Channeler, Medium, Stockbridge MA.' The screen blinked before the results loaded. He scanned the list of entries, but none of them appeared remotely connected to what he was chasing—what Julia had chased. None that suggested they would be the type to reach into the afterlife and do what Julia was after.

He sighed and tried once more. The smiling face of Layla approached him before he could, placing the unappetising plate of toast and sliced banana before him and departing wordlessly. He stared down at the plate with disinterest and brought his attention back to his phone, tapping in 'Resurrection ritual Stockbridge MA.' It came up with a warning about misinformation, along with no results.

Ron leaned back and rubbed his hand over his face. It felt like the town itself was resisting his efforts. It was as if Julia was the only one meant to see what had called to her, and no one else.

He set the phone down, the screen fading to darkness as it faced the ceiling. Next door, the laundromat drums thudded softly.

He was looking in the wrong place. But what other place *was* there?

He picked up the toast and took a bite, chewing it languidly. He would have to defer to the detectives. They undoubtedly had far greater access and resources to rely on that would hopefully find the answers he so desperately needed.

CHAPTER THIRTY

Millie sat down with Bob an hour before the scheduled interview time with Ron and reviewed the plan for questioning. Bob was thorough as usual, but the lack of results from the Mathews and Holloway houses clearly frustrated him. The reports were still a day out, and so far, nothing had come up as being useful. Still, if something did turn up, they could always get Ron back in. They were also still waiting for the toxicology results from Mary Hinsworth. They were due by week's end and might yet provide further information they could follow up on.

By the time they were done, Ron had arrived, and Bob and Millie went to meet him at reception. He cut a sorry figure. His dress shirt was creased and untucked, with no tie. His hair was wild, showing no traces of product to smooth it down. Stubble lined his face, which hung loosely, making him look years older than he was. Deep bags lined his bloodshot and haunted eyes.

"Mr Mathews, thanks for coming. I'm sorry for dragging you down here so soon after your wife's passing, but it's procedure, you understand," Bob said gruffly. He really wasn't good with people who had been through trauma.

Ron stared at the floor, shuffling his feet and nodding uncomfortably.

"We really appreciate you coming in. I know... this isn't easy," Millie said gently, glaring at Bob, who gave a shrug back and shot her a grin. "Detective Jordan's going to walk you through a few questions, all right?" Millie continued, gesturing toward the door.

"Okay," Ron said, his voice barely above a whisper.

"Would you like a coffee or tea before we start?" Millie asked, her voice full of concern at Ron's frail appearance.

"No, thank you," he replied, his voice tight with tension. "I'd rather just get this over with, if that's okay."

Bob gave a curt nod. "Then that's what we'll do. This way, please, Mr Mathews."

He led the way to the security door, swiping his keycard, pushing and holding it open as Millie and Ron passed by.

They walked in silence down a short corridor, the fluorescent lights humming above accompanying them. Near the end, they paused before a closed door.

"This is where I leave you in Detective Jordon's capable hands," Millie said, giving Ron a reassuring smile.

Ron nodded and inhaled slowly as if in preparation as Bob opened the door, revealing a brightly lit room. He stepped inside, Bob following on his heels.

Millie left them and headed toward and through the next door up the corridor, sitting down to view the room through the mirrored glass. Like the typical viewing rooms that were shown in the movies, one of the few things they got right, the interview room was sparsely decorated, only containing a metal table, a box of tissues, and two chairs.

Bob gestured for Ron to take a seat opposite the mirror, giving Millie a clear view of his now sweat-lined pale face. Bob remained standing and paced, shuffling a manila folder and leafing through it in a tactic that Millie knew was meant to make the interviewee more nervous.

He let it drop to the table with a slap and headed toward his seat, where he picked up an archive box from beside it. Millie frowned, puzzled. This hadn't been mentioned in the briefing. He placed it on the table slowly as he watched Ron's reaction and pushed it aside before he dropped into the seat to face him.

"Just letting you know as a courtesy, we will be recording this interview," he said, pointing at the cameras positioned around the room and behind him through the mirror.

Ron followed his fingers and looked at the cameras nervously before turning his attention back to Bob.

"Okay, let's go over what happened," Bob said, reaching for the manila folder and pulling it open once again. "Start with the moment you woke up."

Ron blinked, lowering his eyes to focus on the table. He swallowed. "Julia and I... we'd fallen asleep after. Well... you know..." Ron's face flushed slightly as he flashed a glance at Bob and the mirror behind where Millie was sitting. Millie felt a brief wave of secondhand embarrassment for Ron as she watched Bob nod, encouraging him to continue.

"I woke up sometime later from what I thought was a nightmare. I heard screaming. Julia's screams. She sounded so terrified..." His eyes welled up with tears, and despite trying not to, Millie felt a pang of heartache for him. Try as she might, something about Ron ruined her objectivity.

"What time was this?" Bob said, studying the information in the folder carefully.

"I... I don't know. I wasn't paying attention."

Bob nodded. "Continue," he said simply.

Ron blinked back his tears and wiped his hand across his nose. Wordlessly, Bob pulled out a tissue and handed it to him. Ron nodded gratefully and took it, blowing his nose.

"I ran toward the stairs. I could hear voices, but something wasn't right with one of them."

"How do you mean?" Bob asked.

"One of them was obviously Julia, but the other?" Ron shuddered as he shook his head.

"At first, I thought it was Mary. It sounded almost exactly like her, which was impossible. Then... it changed. The voice was low, almost gravelly, like a voice dragged through mud. Every word made me sick to my stomach, as if they were said by something that wasn't meant to be heard. Like something evil was trying to wear Mary's voice like a mask."

Bob looked sceptical. "Did you hear what the voice said?"

"I had just reached the top of the stairs when I caught the last part of it. Something like, 'Give your mother a kiss.'"

"Jesus," Millie whispered. A chill shot through her spine as she stared at Ron through the glass. This was no performance. There was nothing but pure recollective fear in his body language, and it was written all over his face.

Bob nodded slowly, his eyes watching Ron like a hawk. "And then what happened?"

"I ran the rest of the way downstairs. I called Julia's name but—" He faltered, and tears flowed down his cheeks as his face twisted in grief, his breath becoming harder to draw. "I saw that thing... A monster... It looked a bit like Mary but wasn't. It couldn't have been. It hardly had any skin on its head. It still had her hair, but it was thin and ragged. She had this long tongue, thick, slimy, dripping with something. And her eyes... Oh, god, her eyes..." His breathing was rapid, almost to the point of hyperventilation.

"Do you need a minute?" Bob's eyes narrowed as he studied Ron's face, his expression giving away nothing.

"No." Ron drew in a few deep, shaky breaths and shook his head. "I just want to get this over with. Its eyes... they were huge. Like too big for their sockets and pure blue. They were radiating light, almost like a torch."

Bob nodded, folding his arms over his chest. "Anything else?"

"It was hunched over like someone ancient. Its skin was slimy and runny, like it was rotting. It smelled like it, too. It was awful. Like rotting meat left out in the sun for months."

"What was it doing when you saw it?"

Tears spilled freely from Ron's eyes, and he reached for another tissue. He dabbed at his face and wiped his nose before continuing. "It... It had its hands on both sides of Julia's head, pressing inward. I heard a crack and..."

He broke into heavy sobs, and all Millie wanted to do was to run to him and wrap him in a hug. She knew by the way she was reacting, *had* been reacting to him, meant that she was falling for him, or at the very least had feelings. A bad sign, given the need to remain unbiased, and it was also inappropriate. She sighed and gazed at Ron with sadness, watching as he slowly brought himself back under control.

"It looked up at me when it saw me. Only briefly before it concentrated on Julia again and then... Then her head exploded." He sat back, his body racked with silent sobs, a blank stare fixed on the table before him. His body language was like a soundless scream. His stooped form, haunted eyes, and trembling hands spoke of someone overwhelmed by the trauma of what they'd witnessed.

"What happened to the thing? Mary?" Bob prodded gently. His tone of voice was almost sympathetic, which was a surprise to Millie. She couldn't recall the last time he had shown any sort of tenderness during questioning.

Ron's eyes darted upward. His hands twisted in his lap as if he were unravelling something. "It looked at me. Gave me this hideous smile. It was like it saw through to my soul. Then it... it disappeared, right in front of my eyes. One second it was there, and then..." He let out a breath that sounded thin and defeated. "It just... faded. Drifted away like smoke. Like it was never there at all."

Bob's brow furrowed, disbelief with a hint of curiosity etched on his face. "Are you sure you weren't hallucinating? Did it run? Was someone else there? Did you hear, smell, or see something?" Bob pressed, trying to make a semblance of sense out of something that seemed well out of the range of reality.

Ron shook his head emphatically. "I thought I was hallucinating, too. I've been trying to work out what other possibilities there were, but nothing can explain what I saw."

"Did you take any drugs? Any alcohol?"

Ron hesitated, a somewhat guilty expression forming on his face. "I... I've been drinking pretty heavily the past week or so, since... since Julia came back from the hospital," he sighed heavily. "She was just so different. I could tell she blamed me for how things turned out between her and her mother. The fight she had with her at the end. She probably already told you about that when you interviewed her, right?"

Bob nodded and leaned forward in his chair. "You say you've been drinking. Were you drinking last night, Mr Mathews?"

"No. Not last night. Last night was different."

"How so?"

Ron massaged his temple slowly and grimaced. "Sorry, I have a horrible headache at the moment I can't seem to shake."

Bob nodded impatiently, gesturing for Ron to continue.

"The house had been a wreck since Julia came back from the hospital. What with me drinking and Julia confining herself to bed..." Ron shook his head and sighed before continuing. "Anyway, she was up, had cleaned up the house, and was waiting for me when I walked through the door. She hugged me. One thing led to another, and we went upstairs to the bedroom. I don't think I need to explain what happened there," Ron said softly, sadness etched on his face at the memory.

Bob leaned back and studied him silently as Ron shifted

uncomfortably under his gaze. "Rather a sudden turn-around, don't you think?" Bob said, suspicion clouding his features.

"Listen, I need to tell you something," Ron said as he lurched forward suddenly, his face taking on a look of urgency.

Bob's eyebrows raised in surprise at Ron's sudden change in mood. "Go ahead."

"Two..." Ron hesitated, his eyes blinking as he searched his memory. "No, three days ago, I came home from work to find the house empty. Julia was gone. I ran upstairs to check if her things were still there because I... I thought she might have left me. Things were so bad between us at the time, I wouldn't have been surprised. But her things were still there. I sent her a message, asking if she was okay and when she would be back, but I didn't hear anything from her. I think it was an hour later that she came home."

"You think?" Bob questioned, trying to coax a specific time from Ron.

Ron's face turned a shade of crimson. "I... I had been drinking, you see, and things are a little... blurry."

"I see," Bob said, nodding slowly.

"Anyway, she came home, and she saw I'd been drinking. She got angry, and that was when she said something strange." He hesitated once more and glanced at Bob. Millie could tell he knew he was under the microscope and was being found wanting.

Bob waited, his arms still crossed, a flat, unblinking stare focused on Ron.

"She said she'd been to see someone. Someone who could bring back Mary. She said it cost five thousand dollars, and she had to hand over a picture of Mary, but she would return in two days."

Behind the glass, Millie's stomach dropped as if a lift cable had snapped. The chilling realization hit her like a physical blow. What she had seen and felt, she hadn't been hallucinating at all. Her skin prickled with fear, each hair standing on end as a cold dread settled deep within her bones. A wave of nausea washed over her as she sat there, staring through the glass at the two men in the interview room.

"Wait a minute, who had she seen?" Bob asked. He uncrossed his arms, his brows knitting, as he leaned forward. "You're telling me she gave someone five thousand dollars and a photograph, and just expected her dead mother to... what? Walk in through the front door like nothing happened two days later?"

"I didn't believe her," Ron said quietly. "She seemed out of it. Like she was drugged or something. She smelt of incense and herbs, and her eyes were kind of... distant. Like she was looking at me but not seeing me."

Bob exhaled through his nose, a sound low and unsettled. The sarcasm he usually reached for stayed put. "Who was it?" he asked. "Who did she go to see?" His voice no longer sounded like a challenge. It sounded like a man hoping for an answer that made sense but already knowing he wasn't going to get one.

"That's the thing. She didn't say. She walked off upstairs, and I knew I couldn't get her to talk anymore after that, so I left her alone." He sat back and sighed. "I tried to find out. I logged onto my bank app and checked the transactions. There was one for five thousand dollars, just like

Julia said, but when I tried to look at it, the app just displayed an error. I tried restarting my phone and restarting the app, but it kept happening. Eventually, I tried calling up support, and even they couldn't work it out. They said they had to refer it to tech support, but it's still not fixed, even now, three days later."

Bob frowned, but his eyes lit up all the same. Millie knew the look well. Here was something he could finally make sense of. Something tangible to follow up on. "Now that," he said, his voice low but steady, "is something I can work with."

He pulled out his notebook and pen, flipping it to a blank page. "Bank name?"

"Crescent Capital Bank," Ron said, sounding somewhat relieved.

Bob nodded, already scribbling. "Alright. We'll get a warrant for the full transaction log and metadata—routing info, timestamp, and recipient details. Whatever's tripping your app, we'll see if it trips up on paper too." His pen paused. "You said support couldn't pull anything either?"

Ron gave a helpless shrug. "Just said there was a glitch and escalated it. No answers."

Bob snorted in a half chuckle, half scoff. "Glitches don't swallow five grand and leave a ghost behind. If someone's covering their digital tracks, they weren't expecting us to dig this deep."

He glanced at the mirror, his eyes searching for Millie beyond it. She could already feel the rhythm shifting. Bob had the sniff of a real lead now. Whatever disbelief he'd clung to earlier was starting to erode under the weight of something far more useful, a trail.

Bob returned his attention to Ron. "I'd like to run you through an alcohol and drug screening, if that's alright with you."

Ron gave a tired shrug, eyes fixed on the table. "Sure. It might still show traces of alcohol, though, if it hangs around in the system after a couple of days."

Bob nodded with a half-smile. "The results will tell us that, if what you're saying is correct." He allowed the pause to linger, making it feel heavy with unspoken meaning.

Millie, still behind the mirror, caught the flicker in Bob's eyes. Not suspicion, exactly, but on the road toward it.

"Oh, and one more thing before we wrap things up here," Bob said, his eyes flashing with anticipation as he stood up, pushing the chair back with a sharp scrape. He flipped the lid off the archive box and picked up something from inside, letting it drop onto the table with a loud thud.

It was an old photo album. Ron's eyes drifted to it, and he shifted uneasily before moving his attention back to Bob warily.

"Can you explain to me why this photo album was open on the floor upstairs to a page with a picture of Mary, Ella, and Bryan Holloway?"

Ron frowned, a look of confusion crossing his face. "I know Mary, but who are Ella and Bryan Holloway?"

"Come now, Mr Mathews, you must know," Bob said, as he flipped through the photo album until he landed on a page and pointed accusingly at a photo.

Millie stood up from the chair and leaned forward, trying to get the right angle to see what Bob was referring to. It wasn't clear from her vantage point, but she could just make out three figures, one of them Mary and the other two presumably Ella and Bryan.

"I've never seen them before," Ron said, a shadow of confusion crossing his face. "Julia told me that Mary had a brother and a sister, but she never showed them to me in a photo. Maybe Julia had been looking at that page when we went to bed." He paused, with a puzzled look still on his face. "Why are you asking me about them?"

Bob sighed, his eyes losing their sparkle. "Bryan Holloway was killed a few hours after Julia."

Ron's eyebrows shot up in surprise, and his face became visibly whiter than it already was.

Millie could see the disappointment in Bob at Ron's answers. Despite not knowing about the photo album and this particular line of questioning, she knew he was hoping for some sort of breakthrough, a tell that would indicate he was behind the deaths. This was despite the fact that the officers positioned outside Ron's hotel had stated that he was in his room at the time of Bryan's murder.

"How can... How can that be?" Ron's voice caught in his throat. "Do you know who did it?"

Bob pursed his lips and shook his head before he picked up the photo album. As he did, a single photo that had been loosely tucked between its pages slipped from within and floated to the table like a falling leaf.

Ron's breath hitched. Behind the glass, Millie stepped closer to the pane, her forehead nearly touching its surface. She squinted, trying to make sense of what she was seeing.

The photo showed Ron and Julia locked in an embrace, the sun painting their faces, both frozen mid-laughter and looking at the camera. A moment that hadn't yet known shadows.

"That was... the day I proposed," Ron whispered. "We were at the lake... What is it doing here?"

Bob gave a faint shake of his head. "It was in your wife's nightstand. In the top drawer. You'll get it back when we close the case."

Ron looked down at it, his face crumbling, and then something in the room shifted. The air seemed to fairly crackle, as if suddenly charged, the fluorescent lights flickered, buzzed louder, then dimmed. Ron's breath misted in the air, followed by Bob's, as if they had been transported to the middle of the Arctic.

"Do you feel that?" Ron murmured, his eyes darting around the room.

Bob took a step back, his eyes scanning the lights and the walls of the room. And then, in the corner, where the dimmed fluorescent lights could not reach, something began to form.

It took shape fast, too fast for either of them to process what was happening. Now fully materialized, a hunched shape stepped into the light with a hiss. Its skull was nearly bare, with what little skin remaining gleaming wetly in the light. Strands of hair, stringy, damp, and rotting, hung over its face like curtains in a flooded house. Its eyes, molten blue, glowed from within like stars, pulsing with a knowledge so ancient it defied human understanding. They locked onto Ron with a singular purpose.

A long, immensely thick, and grotesque tongue slid from between its jagged, exposed teeth and curled upward like it was tasting the fear rippling through the air.

Ron stood up from the chair like lightning, and it clattered backwards onto the floor as he stumbled away from the table, trying to put space between him and the creature. "No...oh God. Mary?!"

Bob recovered from his initial shock, and his hand went to his holster, drawing his weapon in one smooth motion. "Stay back!" he warned the thing, but it paid him no notice as it took its first steps on its slow, inexorable approach toward Ron.

Bob didn't hesitate; he fired, the bullet whistling through the air only to vanish into the thing, leaving no wound. The creature grinned and lunged toward Ron.

Bob moved again, driven by a desperate impulse, and threw himself between them.

The blow intended for Ron instead hit Bob, with a savage, inhuman strike that lifted Bob off his feet and slammed him into the wall. His body hit with a sickening thud, an audible crack that could only indicate the snapping of bone, and he slumped to the ground, motionless.

Millie didn't think. She ran out of the observation room and tore down the hall to the interview room. Slamming through the door, she rushed inside, grabbed Ron by the collar, and dragged him out the door and into the hallway. The thing, still staring down at the unmoving form of Bob, turned its head slowly, cocking it at an unnatural angle, and stared at her, as its tongue twitched in agitation.

And then, as if its fun had been ruined beyond repair, the thing unravelled.

The shadows folded in on its figure as it turned to thick smoke and dissipated into nothingness, leaving behind a deathly silence in its wake.

Ron collapsed beside the door, weeping. Millie rushed back inside the interview room and crouched beside Bob's fallen form, two fingers pressed to his neck with trembling urgency. There was nothing. He was gone.

She bowed her head as tears trickled down her cheeks. Her partner. Her friend. The man who'd been like a father to her was now nothing more than a cooling husk. A life of steadiness and fire replaced by forever silence.

"Is... Is he...?" Ron asked, his voice weak and shaky.

Millie nodded, not able to trust herself to speak. Not yet. Her body shook, overwhelmed by the events and the feelings of devastating loss.

She was vaguely aware of heavy boots pounding down the corridor, but the sharp, insistent rhythm couldn't penetrate the thick fog of her grief. Alarmed voices surrounded her, distant and distorted, and it wasn't until firm hands guided her from the room that she realized she was moving at all.

CHAPTER THIRTY-ONE

Chief Thomas Delaney's office – 1 hour later

Millie sat stiffly on the hard wooden seat in Chief Delaney's office. Her uniform was smeared with Bob's blood. Her badge hung from a lanyard around her neck, gleaming dully in the bright, buzzing overhead light. Her eyes were dark hollows, sunken beneath the weight of loss.

The door closed behind her softly, and she heard the blinds being drawn, hiding her from the curious prying eyes of those from the office. Soft footfalls followed as the chief came into view, rounding the corner of his desk and sitting down opposite her in his chair, which had been made more for functionality than comfort.

Millie was barely aware of him in front of her as she took in the chief's service plaques and framed commendations lining the wall above his seated figure. She'd seen them many times before, but they were easier to look at than the concerned face of the chief. The air was filled with unease, a tension that she wasn't used to when being in his presence.

The chief cleared his throat awkwardly, trying to draw her attention to him. "How are you doing, Millie?" he asked quietly, his voice conveying the sympathy and concern he was well known for when it came to his detectives' well-being.

Her eyes finally fell on him and immediately welled up with the familiar onset of tears that seemed like they just wouldn't stop. She closed her eyes and took a deep breath, holding it for a few seconds before releasing it. Reaching for a tissue on the desk, she dabbed at her eyes before answering. "I feel like I'm in a nightmare I can't wake myself from."

Chief Delaney nodded, his own face falling in sadness. He and Bob had worked together the longest of anyone else in the office, going on almost twenty years. The position of chief could have been filled by either of them, but Bob had no interest, preferring fieldwork rather than 'professional babysitting with added paperwork' as he liked to say.

The chief blew a breath out slowly before he reached for a stainless-steel coffee thermos on his desk, taking a sip and setting it down with a gentle metallic thunk. He looked at her sadly and folded his hands on the table. "This will probably come as no surprise to you, but I'm placing you on administrative leave, effective immediately. I'll need you to have a mandatory psych evaluation, standard protocol, and all, you understand."

Millie gave a single nod. Her mouth moved to try to form words that never came.

The chief sighed before continuing. "I need to ask, what happened in that room?"

She looked down, her brow furrowing. "You wouldn't believe me."

"Just try. I need to hear details from your perspective," he said, his voice soft but firm.

Millie exhaled shakily as her eyes drifted to the recorder on the desk, its red light glaring at her as if in accusation. "Bob was performing a standard interview with Ron, trying to get details of what he saw last night, determining if he was responsible for his wife's death. He was just about to wrap things up when..." She halted, her breath catching in her throat as the memories flowed through her mind.

Delaney nodded in understanding. "Take your time," he said encouragingly.

Millie gave a short nod and dragged in a breath as she fought to compose herself. "The lights in the room, they flickered and dimmed, and there was a... darkness that formed in the corner. It solidified, and the thing that stepped out... It was... Mary Hinsworth. But wrong. Like the corpse she had been, but alive. Twisted. A perverted form of her that wasn't human. I've seen death, Chief. That thing... it was like it was wearing death like a second skin, using it for its own purposes."

Silence filled the room as the chief stared at her, speechless. He had only ever known Millie as a strong, confident detective with sharp instincts and a work ethic that was the envy of many. She knew she must be coming across as if she had a psychotic break. As if she were delusional.

Chief Delaney finally nodded slowly. "I'm familiar with the Hinsworth case, a curious one indeed that I know had

Bob baffled, and as you know, Bob hated an unsolved mystery." He sat back and drummed his fingers on the table, his face taking on an unreadable expression as he continued to stare at her. "The footage from the interview room turned out to be corrupted. One minute, Bob was talking to the suspect, wrapping things up as you say, and then static. One continuous stretch of grey snow. I have the techs on it, but for now... there's nothing we can see. They did manage to recover some sound, though. A muffled cry from Bob, a thud, and his screaming."

She blinked, surprised. She had expected that the tape would show nothing, but the sounds captured were new.

"Listen," he said, leaning forward again and looking at her with resignation, "we'll continue to look into this, but for now, I'll need your badge and sidearm," he said gently.

She nodded, her hands trembling as she reached up and slipped the lanyard over her head, setting it and her badge on the desk with a heavy clink. She hesitated with her weapon, then handed it over reluctantly.

"Get some rest," Chief Delaney said as he gathered her weapon and badge, sliding them into a drawer, which he locked securely. "And talk to someone. Bob would've wanted..." He choked on the words, barely getting them out. "He'd want you to come through this."

Millie struggled to contain an outburst of sobs as she stood. She nodded wordlessly and walked out, each footstep echoing like a gunshot down the empty hall.

CHAPTER THIRTY-TWO

Three days later

Making the last few adjustments to his tie, Ron placed both hands on the cool, smooth marble of the bathroom unit and stared at his reflection in the mirror. He looked terrible, but he supposed everyone would after what he'd been through. His eyes were ringed in shadows from sleepless nights, his skin a sickly pale white, a testament to the diet of alcohol he had been on the last few nights. Tears began to glisten in the corners of his eyes once more, and he quickly wiped them away. There would be plenty of time for them at the service. Popping open the cabinet, he rifled through the shelves, finally finding the near-empty painkiller bottle. He downed a couple with a few mouthfuls of water from the tap. Hopefully, it would calm his throbbing head that he still had after last night's alcoholic binge enough so he could get through the day.

The last few days had been hectic. After Bob's death, he had been questioned again about what happened, this time by Internal Affairs. If the original interview with Bob had been tense, this one bordered on interrogational. They circled him with questions, reframing and repeating the same lines over and over, clearly hoping he'd slip, revise, or reveal something they could use to make sense of the incomprehensible. But he had no different answer to give. What had happened defied logic and explanation. Had defied belief.

The next day, he was asked to undergo a psychological evaluation. He agreed without hesitation. He had nothing to hide, and he wanted no lingering doubts about his role in Bob's death. No one told him the results, but the fact that he hadn't been hospitalized or charged with obstruction probably meant he had passed.

In between all that, he had been busy organizing Julia's funeral. The few contacts he had—Julia's cousins, whom she had seen from time to time—had managed the invitations on their side, leaving him to organise his side of the family, namely his parents and his younger sister. He had also shot Millie a quick message asking if she could come so he could discuss tracking down the mysterious transaction and the person Julia had seen, though he hadn't heard anything back from her. And early this morning, just a few hours ago, he was given clearance to return home. And now... home is where he was. Except it didn't feel like home anymore.

The house was heavy with Julia's absence. Every room bore her imprint, but none of her presence. It felt like he was trespassing in a museum dedicated to someone else's life. Everywhere he looked was a reminder of what he'd lost. The bookshelf in the corner still held her favourite novels, each spine softened by her hands. In the bathroom, rows of makeup lined the cabinet just as she'd left them—colours chosen for evenings that would never come. The walk-in closet was a quiet graveyard of fabric and scent: her dresses, her coats, her shirts, some still clinging to the faint trace of her perfume.

None of it would ever feel her touch again.

The thought of sorting through it all and deciding what to keep and what to give away felt unbearable. He didn't know how he'd survive the process without breaking apart, over and over, in rooms that now echoed with nothing but the memory of love.

He sighed, wiping away the tears that had resumed their flow down his cheeks with a now-damp handkerchief. He would need to get a clean one before he left the house.

Approaching the bed, he sat on its edge. The mattress dipped unevenly, a reminder that her weight would never grace its presence again. And there, right at that moment, that was the worst part of it all. Sobs wracked his body once more, and he felt himself on the verge of losing himself in them. Something he could not afford to do. He had to leave in a matter of minutes.

He forced himself to his feet and gathered his jacket and a spare handkerchief, exiting the room as fast as he could, as if his memories had become something physical that he could outrun. Downstairs was just as bad. The clock ticked too loudly, the refrigerator kicked on like a threat. Nothing moved, but everything felt on edge. The lounge room had been cleaned, but bloodstains remained on the couch and the carpet. Wherever he went, he couldn't escape what had happened. It was then that he made the decision. He couldn't stay here. Not right now. It was too much.

Grabbing the keys off the hook by the front door, he rushed outside, barely remembering to lock it behind him. He would spend the night at the hotel once again until he could figure out what he would do with the house.

He glanced at his watch and swore. It was almost 12:44 pm. The funeral would start at 1:30, and he was supposed to be there half an hour early. He would be almost 15 minutes later than he should have been. Jumping in the car and getting onto the road was a relief. Despite the grief that awaited him ahead, it was somehow better than being mired in misery and longing for what would never be again, though that was something he would have to come to terms with in the days to come.

He was greeted at the chapel with sympathy and understanding. Despite his late arrival, the final details of the service were nailed down quickly, and before he knew it, the chapel was half-full. He greeted each newcomer with a soft murmur. Faces filled with sympathy and sadness swam by before his eyes as he went mechanically through the motions. Finally, the time came for the service to start. He walked down the aisle, to the accompaniment of sobs, passing shaking hands, dabbing at moist eyes with crumpled tissues.

The service blurred past him. Kind words were spoken, true and heartfelt, but they floated like dandelion seeds and refused to settle. Faces nodded. Many wept. Ron sat at the front, hands clasped, nails pressed deep into his palms, his parents and sister by his side. When they played Julia's favourite song by Ed Sheeran, accompanied by photos of her life, he felt his throat tighten, but no tears came. Not yet.

Afterward, he lingered by the door, receiving and offering unenthusiastic hugs, half-meant thank yous, and empty words like, "She would've loved that" or "She always spoke so highly of you." The world felt thin and brittle, ready to crack at any moment with the weight of genuine feeling, yet somehow, someway, it didn't.

His sister, Mandy, and his parents gave him a tight hug as they passed. Having organized the wake at a local function centre, they had to get there early to get everything settled and make any last-minute arrangements. He would see them there later.

Another face approached, this one like all the others, crumpled with sadness. In her early sixties, it wasn't her kind, gentle eyes and grief-worn face that caught his attention; instead, it was what she held in her hands.

"I thought you might want this," she said, her voice low and deep with feeling. "It was on my mantelpiece and is one of my favourite photos, but I think it belongs with you now."

Ron frowned briefly, trying to place who it was that was offering this picture before it dawned on him. "Ella?"

She nodded warmly as she extended the photo out for him to take. He did so carefully. It was in a frame, slightly faded but bright with memory. Julia, eight years old and laughing, sat between a younger Mary, Bryan, and Ella, flanked by two cousins, Sarah and Andy, all sunburnt and squinting into the sunlight. Sand and sea were captured behind them, joy etched in every crinkle on every face, even Mary's.

He stared at the image, brushing his finger over Julia, and swallowed hard. "Thank you," he whispered, his voice catching. "I've never seen this photo before, but everyone looks so happy."

Ella nodded, her eyes misting. "Julia lit up the beach. Even as a kid."

Ron met her gaze, steady and raw. "Thank you, Ella. For this. It means more than I can say."

Ella gave him a faint, understanding smile. "You don't have to say anything. I know."

Ron's face fell, and his cheeks flushed with guilt when he remembered how much she had gone through. With all of that loss, it was a miracle she had even turned up, let alone managed to be coherent. "Oh, I'm so sorry, Ella. I know you lost Bryan, too. That, on top of losing Mary and Julia. Are... are you okay?"

Ella's face buckled, and tears flowed down her cheeks, but she nodded quickly, wiping at her eyes as if ashamed. "No, but I will be. And don't you worry about me, okay? Just concentrate on yourself. When we lose those we love in our lives, we need to let ourselves grieve. It's one of those few times where you can be justifiably selfish and prioritize yourself, so don't you dare feel guilty, okay?"

Ron nodded as both of them struggled to contain their tears. They exchanged hugs, this one more heartfelt and fuller of meaning than any he had given today before they parted, and Ron was temporarily left alone to stare at the casket at the end of the church, his heart feeling as empty as the church now was.

"Excuse me, Mr Mathews?"

Ron turned around to see the sympathetic smile of

Detective Millie Armstrong. To his surprise, she wasn't dressed in the standard business attire that he was used to seeing her in. Instead, she was wearing a tailored black blazer, paired with a high-neck blouse of soft charcoal silk. Her trousers were pressed, flowing just above polished, low-heeled shoes. Her hair was swept into a neat bun, framing her mournful expression.

"I'm sorry I didn't let you know I was coming. It's been a rough few days to say the least, though I don't need to tell you that," she said softly.

He nodded mutely, unable to trust himself to speak. It seemed that the dam holding back his grief was finally about to burst.

"It was a lovely service, I'm sure Julia would have appreciated it," she added, giving a respectful nod toward the chapel where Julia's coffin was visible off in the distance. "I'll keep this short, okay? I know you need to go to the wake. Listen, I know you want me to look into tracking down who Julia saw, but I'm afraid I've been put on administrative leave."

"What... what does that mean? Are you in some kind of trouble because of what happened?" Ron asked, managing to put aside the wave of grief that threatened to collapse onto him to focus on what Millie was saying.

Millie sighed and looked away, staring into the gardens surrounding the chapel. "The situation at the office is still being investigated. The camera footage is missing the section where Bob was killed. There was only some audio captured, and it's not enough to explain what happened. Our accounts were a little too unbelievable for the powers that be to believe. So, I'm in a holding pattern right now.

What that means is that I no longer have the resources to trace the transaction that Julia made."

Ron's face fell at the news, and he lifted a hand, sweeping his hair back with a sigh. "So, I guess that's it then," he mumbled, his lips trembling slightly. An onset of frustration, sadness, and hopelessness hit him, and all of a sudden, he felt his legs weaken. It was as if he had unknowingly put all his belief into this last avenue for discovery of what had happened. Now it seemed that avenue was no longer open to him.

Millie turned back to face him, her expression softening as she saw the last of the hope drain from his eyes. "No, Ron. It's not over," she said, her voice quiet but firm.

He looked up, blinking in confusion.

"I may be in a holding pattern officially, but I'm not finished," she continued. "Julia's transaction, whoever it was she saw, matters too much to just let it go." Millie's eyes misted over with her own tears. "We've both lost someone now over this, not to mention the others this... thing has killed. I need to put a stop to it." Millie paused, her expression hardening with determination. "I can't access what I need to, but I know someone who can." Millie offered the faintest of smiles, one that didn't quite reach her eyes.

"I'll talk to her tonight."

The weight in Ron's chest lifted slightly, a flicker of something, maybe expectation, maybe just simply warmth cutting through the grief. "Tha... Thank you," Ron managed with a weak smile. "Listen, I have to go to the wake, but please let me know if you find anything."

Millie nodded and hesitated before stepping forward, enveloping him in a quick, awkward hug. "I'm so sorry for your loss," she whispered before she let go and turned to head back toward the parking lot.

Ron stood there and watched her go, a mix of surprise, unexpected warmth, and relief washing over him. He could feel it now; there was something between them. He couldn't deny that he felt a small spark at her hug. That thought was enough to rain guilt down on him. Here he was at his wife's funeral, and he was thinking about another woman. He couldn't help but feel disgusted with himself. Shaking his head, he headed toward his own car as he prepared to brace himself for the onslaught of well-wishes sure to head his way at the wake.

CHAPTER THIRTY-THREE

The next day

"Lucy Marie Jackson, no running near the BBQ, please. We don't want Lucy steak for lunch today, thank you," Ella Sinclair called out in warning, the warmth in her voice softening the threat.

Lucy slowed down obediently to a fast walk as she passed close by the BBQ where Mike, her father, waved a pair of tongs at her to try to get her attention. She grinned and cast a look over her shoulder at her sister, Sarah, who was in pursuit of her and pulling a face. Lucy, at five, and Sarah, at six, were full of energy. Far fuller than Ella could remember being at that age.

She laughed at the pair's antics as she returned to put the final touches on the chicken salad she was preparing. Her daughter, Belle, stood next to her, shaking her head with a wry smile as she cut up and put onions aside for Mike to use for the BBQ.

"She's grown so much lately. She must've had a growth

spurt," Ella remarked, as she peppered the salad with croutons. She sighed and shook her head. "Time goes too fast."

"Tell me about it," Belle replied. "I can't keep up with how fast things move. Buying new clothing, new toys, trying to understand the latest trends and phrases..." She shook her head in amusement. "I feel so old, and I'm barely thirty." Belle and Ella shared a chuckle as the pair took a break and leaned back against the table, watching Lucy and Sarah as they ran circles around the backyard, exchanging tags.

The spacious yard was bathed in sunlight, with only a few clouds casting their shadows on trees that were mostly bare except for a few golden leaves clinging for dear life to their branches. The air bore a crispness about it, a sign of the approaching winter. This close to it, it was often difficult to get days like this, but it was like the gods had gifted this day to them. A day to share with family, a day to treasure because no one ever knows when a seat at the table might fall empty. Ella shook that morbid thought off. Losing both her brother and sister in the space of a few weeks had gotten her normally composed self feeling her mortality more than ever.

"It's a shame Andy and Billy couldn't make it," Ella said, her face dropping, her eyes wrapped in sadness. "But it's understandable. They were both so close to Bryan." She looked away as her eyes brimmed with tears.

Still, warmth stirred in her chest, a sunbeam briefly pushing away the shadows of her sorrow, as she pictured their faces. Andy, Bryan's son, was a mechanic and owned his own business. On top of that, he had bought some old, classic cars that had seen better days and was restoring them at his home. Billy, Andy's son, who was seven, was obsessed with video games as most boys were and spent most of his spare time playing them. His mother had passed away in a car accident a few years ago. They had been close to Bryan, visiting as often as they could. Though Bryan had been an artist, he had shared Andy's passion for car restoration, for bringing broken things back to life. He had adored Billy, whom he tortured with dad jokes and pranks, much to Billy's delight, who returned his adoration tenfold.

"Andy has never been good at dealing with emotions. He'd prefer to ignore them and drown himself in work," Belle said, her voice coloured with frustration. "The worst thing is, he's teaching Billy to dismiss them too."

"Don't be too hard on Andy," Ella said gently. "Bryan was never one to dwell on emotions, either. The apple doesn't fall far from the tree, as they say," she said with a sniffle, managing a small smile as she blinked away the tears at the corners of her eyes.

She turned back to examine the table. "Now, I think we're almost ready to go. We just need to wait for Mike to finish with the meat and then... Oh... wait, I forgot the mayonnaise for the salad," she said, noticing the missing bottle. "I'll be right back."

She turned and headed toward the double sliding doors leading into the house, closing them behind her. She hummed to herself as she neared the fridge before she felt the all too familiar pang of her bladder. With a sigh, she diverted her path and headed instead down the hallway toward the bathroom. Though grateful for her life's journey so far, the aches in her joints and frequent bathroom trips were a constant reminder of her age. *That, and seeing the relentless energy of my granddaughters*, she thought with a smile. She pushed open the bathroom door and headed toward the toilet. Moments later, as she turned to the sink, the bathroom door lock engaged behind her with a sudden, sharp click, making her jump.

"Lucy? Sarah? Is that you?" she called out, a tone of exaggerated indignation in her voice. She listened for the telltale giggle and pattering footsteps of the girls, but none came. The only sound was that of the toilet cistern filling itself after its use.

"It better not be, otherwise one of you will be getting attacked by the tickle monster when I come out," she called. She could already picture one of the two girls outside, trying to hold in a giggle. She shook her head with a smile and turned on the tap, pumping soap into her hands and rubbing them together under the cool water.

Finishing up, she turned off the tap and dried her hands with the washcloth beside the sink. She examined her reflection in the mirror wistfully, noting the ever-deepening lines creasing her face. A testament to a life well lived but noteworthy, a reminder to live the life she had left and fill it with as much joy as she could.

A flash of movement behind her in the reflection caught her attention, something indeterminate that her vision, dulled by the years, couldn't quite catch. Her curiosity piqued, she leaned closer to the mirror, the corner behind her swallowed by an unnerving darkness, its contents hidden within. A sudden biting chill permeated the room, making every exhalation misty. Ella watched, mesmerized, as frost spread across the mirror like a flash of lightning. Then, icy tendrils formed and extended across the glass, their edges sharp and crisp.

Behind her, the darkness grew, expanding ever outward, as black tendrils extended out of the pure black, their every motion exploratory as if they were searching for something. Then, there came a deep, tortured growl as a form grew, fed by the shadows like reality born from a nightmare. Mary, a macabre, twisted version of her, stepped out into the light, her unnaturally bright blue eyes burning like beacons of pure evil. She grinned at Ella, her grotesque face with mouldering patches of skin stretching and parting over her skull as a large, thick, and lecherous tongue snaked out from between her lips and hung loosely over the few broken teeth that remained on her lower jaw. She took a slow, shuffling step, her decayed body shuddering as if protesting with every movement, struggling to contain the demonic life that was making use of its body.

"Ellllllllaaaaaaaaa," she groaned in a voice that contained two within the one. One recognizable as Mary, the other dripping with corruption.

"You're not Mary," Ella whispered, her voice partly horrified but also full of pity for what Mary had become. She spun to face the creature who was once her sister, but now no longer, her body possessed by something foul not belonging to the world. "Get out of her. Leave her be. You have no right to use Mary as your plaything. Your toy for your twisted games. I see you, demon."

The demonic creature hissed, its eyes flashing in anger as it took another step closer. Its body trembled with unbridled rage. It was unused to a human standing up to it, resisting the fear and intimidation that it usually imbued in its victims.

"Get it over with then, but know this. You have no power over me. What you are will always be less than what is to come. Your darkness is nothing but a speck in the light of God, and it will be extinguished. Things such as you have no place in the world. Your time will come soon." She grinned at the creature as she stepped forward to meet it, spreading her arms wide. "Come to me, sister, embrace me one last time. Like you used to do so many years in the past before things soured."

For the first time, the creature faltered, uncertainty replacing its former confidence. It shuddered, its body convulsing with tremors as the unnatural glow in its eyes died away, revealing Mary's own eyes, filled with a poignant mix of sorrow, love, and regret, only to vanish again in the reappearance of the cold, blue light. A snarl erupted from the depths of its throat, both animalistic and feral.

Undeterred by the agitated demonic creature, Ella continued her path toward it, her arms wide, radiating love in the face of overwhelming hate.

The demon drew itself upward, abandoning its pretence of Mary's hunched form, and swept its arms down, its distended, razor-sharp nails carving through Ella's arms with ease. Blood arced from the stumps of flesh as her severed limbs fell to the floor with a sickening splat.

Ella's body screamed in agony, her exposed nerve endings sending waves of pain, but she refused to vocalize it. She wouldn't give this thing that had stolen Mary's body the pleasure.

She gritted her teeth, her body shuddering, her

lifeblood spilling to the floor, and stood her ground as the demon loomed over her. "Finish it, you fucker," she managed between small gasps of breath, every inch of her fighting her instincts to scream.

The creature growled, its tongue whipping around in its mouth in agitation as it wrapped its unnaturally long arms around her in a macabre embrace and pulled Ella to its body. The pressure increased steadily, as if the demon wanted to pull her into itself. She let her body relax even as the bones in her back bent and cracked. Even as her spine collapsed under the pressure of its unrelenting grasp. She grunted as her upper half fell backwards, no longer supported by her spine, which had been separated in two. Stars sparkled in her eyes as darkness closed in on both sides of her vision like curtains. She closed them and pictured Mary, not as the monstrosity that had her in its grip now but as she used to be, before things turned bad between them. She held that vision of Mary in her mind, as well as that of her brother, Bryan, their smiling faces full of love as the last vestiges of her awareness faded away. The demon's claws ripped through her back, tearing her apart, but she felt nothing. Death had already granted her merciful release.

CHAPTER THIRTY-FOUR

The next day – 1:42 pm
Millie's house – Pittsfield, MA

Millie sat in the half-light of her living room, a steaming mug of coffee in her hand as she stared at the rivulets of rain running down the window. It had been raining on and off all day. Right now, it was heavy, each drop landing with an exclamation point as if it were trying to warn Millie of something. Like it knew what she was doing was wrong and was trying to convince her to turn away from the path she was on.

She took a sip of her coffee and glanced down at her phone, willing it to light up with the call she was waiting for. It remained dark for now, but surely it wouldn't for much longer. Since convincing Maggie to help her track down Julia's bank account transaction and phone records the night of Julia's funeral, she had been patiently waiting for news. Maggie had promised her it would take no longer than two days. It had been two days now.

She left the phone on the coffee table and stood up from the couch, approaching the window to stare outside at the rain-drenched landscape. Her house overlooked a street that curved gently downward. A cascade of water followed the slope, the drain barely able to accommodate the water that it contained. The slate rooftops of the houses on the other side were being assaulted with raindrops, a slight puff of mist erupting with each splash. Trees swayed beneath the silvery threads of rain, their few remaining leaves clinging stubbornly to branches as if their lives depended on it. The Berkshire Hills loomed in the distance, soft and muted, like sleeping giants under a wet blanket, as tendrils of mist swept through pockets of trees.

She took in every detail of the scene as if it were evidence. A habit she had formed without knowing. The world outside moved on whilst she was stuck here in limbo. Administrative leave felt like being locked in a waiting room while investigation after investigation marched on without her.

A car passed slowly and steadily, its tyres carving a path through the water on the wet asphalt. It wasn't one she recognized.

She took a sip of her coffee and realized it was now cold. She had lost track of time again. Another common occurrence since being stuck at home.

Millie exhaled with a slow breath, her eyes tracing the path of a single robin, which touched down on a branch of a tree across the road. Rain beaded on its feathers, and it puffed its chest as if in defiance of the drizzle.

"They're all out there trying to make sense of things while I'm in here staring at a bird and drinking a cold coffee," she murmured, shaking her head at the injustice of the situation.

The robin flew off, and her phone on the coffee table vibrated, its screen displaying Maggie's name in a radiant glow. It almost felt orchestrated. She rushed over and answered before the second ring. "Hey Maggie, how's the investigation going? Any news?"

Maggie's breath was slow on the other side before her voice arrived, cautious and low. "Millie... I shouldn't even be calling you. They put you on leave for a reason."

Millie rubbed at her temple and sighed, feeling a rush of guilt. "I know, it's just... I can't let this go, you know? After what happened with Bob, I need answers. Whoever or whatever did this needs to pay and to be stopped."

An answering sigh came back through the phone. "I know Millie. Bob was a big part of my life, too."

"I know you're sticking your neck out for me on this. Thank you is hardly enough, but it's all I've got."

Silence was her answer, a heavy stillness that then gave way as Maggie relented. "Listen, I can't stay on the phone long. Things are crazy around here at the moment, especially after Ella's death."

Millie nodded, forgetting she was on the phone. "Did you find anything?"

"Nothing beyond her body so far. It was torn apart, Millie. I've never seen anything like it. It's lucky the five-year-old granddaughter, Lucy, thought the blood she saw spilling out from underneath the bathroom door was juice or strawberry topping. She'd be traumatized for life otherwise."

Millie felt queasiness coil in her gut. "Keep me informed when you can, okay?"

"I'll try, but no promises."

"Thanks. How did it go with the bank transaction and the phone records?"

"Okay. So, that bank transaction? It's still showing as an error. The bank hasn't been able to work out the problem, and neither have our tech guys. Someone has really gone to a lot of trouble to hide themselves."

"Shit," Millie muttered, frustrated.

"But I've had more success with the phone records, although there was some weirdness involved there, too."

"How do you mean?" Millie asked, her heart racing at the thought of a potential lead.

"Okay, so at 11:34 am on the 11th of November, Julia sent one message, but there was no recipient listed."

"No recipient? How is that possible?"

"I don't know. I pulled the raw data from the carrier. Same thing. Timestamp, message size, even tower routing. But the destination field is null. Not redacted. Not encrypted. Just... absent."

"Okay..." Millie said slowly, trying to make sense of what she was hearing. "How about the message itself? What did it say?"

"It said, 'Hi there, I just saw your video and would like some more information on contacting the recently deceased.'"

Millie's hand trembled, clutching the phone as a jolt of shock, sharp and sudden as a lightning strike, coursed through her.

"Millie, are you okay?"

Millie's head swam, the ringing in her ears drowning out most of Maggie's distant voice on the phone. The words had hit her like a physical blow, confirming her worst suspicions: something unnatural was behind it all. It had to be. It was undeniable now.

"Ye...yeah, I'm okay," she said, trying to steady her voice to reassure Maggie. "Was there a response?"

"There was... and Millie... Here's where things get even weirder."

Millie's mouth went dry. "Go on."

There was a pause, like Maggie was debating whether to keep talking. "The response was, '166 Ashen Way, 2 pm. I can help you with what you seek. Bring a photo of your cherished one with you.'" There was another pause before Maggie continued. "Millie... this message... it wasn't on Julia's phone, it was only in the carrier logs. I don't know how that's possible."

Millie closed her eyes, trying to keep her composure.

"I'll send the log to you now, but Millie... just be careful. Someone really doesn't want this trail followed."

"Good. Means I'm getting close. Thanks, Maggie." She hung up. The house seemed colder suddenly. Somewhere behind the walls, the building creaked as if it had heard everything.

Her phone buzzed as the messages came through. She had the address; now she needed to let Ron know what she'd learnt.

She checked her watch: 2:20 pm. If she left shortly after the call to Ron, she could get to the mysterious address with plenty of daylight to spare.

She picked up her phone, searching for and finding

Ron's name. She hit the call button and pressed the phone to her ear. Outside, the rain had softened, reduced now to a fine mist, but the atmosphere still felt heavy and oppressive somehow.

The phone rang almost to the point where Millie was about to hang up and jump into her car, but at the last moment, Ron finally picked up.

"Millie?" Ron's voice was rough and tired. Millie knew that sound. It was the combination of a long night of drinking with little sleep.

"Hey, sorry, did I wake you?"

"Yeah, but I shouldn't have been sleeping anyway. Shouldn't have drunk that much last night either, for that matter," he said, confirming Millie's suspicions.

She paused, swallowing before speaking. "I know it's been a couple of days, but I just heard back from my contact."

There was silence on the other end of the phone before Ron spoke. "Yeah? Any luck with the transaction?"

"No, it's still showing an error. The tech department hasn't made any headway on it either."

"Shit," Ron mumbled, his tone frustrated and defeated.

"But we did find something in Julia's phone records. Two text messages. One sent from Julia, the other from an unknown number in reply."

Ron's breath quickened on the other end of the line, both heavy and hoarse. "What... what did they say?"

"Julia's was sent at 11:34 am. No recipient listed. Just a blank field. But the message went out. It said, 'Hi there, I just saw your video and would like some more information on contacting the recently deceased.'"

Ron didn't respond right away. When he did, his voice was quieter. "She said she had been in contact with someone. This must've been the start. You say there was no recipient listed? No number?"

"No, it's as if it's been wiped somehow. We have no idea how that might be possible, but it's likely a glitch." There was a moment of silence once more before Millie continued. "But she got a response, and it contains an address." Another silence followed. Through it, Millie could hear the rain again tapping faintly against the glass. "I'm going to head there now and check it out," Millie said finally.

"I'm coming with you," Ron answered back quickly.

"Ron..."

"She was my wife. And you're not even supposed to be working on this case anymore. If something happens—"

"I'm not asking for permission."

"I'm not giving it. I'm coming because I need to. And because I don't want you walking into this alone."

Millie's breath caught. There was something in his voice, something raw and unguarded. "Okay," she said finally, the word hanging heavy in the air. "I can pick you up in about thirty minutes."

"I'll see you then. Oh, and Millie?"

"Yeah?"

"Thank you. For everything."

Ron hung up, and Millie dropped the phone slowly to her lap, her eyes lingering on its darkening screen. The silence that now blanketed the house following the call didn't feel empty. It felt like it was waiting.

CHAPTER THIRTY-FIVE

Ron took a sip of his lukewarm mug of coffee and glanced down at his watch anxiously. After he had gotten the call from Millie almost thirty minutes ago, he had dragged himself up from the bed, taken a quick shower, had a shave, and donned the last of his clean set of clothes from his suitcase. The rest of his clothes remained in a pile on the floor, still unwashed, abandoned there in favour of the far more attractive prospect of the whiskey he had consumed since returning to the hotel. He knew he was in danger of falling into alcoholism. Hell, maybe he already had, judging by the amount of it he had consumed over the last few weeks.

His stomach was rejecting the coffee, rejecting its bitter taste, crying out instead for the warm amber liquid in the quarter-filled bottle on the coffee table. He winced as he surveyed the state of his room. The table was littered with empty bottles, empty takeaway containers, and crumpled napkins. The air was stale with the smells of old food and cheap liquor. It was only now that he had something to focus on, a glimmer of hope for an answer as to what had happened to Julia and those connected with her mother, that he realized how far he had fallen.

Rising to his feet, he gathered the empty bottles and placed them in the recycling container underneath the bench where the microwave sat. He had just finished tossing the takeaway containers into the bin when there came a knock on the door.

Eying the dirty laundry pile next to the bed in disgust, he made his way to the door, hoping Millie wouldn't judge him too harshly. He opened the door and blinked against the sunlight that bore down on his eyes, temporarily blinding him.

"Hey," Millie's voice said as her silhouette came into view, his eyes slowly adjusting to the brightness. "By your reaction, I'm guessing you haven't seen much sunlight the last few days," she said, as Ron continued to blink, her face gradually coming into focus.

"You could say that," Ron admitted. Up until now, he hadn't realized just how dark the room was, having closed the curtains after he had returned to the room after the funeral. They hadn't been open since.

"I'd invite you in, but the room is in a bit of a state," he said sheepishly.

She laughed and nodded, a knowing smile on her face. "Don't worry, my house is in dire need of attention as well. Are you ready to go?"

Ron nodded. "Oh, wait, let me just get my coat." He ran inside and picked up one that he had thrown across the back of a chair, praying it wasn't one of the dirtier ones.

The pair was silent on the way to the car, both of them

consumed by thoughts of what lay ahead of them and the answers they hoped to find.

As they pulled out of the hotel parking lot and headed onto the main road, Millie filled him in on the details of the phone messages and, to his surprise, the investigation up to now.

"Ella's dead?" Ron asked, his heart sinking at the thought. Though he didn't know her well, the last interaction he had with her stuck in his mind. Mary, or the thing that she had become, was clearly on a warpath.

Millie glanced at him, her expression etched with concern. "Are you okay?"

Ron took a slow breath and looked out the window. "I don't know how I'll ever be okay," he whispered softly, doing his best to keep his composure.

The light touch of Millie's hand on his thigh startled him, and he jumped, his leg jerking involuntarily. She took her hand off quickly.

"Sorry, I was just..."

"No, it's okay. I was just surprised, is all. I'm wound up too tight," he said with a short, strained laugh.

"Yeah, I know the feeling," Millie replied, her voice containing its own tension.

The pair was silent for a few minutes as the landscape outside changed from the township to the narrowed roads of its outskirts. The rain had stopped, but the sky remained a heavy, brooding grey, pregnant with the threat of more rain. Here and there, shafts of sunlight pierced the clouds, illuminating patches of trees in fleeting bursts of golden light as they sped past, creating an almost magical look.

"So Mary... or whatever that thing is, is targeting her

family then," he said to break the silence, which was becoming increasingly uncomfortable.

"It seems so," Millie agreed as she adjusted the phone on the holder, angling it toward her a little more.

"The question is why? What does she gain by doing it?" he asked with a frown. "And why go after me?"

Millie glanced at him before returning her attention to the road ahead and exhaled slowly. "Things of a demonic nature, like Mary or what she has become, rarely work off logic. They thrive on chaos, on causing as much pain, suffering, and hurt as they can. I think whoever Julia contacted knew this when she brought back Mary."

Ron stared at her, feeling the blood drain from his face and freeze in his veins. "How... how do you know all this?"

She threw him a quick, calculating glance, as if she were weighing up whether to go ahead with what she was about to say. "Well... I don't, really. It's more of an educated guess. I grew up in a house with spiritual beliefs, mainly inspired by my grandmother, who lived with us. I didn't follow those beliefs at the time, and my mother and grandmother knew that. Still, I used to love the spooky stories she would tell me about her experiences, about those she helped. Ghosts, demons, creatures, superstitions, she would tell me about them all. It was, I guess, her version of a bedtime story. I thought it was all made up at the time. I mean, who wouldn't you know?"

Ron nodded, giving her space to continue.

"But there was something about the way my grandmother told those tales, like they were true. Like she believed every word of what she was saying. It was only later, when I got older, that I realized that she did. She was referred to as a Wise Woman."

"Okay, so by Wise Woman, I'm guessing you mean not just someone who knows a lot," he said sheepishly.

Millie laughed and shook her head. "No, she was someone who people went to when they felt like they needed a spiritual touch, whether they came seeking advice on hauntings, spirits, folklore, and even things such as dealing with grief. She was deeply in tune with the human spirit and gave those who sought out her help what they needed to hear or ways to deal with whatever affliction they faced."

Ron nodded. "So, you grew to believe in her beliefs as you got older?"

"No, not exactly. I never had experiences with the unknown or supernatural to give validity to my mother and grandmother's beliefs, but..." she said, trailing off mid-sentence as her lips pursed thinly. "I was open to belief. Always have been. And this case... well... I think we can both agree, is far beyond what either of us can explain."

"You can say that again," Ron muttered. "Unless we're both hallucinating, or going crazy."

They shared a tight grin before Millie slowed the car down, glancing between the GPS on the phone and the road outside.

"According to this, we should be coming up on Ashen Way."

The pair looked out the windows, scanning their surroundings. Trees lined both sides of the road, their limbs coming dangerously close to overhanging it. Lumpy shapes between the trees on one side caught Ron's attention. It wasn't until they were almost upon them that he recognized the shapes as gravestones, old and worn, their grey surfaces slimy with dampness and partially hidden by twisting weeds and gnarled vines.

"There!" he exclaimed, pointing to a tall, weathered sign barely visible through a gap in the trees, a glimpse of a dusty road next to it.

Millie slowed down further and switched on her indicator as they reached the concealed road and turned into it. Unlike the paved tarmac of the road they'd left, this one was a mix of dirt interspersed with grass, still slick from the recent downpour of rain. Mud splashed up behind them as the car fought its way along the forgotten road, its chassis protesting with each jarring bump and shudder against the pothole-filled surface. There were no signs of civilization here at all. Trees and shrubs choked both sides, the occasional fallen tree branches and sticks crackling and snapping under the car tyres. Ron frowned as he peered through the window, the car slowing to a near crawl as Millie struggled to navigate the barely drivable road.

Then a flash of white through the trees caught his attention. It was a rough structure, partially collapsed, with patches of pale, creamy paint cracked and peeling from aged, rotted boards. The section still standing hinted at years beyond easy estimation.

"Are you sure we're on the right road?" Ron asked doubtfully as he continued to survey both sides.

"According to the GPS, we are," Millie said, her own doubt clear in her voice. "It should just be up ahead."

Ron squinted at the GPS, the blue dot pulsing against the skeletal outline of the road, as if it, too, were uncertain.

"This is it," he muttered, just as the robotic voice declared, 'You have arrived at your destination'. Millie eased the car to a halt.

Ahead, the road reached a dead end as if it had given in to the overwhelming power of nature that closed in on it.

They scanned the wilderness before them. On the opposite side of where the GPS indicator pointed, partially obscured by the trees, lay the ruin of a bridge, its wood sagging and splintered like a carcass left too long under the sun. It hovered over a gully, once overflowing with rushing water, now choked with gnarled weeds.

Ron frowned. "There's nothing here."

There was no shop, no paths, no sign of human habitation at all. Not even a landmark that might have tied Julia to this place. Just the quiet hush of a no-man's-land that had long since been forgotten and maybe wanted to stay that way.

CHAPTER THIRTY-SIX

4:05 pm

Belle stared vacantly at the sink, watching the small dollops of water form on the faucet and drop. Each one seemed to fall in tandem with her own teardrops, as if they were one and the same. As if her house was grieving right alongside her.

First, it was Bryan, now her mother. Both gone in the space of a few short days. No suspects, no valid explanations, just a generic line fed to her by the police that their deaths were still being investigated. The impact of what had happened had only now just sunk in. Only the fact that her daughters needed her had kept her going, but even then, she had just been operating on autopilot, a shell of the person they needed her to be. She was thankful for her husband; Mike had stepped up in that regard, keeping them occupied and taking over some of her duties to give her space.

"Alright, I think I've finally worn the girls down enough. They're watching cartoons in the playroom upstairs. I have no idea where they get their energy from, but I'd sure like some of it." Mike's loud voice startled her as he walked into the kitchen, collapsing onto the seat opposite her with a heavy sigh.

"I'm sorry. I should be helping with them. It's just... I feel so empty inside right now. I can't, I just can't." Her lips trembled as she looked at him, her face slack with grief. Seeing his exhausted face, drawn and full of concern, only made it harder for her to contain her tears. She felt like a failure, like she was letting both him and her girls down.

"Hey," he said softly as he leaned forward and took her hands in his. "You don't have anything to be sorry about, okay? I've got this. Please don't worry about me or the girls. You need to look after yourself right now."

Just as he'd finished, two screams, those of Lucy and Sarah, travelled downstairs from the direction of the play-room. Mike stood up with a groan and shook his head. "I'd better go see what trouble they've gotten themselves into now. I'll be back in a sec," he said, his heavy footsteps clomping down the hallway and then up the stairs. The girls' high-pitched screams and shrieks continued to pierce the air, causing Belle to frown. There was something different about those screams; a raw, guttural quality that set them apart from the girls' usual playful shrieks. They sounded almost terrified.

A sharp clicking sound, like that of a tiny hammer hitting metal, startled her, drawing her attention to the stove. Her breath hitched, her eyes widening as she watched the dials rotate independently, followed by a sudden whoosh of gas igniting into flames. With a gasp, she shot upright, her chair toppling backward and falling to the ground with a loud clatter.

She staggered toward the stove, the smell of gas filling the kitchen along with something else. Something rotting. As if the contents of the kitchen drain were belching up years of old food and scraps caught in its pipes. She twisted the knobs on the stove, her fingers trembling as she turned them back to the off position, but nothing happened. The flames remained, some even rising higher, as if in defiance of her attempts.

"Mike, I need help," she called out in desperation, continuing to twist the dials in panic as the heat in the kitchen began to build.

From behind her, a voice, low and full of malice, slithered like a snake, chilling her to the bone despite the heat. "Beeeelllllllllle wheeeeerrreees yoooooouuuur sunsssscreeeeeen? Hooooowwww mannnnyy tiiiiiimmmmmessss doooooo Iiiiii havvvveeee tooooo telllllll yooouuuuuu." She spun around and froze in terror, her eyes locking onto a grotesquely twisted form that loomed only an arm's length away, its chilling proximity filling her with a nauseating dread.

Intense blue orbs stared into her eyes, keeping her rooted in place with fear as the creature extended a decayed arm toward her, its bony hands with talon-like fingertips cupping her face gently and giving it a grandmotherly squeeze.

"Get the fuck away from her," Mike growled from the kitchen doorway. Fear was plainly visible in his wide, unbelieving eyes, but his rigid posture was another story. He clenched his fists threateningly as he took a step forward.

The thing hissed as it swung its head toward him. Belle took the opportunity to slide sideways away from the creature, but it sensed her movement and refocused its attention back on her.

With a roar of furious anger, Mike launched himself at the thing, but before he could land a blow, it effortlessly flung its arm and connected with his ribs, sending him sprawling across the kitchen table and into the wall with a bone-jarring thud. A deafening crash shook the kitchen. Plaster fragments exploded from the wall, leaving behind a deep, ragged dent as Mike's body fell to the floor from the rebound with a heavy thump.

"Mike, no!" Belle screamed, watching the scene play out but helpless to do anything about it.

"Mommy!" Lucy and Sarah's voices cried out in near unison, drifting from the base of the stairs into the kitchen entrance.

"Girls, run! Get out of here, go next door and get help!" Belle shouted, forcing every ounce of urgency she could into her voice, praying they'd listen before it was too late.

"But Mommy—" Sarah began, her voice shaky, before Belle's sharp words cut her off.

"Go! Go now, and don't look back!" Belle screamed as she reached for a knife in the chopping block on the bench beside her, but she hadn't even gotten a grip on the handle before the thing struck.

The creature's eyes flashed with excitement as its hand lashed out, its icy fingers curling around Belle's throat in a vice-like grip. She was yanked backward with brutal force, dragged toward the hungry glow of the burners. Heat licked at her back, the air vanishing from her lungs as she kicked out weakly at the fiend, its thick mucus-covered tongue lashing wildly in anticipation. Her vision blurred as her lungs screamed for air. Her legs gave way, but the thing's grip kept her from falling, suspending her in mid-air. Then she heard it. The front door slammed shut. The sound reached her ringing ears like a lifeline. Her girls were safe.

Relief filled her chest, fierce and pure. Even as her body fought for breath, even as the flame's heat edged closer, Belle let the fear slip away. Her eyes, vision filled with blinking stars, fell onto Mike's sprawled form, noting the rise and fall of his chest. At least he would live to look after the girls. This thing... this monster that looked vaguely like her Aunt Mary, whom she hadn't seen in years, was clearly just after her.

The demonic thing grinned at her. What remained of the thin, decayed skin on its face stretched and tore into ragged ribbons, revealing gum-pink muscle beneath, slick with ichor. With its grip iron-hard, it pushed her head down toward the burners and the naked flames with force.

The heat met her face with a hiss. Her skin blistered instantly, curling and splitting like parchment caught in flame, sloughing from her cheeks in wet clumps that sizzled as they fell.

The unbearable stench of her own burnt flesh filled her nostrils, followed by the greasy reek of burning fat, the pungent odor of singed hair, and the dry acrid smell of scorched bone. Her scalp ignited, flame spreading from strand to strand like kindling soaked in oil.

She tried to scream, but nothing came. Her lungs had collapsed under the unrelenting pressure of the creature's grip and her failed attempts at drawing in breath. She felt her eye boil before it ruptured, bursting and casting its juices across the surface of the stove with a violent hiss and resultant steam. Light turned to black.

And then came the voice once more, slithering around her consciousness as if the creature was speaking directly into her mind. "Thiiiisss... iiisss... whaaat... haaapppnnnsss... wheennn... yoouuu... dooonnnn't... liisssten... tooo... Auunntiiiieeee... Maarrryyyyyy..."

Each syllable was dripping with evil, echoing around a mind already well on its way to sinking into silence. And then, it did.

CHAPTER THIRTY-SEVEN

"Now what do we do?" Ron said with a frustrated scowl.

Millie was silent for a moment. This situation was way beyond her limited ability to understand. They needed help, and she only knew of one person who could possibly give it.

"There's only one more thing I can think of," she said, swinging the wheel around to do a U-turn and pressing down on the accelerator. "Let's visit my grandmother. She might have some idea of what we're dealing with here and what to do."

Ron nodded, his frown easing a little. "How far away is she?"

"Luckily, she still lives with my mother. Back where I grew up in Lanesborough. It should take half an hour to get there."

"Okay," Ron said, hesitating before continuing softly. "Thank you."

She looked at him, confused by his shift in tone. "For what?"

"Doing this. Allowing me to come with you. Helping me. All of it," he said earnestly. He placed his hand on her thigh before he withdrew it quickly. "Oh, sorry. I didn't mean..."

"It's fine. You don't have to apologise. It was... nice, actually," she said, surprising herself with the boldness of her words. She felt her cheeks burn with embarrassment as they sunk in, and immediately she chastised herself for them. Ron was grieving for Julia, and here she was trying out a line on him.

Ron let out a small, strained chuckle, and she glanced at him out of the corner of her eye. His face was flushed too. She felt her heart rate quicken. Perhaps there could be a chance for something between them after all in the future. She forced herself to concentrate on the drive ahead. This was no time for daydreaming. For all she knew, the demon could already be targeting its next victim. It needed to be stopped.

The drive was a blur of green fields and distant mountains, passing in quiet contemplation before giving way to concrete and steel as they drove through areas of civilization. Rain sprinkled down, pausing intermittently, like a hesitant dancer as daylight gave way to the artificial glow of the headlights of cars.

The road narrowed as they turned off the highway, trading the well-maintained asphalt's gleam for the aged patchwork of worn and cracked pavement. They wound through the streets, heading steadily in the direction of the older part of town. With one more flip of the indicator, she turned down a street that was as familiar to her as her own hand. It was like time had stood still here; everything was exactly as she remembered. Tall maples lined both sides of the street, their skeletal limbs waving gently in the fall breeze. The houses drifted by slowly, offering glimpses of weathered clapboard siding while porch swings swayed.

Millie eased off the gas as her eyes darted between the road and the houses, their driveways stained by decades of tyre tracks and oil. Here and there, mailboxes leaned at odd angles, some desperately needing a fresh coat of paint, their colour fading to mottled grey and flaking what little remained on their surface. The silence here was different, like it had a personality of its own. It spoke of the quiet wisdom and deep patience that only age could provide.

Ron shifted in his seat. "It's like time forgot this place," he said, giving voice to Millie's thoughts.

She didn't answer. They were approaching her mother's house just ahead. One of the better-maintained homes in the neighborhood, the house was presented in a squat colonial style. Hugged by bare birch trees, the porch light shone like a beacon in the fast-approaching dusk. Curtains stirred in the front window, a sign someone had noticed their approach. Being the only car driving down the road and the quietness of the area, it was no surprise.

She parked the car and switched off the engine. The ensuing silence was almost deafening.

Then her phone rang, making her almost jump out of her skin. It was Maggie. By the end of the phone call, Millie's face was ashen, her stomach churning with a nauseating unease. She hung up and stared at her mother's house for a moment.

"Did I hear that right? Someone else has been killed?" Ron asked, looking as though he was already dreading the answer.

Millie nodded slowly, a grimace twisting her face. "Ella's daughter, Belle. Her face was burnt to a crisp, cooked by the stove burners."

"Jesus," Ron whispered, his face whitening slightly.

"We need to put a stop to this," Millie said, her face hardening with determination. "C'mon, let's see what my grandma has to say."

Sliding out of the car, she strode toward the front door and waited for Ron to join her before knocking. Not for the first time, she scanned the porch roof, hoping to see evidence of a security camera she knew wouldn't be there. She knew it was the detective in her, but she wished they had listened to her and given in just this once for security reasons, but both her mother and grandmother favoured the discretion of her grandmother's clients. Besides, they were adamant that nothing would ever happen to cause them to need it, and luckily, so far, they hadn't.

The door opened to her mother's still remarkably youthful face. With just a scattering of silvery grey hairs at fifty-four, Candace could easily pass for someone in her forties. Her face lit up with a smile at seeing Millie, and she stepped forward to give her a hug.

"Millie, darling, I've missed you. It's been too long," she said with warm, genuine feeling. She hung on just a bit longer than necessary before letting go and stepping aside to let her in.

"And who's this strapping young man? Did you forget to tell me something?" Candace's eyes scanned Ron from head to toe before her gaze landed on Millie, a teasing smile playing on her lips, eyebrows playfully raised.

Millie blushed furiously, keeping her gaze on her mother. "No, Mom, he's just a friend. Ron, meet my mother, Candace. Mother, meet Ron."

"A pleasure to meet you," Ron said with a smile, extending a hand to shake hers, his own cheeks slightly flushed.

Candace giggled and took his hand in both of hers. "Oh my. Millie, if you don't want him, I'll take him," she said, her playful smile extending wider as she gave Ron a wink.

A nervous flutter filled Millie's chest as Ron's laughter rang out. She felt her mouth work uselessly, unable to form a coherent thought or word.

"Now that the pleasantries are out of the way," Millie said, glaring at her mother pointedly, "we really need to see Nanny Mae."

Candace instantly sobered and looked at her with pursed lips. "You're not here for a social visit, then. Something of the spiritual nature come up in one of your investigations?"

"You could say that," Millie said with a short nod.

Candace sighed. "Well, I guess I'm not going to get anything else from you. She's in her room." With a sweep of her hand, she indicated the hallway on the other side of the living room. "Will you be joining us for dinner?"

Ron and Millie looked at each other, each mirroring the other's slightly nauseous expression.

"No thanks, we really need to move on this case right away before someone else gets hurt."

Candace nodded in understanding. "I see. Well, another

time then. Do make sure you bring this one back with you when you do," she said with a giggle, giving one of Ron's biceps a gentle, playful squeeze.

Ron chuckled, shaking his head as Millie shot another glare in Candace's direction before she took the lead, heading down the hallway.

The polished floorboards creaked with each step they made, a familiar sound that took Millie back to her childhood. She felt instantly at ease here, safe in a way she'd never felt since she'd moved out on her own. She blamed that on her job. After all, it was difficult to feel completely safe as an adult woman living by herself when she had been part of so many investigations that showed the depravity of human nature. Here, she could forget all that and lose herself in the warmth of family life in a neighborhood she had always loved.

The scent of incense drifted from the room directly ahead at the end of the hallway. The door was open, letting the curls of the fragrant smoke drift out into freedom.

"Nanny Mae?" Millie called out, giving her grandma a warning so as not to startle her before she walked in.

A low voice answered, soft but steady. "Come on in, baby girl. I've been expecting you."

Millie stepped into the room almost reverentially as she looked affectionately toward the aged woman seated in a rocker near the window. The room looked the same as it always had, as if it had been frozen in time since Millie's childhood. Along with the rocker her grandmother was seated in, there was an antique wooden armchair in the corner of the room, with a colourful crocheted blanket draped across its back. An old wooden shelf next to it was cluttered with flickering candles, glittering crystals, and various bottles of oils. The walls were adorned with beautiful pictures of landscapes, creating a calming and peaceful atmosphere. Various trinkets and religious paraphernalia from native cultures hung in between on the spare patches of walls. The lights were turned off, abandoned in favour of the candles lining the shelves and on an ancient dressing table, complete with a gilded mirror. Their flames swayed gently as Millie and Ron passed to make their way toward her.

Nanny Mae was dressed in her usual linen blouse, with a shawl embroidered with symbols of crescent moons, moth wings, and sacred herbs resting on her shoulders. A strand of amber beads around her neck caught the glow of the candlelight. At eighty-four, she emanated presence, the type that stills a room without demanding it. Her hair was pulled back into a loose bun, held in place by a velvet ribbon the colour of thunderclouds. Deep laugh lines framed her eyes and mouth, softening her features and giving a glimpse into a lifetime spent listening closely and loving fiercely. Her eyes, pale and lucid, seemed to shift between shades of cornflower blue and storm grey—eyes that looked through things as much as at them.

Even in the short silence since she had spoken, there was movement about her—the gentle shake of her rocking chair, the rustle of dried herbs suspended near the window, and the faint chime of the charm bracelet she wore. Each item was filled with meaning, be it a memory, a protection, or a promise.

Millie seated herself in the armchair opposite Nanny

Mae while Ron stood awkwardly by the bookshelf, unsure of whether to cross his arms or keep them by his side.

Nanny Mae smiled at her, a smile so full of love and warmth that she felt her heart ache.

"Love looks good on you," she said knowingly, her eyes twinkling with amusement as they shifted toward Ron.

"Oh, god, Nanny, not you too," Millie groaned, her cheeks flushing a fiery red, quickly averting her eyes from Ron as he looked at her, his previous look of confusion now changed to one more akin to thoughtfulness. A nervous silence filled the gap between them.

Nanny Mae sat back and cackled. "Life is too short to not show what you feel, girl."

Millie's throat tightened, words catching there like fish-hooks, fear of further embarrassment silencing her, but luckily Nanny Mae continued, rescuing her from the awkward silence. "Now, all merriment aside, tell me what ails you. I feel you bring tidings not nearly as pleasant as those of affection."

Millie nodded, clearing her throat nervously before she began a slow, meticulous explanation of the case, guided by Ron's input, taking particular care in describing the Mary creature's horrific appearance, its actions, and its victims. Once she was finished, there was silence, broken only by the gentle creak of Nanny Mae's rocker as she sat back with a pensive look on her face.

"This demon," she murmured. "It has been bound to Mary's body, either forced into servitude or promised something in exchange." She leaned forward, eyeing Ron intensely. "You said Julia met with someone. Gave them a photo of Mary?"

Ron's face creased in thought as he nodded, clearly intrigued by her every word.

She closed her eyes, her brows furrowing as she spoke. "The photo is the key. This demon… it's tied to the image, the echoes of presence." She opened her eyes once more, focusing again on Ron. "Do you have any other photos of Mary? Any of her with her family at all?"

Ron hesitated, lost in thought, before his eyes widened and he nodded. "Yes, in the photo album from Mary's house."

"Is that the one Bob had at the police station?" Millie asked eagerly, recognizing they were on the verge of a breakthrough.

"Yes, that's the one. They gave it back to me as they decided it wasn't worth keeping as evidence."

"Then that is how it chooses its victims," Nanny Mae said, nodding slowly. "Every person it's been photographed with becomes a link."

Her words left a chill in the air, and Millie thought back over the victims. Julia, Bryan, Ella, Belle. All related to Mary. Bob was the outlier, but he was a victim of circumstance, trying to protect Ron. Millie frowned. "Wait a minute. If Mary is targeting those she's been photographed with, why did she go after Ron?" She turned to look at him. "You weren't in any photographs with her, were you?"

Ron's face fell, and he shook his head. "No."

"It's not just who you're pictured with," Nanny Mae murmured. "It's who you're bound to." She leaned forward, her voice low and steady. "You were in a photo with Julia. And Julia was in dozens with Mary. The demon doesn't just follow faces, it follows blood. It traces emotional lineage like a thread through fabric. If the host is captured in a photo with someone, and that someone is deeply connected to another—by love, by grief, by family—it can leap."

Millie's brow furrowed. "So, it's like a spiritual contagion?"

"Exactly," Nanny Mae said. "Julia was the bridge. Her love for Ron, her bond with her mother, it made Ron visible to the demon. It saw Ron through her eyes."

Ron's hands trembled. "So, when it killed Julia... it marked me too."

Nanny Mae nodded. "It will circle back to you once it's finished with her family, and it won't stop."

The room fell into a heavy silence, the growing fear within almost palpable. Outside, the wind stirred the branches near the window like restless fingers. Inside, the candle flames on Nanny Mae's desk wavered, casting long, uncertain shadows.

Millie spoke first, her voice soft, feeling overwhelmed by what she had heard. "So, if that's the case, how do we stop it?"

Nanny Mae didn't answer right away. She stood, moving to the shelf where she kept her oldest leather-bound books, brittle with age. She squinted at them, brow furrowed in concentration as she trailed a finger along their spines. "Aha," she said triumphantly as she pulled one free and shuffled over to the desk, laying it gently on its surface. A puff of dust rose with every page turn, a testament to how long it had been since this volume had been opened. Her search ended on a page of carefully written, looping script. She ran her finger over it as she scanned the words, and nodded with pursed lips, her expression grave.

"You don't kill a demon like this," she said, her voice low. "You unravel it. You make it forget itself."

Ron leaned forward, his eyes wide with a mixture of fear and excitement. "How?"

Nanny Mae pointed to the page. "This entry about the creature is old, but it can be interpreted quite easily by those like me to take into account the changes in the world today." She turned to face them. "To make a long story short, you must gather every physical photograph that has the host in it. Every one, leaving no copies behind. You'll need to burn them together, at the witching hour, in a circle drawn with salt and ash from a sacred place."

She moved toward the bookshelf, selecting an old cedar box.

Millie leaned forward, her voice barely audible. "And that's enough?" She took the offered cedar box with a frown.

Nanny Mae's lips pursed. "If done right, yes. But the flame must be lit by someone it's never touched. Someone it's never seen, never marked."

"But we've both been seen by it, so it can't be one of us," Millie said in frustration.

Everyone fell into a gloomy silence. Millie thought of who she knew that could possibly help, and only one person came to mind. "I may know someone who could help, but she's not exactly a believer in this type of thing."

Nanny Mae nodded in understanding. "She doesn't need to be a believer. She just needs to be someone the demon doesn't know. Someone it hasn't touched, seen, or sensed. Otherwise, it'll anticipate the strike. It'll twist the ritual back."

"Okay," Millie said, exhaling slowly.

"Wait," Ron said, his brow knitted with concern. "We don't have the original photo, the one Julia gave to the summoner."

Millie's face fell, the tentative hope she'd been holding onto quickly evaporating. "Shit!"

"Language, young lady," Nanny Mae said sharply, immediately making Millie feel guilty.

"Sorry, Nanny, it's just that it seems whenever we find a potential solution, there's always a catch."

Nanny Mae nodded, her eyes crinkling in understanding. "The complexities of the spiritual world are difficult to get a grasp of, but all is not lost."

"What do you mean?" Millie asked, looking up again, feeling another slight surge of hope.

"If you find and burn all the photos you can find, it'll weaken the demon," Nanny Mae said. "Make it stumble. But it won't fall. It'll retreat, regroup, and wait. You'll buy time, but not peace."

Ron began to pace, his arms still crossed. "Then we need to find the summoner."

Nanny Mae's eyes narrowed. "A task that is not that simple, as you've discovered, but yes."

"And if we can't locate them?" Millie asked, her mind racing to find all the possibilities she could.

Returning to her desk, Nanny Mae slowly closed the book, gathered it in her arms, and placed it back on the bookshelf. "Then you trap the demon. You bind it to a vessel. Not to destroy, but to contain."

Ron blinked, his voice faltering. "A... vessel?"

"A mirror," Nanny Mae said. "One that's never held a reflection of who it belongs to. A new one. You'll need a lock of hair from someone the demon has marked, a drop of blood from someone it tried to claim, and the name the host was first given in love. Then it will need to be wrapped in black cloth and buried in cedar ash when the demon is trapped."

Millie's breath caught. "And once that's done?"

"You seal it with silence," Nanny Mae said. "No one speaks the name again. No one uncovers the mirror. It must be buried in a place where memory doesn't linger—no graves, no homes, no churches. Somewhere forgotten."

Ron looked pale. "And if someone finds it?"

Nanny Mae's eyes darkened. "Then it begins again."

"That doesn't seem like a great option," Ron said with a frown. "We ourselves can control what we do or say, but not those of Mary's family. Especially when there are kids involved with no filters or when they grow up, forget about the silence they need to keep."

Determination coursed through Millie as she nodded. "Then we need to burn the photos and keep looking. It will buy us more time, at least. If worst comes to worst, we try the vessel.

"There is one other thing if you decide to trap it in the vessel."

Ron sighed and rubbed his eyes wearily. "Of course there is."

Nanny Mae's face was grave. "If you find the photo the summoner holds, then the mirror must be unearthed and shattered. You must let the demon back out."

Ron looked horrified. "Let it out?"

Nanny Mae nodded slowly. "The same ritual must be performed, the salt and ash circle reinforced and twice as strong, the photo burned within. Then finally, the photo's ashes and the mirror shards must be scattered in separate running waters, one upstream, one downstream, to prevent spiritual reformation."

"Jesus Christ, it just gets better and better," Ron exclaimed, moving back to lean heavily against the book-shelf, causing the oil bottles on the shelves to rattle together precariously. A grimace crossed his face as he offered Nanny Mae an apologetic glance.

Millie's voice was tight. "What if it escapes before we finish the ritual?"

"Then it will be stronger," Nanny Mae said. "Angrier. It will remember being trapped. And it will come for those who performed the ritual."

"Okay, well, let's hope it doesn't come to that," Millie said, looking miserable. "Let's try burning the photos first and then try to track down the summoner."

Ron nodded, his face clouded with doubt.

"You mentioned the salt and ash. Where do we get those?" Millie asked, her shoulders slumped like she had the weight of the world on them.

"The salt needs to be pure sea salt or rock salt. I don't have any on hand, but you can get it from the Whole Foods Market in Pittsfield. As for the sacred ash..." Nanny Mae shuffled over to the shelf and scanned the bottles, picking one up almost reverentially. "I make sure I always have some on hand. I find I often have need of it." She offered the bottle to Millie, who accepted it with care.

"I think we're all set then," Millie said, exchanging a meaningful glance with Ron.

Nanny Mae nodded and gave her a warm smile. "Just be careful, dear. Demons are unpredictable creatures, and they will do anything they can to try to stop you. It will scream. It will try to leap. But if the circle holds, then it will fade away. Not die, just retreat, but remember, it will be gathering its strength back until it makes its return. You must find the summoner's picture and destroy it before that happens."

Both Millie and Ron nodded, their faces pale and sickly in the soft shadows cast by the candlelight.

Millie gave Nanny Mae a gentle hug, mindful of her age, before she moved to the doorway to wait for Ron. He extended a hand to Nanny Mae, awkward and unsure, but she waved it off with a flick of her wrist. To his surprise and Millie's, she stepped forward and pulled Ron into a brief, firm hug. She leaned in close, whispering something into Ron's ear that made him flush red and suddenly find the ceiling, the floor, and anything but Millie's face intensely fascinating. The two parted, and Nanny Mae gave him a cheeky parting smile before he walked over to join Millie. Wordlessly, the pair walked back down the hall toward the living room, where Candace was seated on the couch, watching the news on the TV with the volume down low.

She greeted them with a smile and stood up to stretch. "Hope everything is okay?"

"Long story. I'll tell you next visit," Millie said distractedly, her mind already working on how to convince Maggie to help with the ritual.

"Are you sure I can't convince you to stay for dinner?"

"Sorry, Mom, not tonight. We have to get to the shops before they close and plan some things out," Millie said, approaching her to give her a hug. "I promise I'll visit soon, okay?"

"You better," Candace said, smiling. "You're welcome too, of course, handsome," she said to Ron, giving him another wink.

They left and headed straight for the Whole Foods Market, the fifteen-minute ride passing in silence, Millie's thoughts tangled in ritual steps and fragile salt lines.

CHAPTER THIRTY-EIGHT

The next day

Ron paced the length of his hotel room nervously for what felt like the millionth time. He'd done it so often in the last few hours that he was surprised he hadn't worn a groove in the carpet. He longed for a walk outside to burn off nervous energy, but the need to be ready to depart at any second kept him stuck in this box.

Sitting down on the bed with a sigh, he thought about what lay ahead. The fate of many, including himself, depended on both him and Millie to carry out the ritual, to destroy the demon, or at the very least, trap it if they couldn't.

After returning from the store with the rock salt they needed, Millie and Ron had wasted no time. They began reaching out to Mary's relatives, asking for any photographs that included her—no matter how old, how faded, or how crowded. Even images with strangers in the background were fair game, as long as the timing suggested Mary might have been nearby when they were taken. Every photo was a potential thread in the demon's tapestry, and they couldn't afford to miss a single one. Luckily, there weren't many of them, but it was still an arduous task to sort through them, one that took them almost to the midnight hour. Mary's relatives were eager to help despite the lateness of their visits, especially after Millie told them it would possibly lead to justice for their murdered family members.

Millie had dropped Ron back at the hotel with a promise to call once she'd spoken to Maggie and convinced her to help. Ron had kept himself busy by gathering the photo album that had been returned to him from the detective's office and then heading home to dig through drawers and boxes for any remaining pictures that might include Mary. He'd grabbed the one off the TV cabinet and found a few more framed photos he didn't even know they had on shelves around the house, which he'd quickly taken.

Then he'd made one final trip to Mary's house, knowing full well the chances of finding more photos were slim. Still, he searched, room by room and drawer by drawer, driven more by hope than reason. But the house yielded nothing. By the time he stepped back outside, he was relieved. Something about the place felt wrong, like it knew he didn't belong and wanted him gone.

By the time he texted Millie to confirm he had all the photos and returned to the hotel, it was nearly 4 am, and though his body ached with exhaustion, his mind was still too wired to sleep. It was now 10 am, and he still hadn't had a wink of rest. His eyes burned, his mind was a whirlwind of fleeting thoughts, and the silence in the room felt heavy and full of foreboding.

He got up again and headed for the container of instant coffee in the kitchenette, dumping a few spoonfuls into the stained mug sitting beside the partially filled kettle. He switched it on and waited for it to boil as his gaze darted between the clock and the door to the room, as though his look alone could make Millie appear.

As the kettle clicked off, a sharp vibration from his pocket startled him. It was his phone.

"Finally," he muttered as he dug into his pocket, his fingers clumsily searching for the phone that seemed determined to evade his grasp. "Fuck!" he said as he finally got a hold of it just as it fell silent. He called back the number, Millie picking up on the first ring.

"I didn't wake you, did I, sleepyhead?" Millie's voice said, sounding surprisingly relaxed. It was a sharp contrast to the tension coiled tight in Ron's chest and his racing, almost panicked thoughts.

"Ha, if only. I haven't so much as had an eyelid closed in rest," Ron answered bitterly.

Millie sighed, her relaxed tone giving way to weariness. "You and me both."

The pair was silent for a moment, and Ron felt his tension ease slightly at the knowledge he wasn't the only one struggling.

"But I do have some good news," Millie continued. "Maggie has agreed to help with the ritual, though I'm pretty sure she thinks we're both nuts."

Ron managed a laugh, feeling the knot of anxiety begin

to loosen. "Yeah, well, who can blame her? I can hardly believe all of this, but here we are."

"Yeah," Millie echoed. "Here we are."

"So, when are we doing this?" Ron asked nervously. The task ahead of them suddenly seemed more real.

"Tonight. As Nanny Mae said, the ritual needs to be done at midnight. It took some convincing. Maggie's got work in the morning, and she's still trying to process all this. Honestly, we're lucky she's on board."

"Yeah, well… she'll believe soon enough. Once that thing shows up," Ron said, a sudden feeling of exhaustion overcoming him. "Where are we going to do this?" he asked. Earlier, he had given Millie a few options to choose from, and she'd wanted to run them by Nanny Mae.

Millie hesitated for a moment. "Ice Glen."

"In the ravine behind Park Street?"

"Yeah. It's quiet, dense with old-growth trees and moss. Feels like time forgot it—like nothing's been touched for a hundred years. Nanny Mae said it's good ground. Old ground. The kind that listens."

"It almost sounds like you've been there before," Ron said, feeling a little surprised.

"I've been there a time or two," Millie said, her voice contemplative.

Ron didn't reply right away. His mind drifted to the thick boulders and the shadows that seemed to rule the location day or night. "Sounds perfect," he said finally. "A place full of shadows suitable for banishing a demon into."

"Exactly," Millie said softly. A yawn came through the speaker. "Nothing to do now but wait."

Ron nodded, forgetting he was on the phone, the

exhaustion finally catching up to him. "We should try to get some shuteye. We need to be on top of our game tonight."

They exchanged quiet goodbyes, and as Ron sank into the mattress, his body surrendered to the weariness he'd been holding at bay. Everything was in place. All that was left now between success or failure was the passage of time.

CHAPTER THIRTY-NINE

Ron woke to the familiar ringtone of his phone, and he groaned, struggling to open his eyes as he grasped for it blindly. The room was dark. He must've slept for hours. Blinking to try to clear the fogginess, he saw the lit-up screen lying next to him on the bed where he'd left it. Grabbing it, he hit the answer button.

"Hello?"

"Finally!" the voice of Millie came through. It was a few moments before he realized the words were coming both from the phone and from outside the door to his room.

"Oh, shit, sorry. Wait a sec, I'll get the door." He hung up and stumbled to the door, pulling it open to the thin, nervous smile of Millie. "Have you been here long?"

"A few minutes. I've been knocking, but you were obviously too out of it."

"Sorry, I was tireder than I thought," he said, trying to contain a yawn.

"Maggie is waiting in the car. I'll give you a minute to get ready."

Not bothering to close the door, Ron grabbed the cedar box containing all the photos of Mary from the photo album and the framed photos he found, and picked up his jacket from the back of a chair before heading back to the impatiently waiting Millie.

"Okay, let's go," he said as he closed and locked the door behind him. Millie nodded and led the way to the car and the waiting Maggie in the backseat.

"Hi, I'm Ron," he said as he slid into the passenger seat, placing the box on his knee before turning to offer his hand. Maggie was dressed in dark jeans, a thick black jacket zipped high, her attire almost perfect to slip into the shadows. Her once jet-black hair was streaked with silver, matching her grey eyes, which were ringed with fatigue, and not just from the night. They carried the weight of years of investigative work and all the unspeakable crimes she had seen as part of it.

Her face bore an unreadable expression as she fixed her gaze on him before her hand closed over his, giving it a firm shake. "Maggie," she said simply. "So," she said after an uncomfortable silence between the pair as Millie dropped into the driver's seat. "We're banishing a demon tonight, huh?"

Ron snorted. Her casual tone made it sound as if it were an everyday occurrence. "Well, when you say it like that, it does sound kind of ridiculous."

"You think?" Maggie replied sweetly.

Ron could see a hint of a smile on her lips as Millie pulled out of the car park and onto the road, heading toward the town centre.

"Truth be told," she added, "I've seen some weird

things over the years. But this... this just might take the cake."

Ron nodded. "Thank you for coming anyway."

"I have to admit, I'm curious about this whole thing, which is why I said yes. That, and it was Millie asking. I mean, she's hard to say no to. Just look at her."

Ron glanced at Millie. Her cheeks had deepened in colour, barely visible in the soft cast of passing streetlights. Her grip tightened briefly on the wheel, eyes forward, trying and failing not to react. The silence stretched, warm and awkward.

Maggie chuckled, but Ron didn't hear it. His gaze lingered on Millie's profile, her quiet concentration, the glint of emotion she tried to hide beneath it. There was something about her, and it was a familiar feeling. One that felt too soon for a heart that was still raw. He turned his head toward the window and stared outside, refocusing his thoughts on the task ahead.

Soon they had entered Park Street, and Millie was easing the car into the small, darkened gravel lot at the end. The tyres crunched over the loose gravel as the headlights fell across the wooden trail sign and were swallowed by the forest beyond. Shadows stretched deep into the trees, the air thick with moisture and pregnant silence.

Ron stared out the window, cradling the cedar box on his lap, his anxiety building steadily. The photos inside barely shifted as they pulled up to a stop, but their presence felt heavier than the paper they were printed on should.

Millie shut off the engine and popped the trunk. "We'll need to carry everything in," she said before she slid out and headed toward the back.

Ron and Maggie followed as she retrieved a drawstring pouch. Inside was the bottle of ritual ash, emanating the faint smell of charred herbs and rosemary. She picked up a worn canvas satchel dusted with faint white grains from beside it and swung it over her shoulder.

"This is Ice Glen?" Maggie asked, rubbing her arms and shivering as she surveyed the area.

"Trail starts just over the bridge," Millie replied, retrieving a couple of flashlights from the trunk and handing one to Maggie before closing it behind her.

Their glow pointed the way to the bridge, and they walked in that direction. Ron adjusted the cedar box and followed, their boots crunching quietly on the gravel as they approached the narrow footbridge. Beneath it, the inky blackness of the Housatonic River flowed, murmuring softly, the moonlight scattering across the surface in trembling fragments. The bridge groaned faintly under their weight, as if reluctant to let them pass.

Beyond it, the path dipped into the ravine. Moss clung to stone like forgotten skin, and tree trunks rose like ribs around them. The canopy above was so dense that barely a sliver of light from the moon penetrated through it to reach the ground beneath.

They continued through until the trees thinned and were replaced by massive boulders littering the landscape. They weaved between them until they found a space that appeared to be ringed by them in a near-perfect circle. A silent understanding passed between them as they stopped, a collective feeling that they were where they needed to be. The air thickened with tension and anticipation.

"Okay, let's get this place ready. Ron, you and Maggie,

find some kindling and wood we can use for the fire. I'll set up the salt and ash circle."

Ron set down the cedar box and joined Maggie, who had already started to gather the sticks and branches she could find from near the few trees that were present in the area. Ron stuck close to her, hampered by the lack of his own flashlight, but still managing to gather a pile of his own.

After a few minutes, they gathered enough kindling and larger pieces of wood, carefully placing them in separate piles inside the salt circle, taking care to step over the lines. Ron retrieved the box and placed it in the circle while Millie added a last few handfuls of ash to the outer circle. After finishing, she stepped back to survey her handiwork.

The salt circle Millie had created was ten feet across, large enough to accommodate the central firewood pile and leave space for the three of them to move within its perimeter without brushing the edges. The circle may not have been perfectly symmetrical, its shape marred somewhat by the uneven soil, but the lines were complete, with not a hint of a gap to be seen.

"Alright, I think that's everything." She blew out a breath and looked at each of them. "Before we start, Nanny Mae said we need to say these things. One of us to each line. Ron, when the fire is lit and the box is on fire, you need to say, 'The face no longer binds. The image no longer holds. Return to the dark, begone.' I'll say, 'From face to flame, the bond is broken. The memory burns. The tether dissolves.' We need to repeat these lines until the cedar box is nothing but ash. Got it?"

"What about me?" Maggie asked. Her voice was level, but the tension in her jaw betrayed her unease.

"I need you to be ready with the salt and ash in case, for any reason, the circle breaks. Remember what I told you about what might happen? If this creature shows up, it will do everything in its power to try to stop us."

Maggie hesitated before nodding slowly and reluctantly. Her expression was unreadable—half scepticism, half something quieter, with perhaps a hint of suspicion. She looked pale under the moonlight, but Ron wasn't sure it was the cold. Maybe it was the surreal weight of being asked to fight something she didn't believe in. Or maybe, just maybe, some part of her had started to wonder what would happen if they were right.

She took the offered satchel with salt and the pouch containing the bottle of ash from Millie and set them down at her feet, giving them a fleeting, faint smile. "Salt and ash. Demon banishment. Just another Friday night."

Everyone laughed nervously before they looked at the gathered pile of kindling.

"Alright, Maggie, you're up."

Maggie nodded once and then crouched down by the pile, extending her hand with the lighter to the kindling. The dim lighting made it hard to see clearly, but Ron thought he detected a slight tremble in her hand, a barely noticeable quiver.

With a strike of her thumb against the flint, a tiny flame burst forth. The kindling it was held under caught slowly, then in almost the blink of an eye, all at once. The fire bloomed orange and gold, expanding rapidly as it hungrily devoured the dry fuel, casting flickering light across their faces. Sparks flew into the air like shooting stars.

The trio huddled around the fire and fed it with the larger chunks of wood. Once they were satisfied it would last, Ron picked up the cedar box and handed it to Maggie, who hesitated before laying it in the flames. For a second, it didn't burn; it resisted, the flames biting hungrily at it but not catching. Then, the air crackled with a low hiss as the box ignited, the flames licking at its sides in an almost hesitant dance.

Millie's voice cut through the moment, strong and steady. "From face to flame, the bond is broken. The memory burns. The tether dissolves."

Ron followed quickly with his own incantation, his eyes flashing nervously around the salt circle. "The face no longer binds. The image no longer holds. Return to the dark, begone."

The wind shifted without warning, and a shriek tore through the clearing. High, ragged, and full of fury. The fire lowered in intensity for half a breath, then surged higher as if it were responding to the challenge. Just outside the ash line, the darkness gathered, limbs twisting and writhing within before it parted, and the demon appeared, its form tall and twisted. It wavered between the grotesque form it had manipulated Mary into and something hideously stretched. Its face was a collage of the burning photos with distorted mouths and too many eyes, expressions layered onto one monstrous canvas like shattered glass.

It hurled itself toward the circle and stopped cold. The salt glowed faintly as the ash at its edges flashed. The boundary held. The demon screamed in pain, its claws extended toward the trio safe in the circle, raking at them in desperation. Its shrieks were ear-piercing, producing waves that carried pressure, nausea, and untold grief turned inside out that crashed into them. Ron and Millie doubled over in pain as Maggie staggered backward. With great effort, Ron stood tall, guiding Millie to do the same. Their voices responded, lost in the sound but still resonant with power the demon couldn't deny.

"From face to flame, the bond is broken. The memory burns. The tether dissolves."

"The face no longer binds. The image no longer holds. Return to the dark, begone."

Out of the corner of his eye, Ron could see Maggie. Her mouth hung open, her body stock-still. She was trying to make sense of what she was seeing. Her eyes were locked onto the demon, scanning for some sign that this was a trick. An illusion. But there wasn't one. Whatever Maggie had believed walking into this clearing, it didn't fit now.

The cedar box was burning, but agonizingly slowly, smoke curling from the tiny gaps of the sealed lid. The demon writhed beyond the ash line, throwing itself against the circle to no avail. Its face transitioned between the forms of Mary and those of the lives it had taken.

Ron heard the voice before he saw her. "Ron..." it said, soft and cracked. "Ron, it's me."

Julia's face appeared. The body was still twisted and deformed, but there she was. Her hair was matted, her eyes swollen red with tears and filled with terror. Her voice hit him in the heart like a jolt of electricity.

"Please, Ron, stop. Don't let them do this. You don't

understand what they're doing," she cried. "You're killing me. Please... take the box out. Please..."

Her hand, broken and too long, reached toward him. The light of the flames flitted across her face, casting it in warmth and shadow, and, for a moment, Ron saw her as she used to be. Laughing in the sun, looking at him in the way only she did, with a mug of coffee in her hand.

His body moved before he knew it, his knees bending, hands reaching toward the cedar box that was now half-devoured within the flames.

"Ron!" Millie cried, lunging toward him and grabbing his arm hard enough to leave bruises. "That's not her. Look again. Look!"

The demon snarled, its illusion fracturing. Julia's features stretched, then warped, her eyes replaced by the familiar, dark, intense blue of the demon's. A gaping mouth formed where her cheek should have been, its flesh giving way to bone. Then came another scream, this one deeper, older. The cedar box, fully enveloped in flame, collapsed inward, the wood giving way as a final flare of flame rose as if in triumph. The thing recoiled as ash burst upward in a spiral, and the demon screamed its last, its many mouths splitting apart, its limbs folding into shadow. Its face changed from one to many to match the pictures consumed by fire, each one distorting as they broke apart, spinning away like torn photographs caught in a storm. The mouths vanished, the eyes closed, its flesh scattered like scorched silk, and then it was gone.

The clearing fell silent except for the crackling of the slowly dying fire. The circle had held. Ron hadn't moved.

Millie still clutched his arm. Maggie kneeled in stunned quiet, and slowly, the sounds from the forest returned.

"We did it," Millie whispered softly. Ron stared silently at the spot where the demon had stood for a few more moments before he turned to Millie and drew her to him in a hug. Tears rolled silently down his cheeks. It wasn't over, but they had time now. Time to track down the summoner, get that last picture, and destroy this demon once and for all.

CHAPTER FORTY

Three months later

Millie opened her eyes, blinking slowly, adjusting to the morning light that bled in through the warped Venetian blinds that slanted in and fell in uneven bars across the threadbare carpet and onto the uncomfortably hard bed.

She had almost forgotten what waking quietly felt like. No texts. No ticking clocks. Just the subtle shift of sheets as Ron rolled slightly in his sleep next to her. She lay still, listening to his breathing, eyes on the unmoving ceiling fan above. It had been three months since Ice Glen. Since the burning. Since that scream. Since grief had tried to wear a face.

The pair of them had maintained close contact after the ritual when they returned to work, constantly sending texts to each other, phone calls that lasted late into the night, coffee meetings during work breaks, all to exchange findings and notes on what they had found relating to the summoner. In that process, they had naturally grown closer, and as time passed, things progressed into intimate territory. They had taken it slowly; the loss of Julia was still painful to Ron, but together they were working through it.

It was two months later that Millie had finally found a trail they could follow. She had gotten lucky and come across someone mentioning a photo album that was left behind in a house in Pennsylvania when a couple moved in. One of them posted on a forum about it mysteriously flicking through pages on its own and opening to a picture. This kept repeating until it eventually stopped. Photos had been posted of each person the pages had rested on. Millie had come across this information too late. She had managed to find out that the people in the photos had died in mysterious circumstances, the whole family over a period of a few weeks. The pair had immediately taken leave and headed there, trading relative normalcy for motels, gas station maps, diner booths scrawled with notes, and the flickering half-trail of someone who'd conjured a demon to fill a hole that shouldn't be filled. Once the investigation led to a dead end, they came across more and more connections to the summoner.

A cemetery caretaker had reported a man burning pictures alone after midnight in Connecticut. A ritual circle was found half-intact in a public park with candles arranged in a spiral, blood droplets leading away from the site in Illinois. A local librarian recalled a woman checking out obscure folklore texts, titles like *Grief Binding and Memory Flame* and *The Bone Thread,* in Michigan. They had followed all the leads to their conclusion and now, finally, here to Indiana, in the same motel where the manager swore a woman had checked in multiple times over the last week under three aliases and disappeared, leaving behind only a bloodstain and a photo half-burned. Millie wasn't certain, but she felt they were getting close now. This was the freshest lead yet, having only been reported a few days ago.

Millie sat up, reaching slowly beneath her pillow for her journal. She'd used it since they started attempting to track the summoner down, noting every lead, every half-promising one, anything that could potentially help them. It was also filled with the dreams Ron had been having since the demon's temporary banishment. Worryingly, they had been increasing as time went on, pointing to the impending reappearance of the thing. She glanced at him, his brow furrowed in sleep, his shoulders tense even resting. There was no doubt. He could feel it too.

She sighed softly and opened the journal, frowning when something slipped out from between its pages. She picked it up and froze, her expression turning to one of horror. It was a photograph. Of Mary. Smiling.

"No," she whispered, the blood draining from her face, her heart hammering against her ribcage.

"Ron, Ron, wake up. You have to get up. Now!" Millie screamed.

Ron sat bolt upright beside her. "Mills?" His voice was groggy, his face full of confusion.

She didn't answer. The photograph pulsed in her hand. Ron's eyes were drawn to it, and his face transformed into terror.

And then the room changed. The light dimmed, the air grew heavy. A thick pressure built behind Millie's ears.

Shadows gathered and drew themselves toward the wall, where a maelstrom of whirling darkness formed. Then the pressure released with a sigh, and the demon stepped through.

It was flickering in and out of reality, partially formed, like it was struggling to remember itself. Its face was half twisted, phasing through fragments of expression. Mary's calm, her anguish, her rage, all layered one on top of another in a blurry amalgamation of her states. And then it screamed.

Ron scrambled out of the bed as it swept toward him. Millie shot out the other side and ran toward the kitchenette, making it to the sticky linoleum of its surface just as she heard Ron's panicked yell, and a heavy thud like a body hitting something hard.

She didn't turn. She couldn't. Not now.

Her eyes scanned the small kitchenette in desperation. They hadn't been here long enough to be familiar with the place. There were cabinets above the counter, a microwave below, and drawers below that. She ran toward them, her trembling fingers yanking open the top drawer and pushing aside menus and battered forks and spoons until she saw it. A cardboard matchbook complete with a faded motel logo. She grabbed it, praying that what remained inside would still work.

Behind her, the demon roared in a cacophony of sounds that seemed to writhe and twist. There was Mary's fury there, Mary's sobs. Her rage overlapped with Julia's begging, layered into one dissonant scream that shattered the kitchenette light in a burst of sparks and glass.

Millie spun and ran back into the room.

Ron was trying to crawl away, blood on his temple where he'd hit the dresser. The demon loomed over him, its body a stuttering mess of limbs transforming between form and memory, faces blurring, flesh bending wrong.

She tore a match free and lit it. The flame danced, weak and orange.

"No!" the thing screeched, not with its own voice, but with Julia's.

Millie pressed the photo to the flame. It curled slowly before it caught, but time betrayed her.

The demon turned to Ron in a swift and sudden movement. A shriek split the air, and its claws shot forward, thrusting into his chest and out his back in a shower of gore before he could scream. His body jerked once, his eyes drifting to Millie in a last desperate plea, then went limp as the photo in Millie's hands fell to the floor and continued to burn.

The thing howled, its many mouths splitting in agony as the flames ate the picture. Ron's body collapsed backward, his eyes wide and unseeing. The demon began to unravel, its skin folding inward, its eyes flaring brightly blue, staring at her as it crumbled into ash and light.

Millie stood there in silence. Her hands trembled, and her knees hit the scorched motel carpet. She screamed, raw and unfiltered. The sound of grief cracked wide open.

Ron was still, his body lying against the wall in broken silence, his eyes unseeing, his chest splayed open. The image was unbearable. This wasn't a stranger. This wasn't just any casualty from a case. This was Ron, the man who had captured her heart. The man she had dared to envision a future with. The man she loved but never got a chance to say the words to.

She crawled to him with numb hands. Her fingers reached out and hovered inches above his face, as if she could coax him back to life with her touch alone.

"No," she whispered. "No, you don't get to do this. You don't get to leave me here. Please, Ron. Please, no." Her voice trembled, then broke.

The room was still thick with the smell of sulphur and ash, the remnants of the demon's disintegration lingering in the wallpaper, in the carpet, in the air, in her lungs.

She pressed her forehead to his, tears dripping down onto his cooling skin. His blood stained her clothing and the palms of her hands, but she didn't notice. Didn't care. She clutched his shirt, her knuckles white.

Her scream returned, sharper, broken, and feral. It filled the room before it faded, her face twisting, her grief transforming into fury. Into a promise.

Then she fell silent. Her eyes rimmed with tears, her breathing uneven. This wasn't over. She didn't know how she would find the summoner, but she wouldn't rest until she did. Not now. Not ever.

EPILOGUE

Lilith Darkmoon sat still in the back room of her shop as reality shivered. Outside, the world twisted.

Beyond the Veil, once nestled in a dying Indiana town, folded inward like a spider poked with a sharp object. Space warped, and shadows bent. When the tremors eased, the storefront had repositioned itself, quietly and undetected, into a forgotten corner of southern Missouri. Once a thread had reached its conclusion, a move was necessary. Safety was paramount, and she couldn't risk being tracked down. Not now.

She exhaled. The air smelled of ozone and sulfur. A sharp wave of pain rushed through her body. The demon's death, though a necessary sacrifice, was no less painful. It had been one of the few babies she had managed to summon to the earth with her limited power, after all.

Its host, Mary, had been marked years ago, manipulated by Lilith to further her penchant for selfishness, control, and emotional manipulation. Lilith had whispered to her, softened her from within, preparing her for the demon that would claim her as its vessel on her death. The advanced state of decomposition of her body, its prematurity, was no accident. It was the toll of years of spiritual erosion, the rot of surveillance. Mary's flesh had unravelled under the weight of her dark attention, which suited her demon perfectly. It had preferred a corrupted host in body and soul, and that's exactly what it got.

The candle on the table in front of Lilith flared violently, its flame doubling, then tripling in size as the runes etched on the floor she sat within pulsed with crimson light. Ron's soul joined the hundreds of others already reaped, spilling into the undercurrent where they lay, waiting for Lilith to utilize in the ceremony that would soon be performed.

"Another offering accepted," she whispered. Her smile was soft, beautiful, but terrifying to behold, both ancient and absolute. She placed her teacup down gently, and the liquid inside rippled.

Closing her eyes, she slipped effortlessly into the shadows, where the echoes of her children waited, their full demonic power held back only by a veil not yet torn. But soon. Soon, she would have enough souls to tear a hole through the fabric of reality. They would enter into this world, not as whispers, not as summoned shades, but whole, entire. A legion that would rid this world of the human vermin that inhabited it.

"The Veil is thin," she whispered, her voice echoing across dimensions. "The gate trembles. Soon, the seals will break."

Her children howled and reveled. She could hear them

as her heart throbbed in a discordant rhythm, in a twisted parody of a hymn.

"Let those who grieve mourn their dead. Let them bury their broken. Let them believe it is over." She smiled, and the shadows smiled with her. "For I am Lilith. First wife of Adam. Mother of monsters. Queen of the Damned." She raised her arms and smiled a terrible smile. "And you, my beautiful children, will walk the earth and reign supreme."

The shadows returned to their places, content to remain patient for now. The runes on the floor dimmed. And the world above turned, unaware that its reckoning was near.

ACKNOWLEDGMENTS

A novel of this length doesn't get into the shape it is without a lot of hard work, and I'm thankful, once again, to have Stephanie Huddle's expertise to cast a critical eye over my words, and make them better. She is a fantastic editor, and I'll be forever singing her praises.

The fantastic, eye-catching cover art was, once again, created by Adrian Medina, an exceptional artist who is such a pleasure to work with.

The formatting of a book goes a long way to enhance the experience of turning its pages, and my formatter, Jyl Glenn, is an expert at making my books shine.

And to my group of talented writers in the Scribes group—thank you so much for your support, friendship, and encouragement in everything I do.

ABOUT THE AUTHOR

A horror fan since childhood, Ian embraces his inner geek with pride, his dedication displayed in the intimidating collection of horror novels and video games that threaten to take over his living space.

He is mad for all things Alien, Star Wars, and cats, his furry companions always there to keep him company as he scribbles down his latest ideas.

He's a father in Melbourne, Australia, sharing his home with his partner, two stepdaughters, and four cats. The sheer number of furry and human companions in his life might be enough to drive anyone a little crazy.

You can follow his writing journey on Facebook at - Ian Gielen - Author

Horror Novella:

Saving Tommy

Horror Novel:

Unholy Blood

Horror Collection:

Echoes of the Damned

Anthologies:

Devour the Rich (Published by Above the Rain Collective)

Cryptid Codex (Published by Crimson Cult Media)

Warning: Wicked Web (Published by Crimson Cult Media)

Invasion of the Saucer-Men from Mars! (Published by Specul8 Publishing)

Attack of the Colossal Creatures from Planet X (Published by Specul8 Publishing)

Books of Horror Community Anthology Vol 4 Part 1 (Published by Books of Horror)

Petting Boo! (Published by Wicked Shadow Press)

Christmas of the Dead: Krampus Kountry (Published by Wicked Shadow Press)

Apocalyptales: Judgement Day (Published by Wicked Shadow Press)

Flash of the UnDead (Published by Wicked Shadow Press)

Flash of the Dead: Requiem (Published by Wicked Shadow Press)

Femme Fatale Flashes (Published by Wicked Shadow Press)

Masks of Sanity: The Monster Within (Published by Wicked Shadow Press)

Children of the Dead: Lost Lullabies (Published by Wicked Shadow Press)

Halloweenthology: Trick-Or-Treat (Published by Wicked Shadow Press)

Flash of the Dead: Halloween '24 (Published by Wicked Shadow Press)

Halloweenthology: Friar's Lantern (Published by Wicked Shadow Press)

Blink of an Eye (Published by CultureCult Magazine & Press)

Merry Creepsmas: The Green Book (Published by Wicked Shadow Press)

Cooks of Horror

Sleeve of Hearts